QUIET WAR

Book 1: Farewell Amity Station

FRANK KENNEDY

Dedicated to everyone who knows they can do it better.

A note from the author:

Farewell Amity Station is set in the universe of the Collectorate, which includes at least three other series. Reading them is not a prerequisite.

1

Collectorate Standard Year (SY) 5370
Philadelphia Redux
Planet: Earth

THE BRAT NEVER LISTENED before he ran. Trevor thought a leash would do the trick. It worked with Fritz, a dachshund equal to the brat in age and cunning. But Mum, ever the stickler, forbade Trevor from treating his little brother like a pet.

She did, however, insist he keep a constant eye on the rambunctious little fool while she tended to her work. They were two months behind on rent, living beyond their means in Earth's largest metropolis.

Didn't help that the war took Father a hundred light-years away. Every time Trevor broached the subject, water pooled in her eyes. She heard nothing since the Swarm invaded Collectorate space.

And now, rumors spread of enemy cruisers in the Sol system, preparing to run the orbital blockade.

Trevor never saw the city so still. Beneath giant glass towers, the streets and parks were empty but for secure drones and a few defiant citizens who refused to shelter in place.

Such a lovely spring day. Not the wisp of a cloud. Templar Park beckoned, twenty levels down. The brat could play until drained of his boundless energy. Trevor could take out his tablet and write stories about great sea adventures set long before humans took to the stars.

Trevor resisted the allure and closed the curtains.

"Fritz needs to go," the brat said, entering Trevor's bedroom.

"He can hold it, Connor."

The brat played with the doorknob.

"No, he can't, Trev. His bladder is all full."

Trevor smirked. He knew his brother's game.

"I took Fritz for a diddle before you got up. He's fine."

Connor twisted his lips into a squishy mess that usually preceded a tantrum. Trevor didn't want to hear it.

"Look, Connor. Just take Fritz to the water room and set him in the shower well. He's done it there before."

The brat gnashed his teeth and hugged the door like a dance partner. There followed the familiar first moan.

"That's nasty, Trev-or. We need to take him outside."

"No. The city's on lockdown. We have to make do. Mum's orders."

Connor threw back his head and pulled the door shut.

"I hate you."

Trevor heard him run down the hall and bang on Mum's door, but she'd invariably tell him to go away. No one disturbed her work. She appeared only for Trevor's kiosk meals and to pee.

She slept beside her workstation lately. The job's demands were endless, she confessed to Trevor. It wasn't fair, but her bosses were former Solomons and had no problem making a Chancellor pay for the sins of her caste.

"It's a long road," she told Trevor. "The hard feelings will end, but it will take time."

"Mum, the civil war ended six years ago."

He was six when the Chancellory surrendered. He never understood what it was all about or why so many had to die.

"Their grievances go back centuries, Trevor. If our roles were reversed, I ..."

She rubbed her eyes and yawned. Trevor watched her age years in a matter of months.

"Until Father returns, I need you to keep on top of things around here – starting with your brother. Promise?"

"I will, Mum."

Trevor did his best for the three months since he made that promise, but he also had the advantage of a new dog and Templar Park to keep Connor preoccupied. The lockdown crippled his strategy.

The tantrums were the worst. Normal for a five-year-old perhaps, but insufferable to a sitter who was twelve. Trevor couldn't lock the door and leave the brat to his own devices. The risk to property and life were too great.

If Mum only took the time to see how Connor had deteriorated. The little boy knew his world had turned upside down, but no one told him why, or when it might right itself. Even Trevor didn't have the answers.

He glanced outside the curtains again and sighed.

It was almost time for luncheon. If he made Connor's favorite wrap and read to him afterward ... OK, that was good for maybe two hours. Then he'd need a new plan.

When would it end?

Fine. Lunch.

He passed by the brat's bedroom en route to the kitchen. The door was flung open. No sounds from inside.

"Connor? Ready for a bite to eat?"

The bed linens had been slung about the room, and a helping of dog toys lay atop the exposed mattress.

Great. A full-on tantrum. It'd been a week since the last time Connor destroyed anything of value.

The pillows were still intact. Good sign.

"Connor? Where did you ...?"

Trevor felt a deep, horrifying pit in his belly when he returned to the corridor. He had a clean view through the living room to the front door, which was propped open with a plush toy.

"Cudfrucker. The little bast ..."

3

He stood outside Mum's door.

No. He wasn't going to raise the alarm. She gave him one job: Keep Connor safe.

Trevor raced into his bedroom and grabbed his hand-comm. He linked in to Connor's amp and tracked the boy's movement. The brat was descending – already ten levels down the lift.

"Don't care what Mum says. I'm going to beat your ass till it's purple this time."

He cursed himself for the thought and dashed from their flat. The lifts were close, but none tracked near Level 20. Why busy now? It was lockdown. He didn't need assholes making life more difficult.

"Hey, Trev, whatcha doing there?"

Cud! Thomas Quinlan. Sixteen, built like a small mountain, and always up for a little Chancellor beat-down.

Trevor matched the Solomon boy eye-for-eye, his Chancellor genetics already sprouting him to six-five with a few more inches to go. Yet he ignored the caste training techniques – Mum couldn't afford to send him to Tier-Up class anyway – and had become gangly. Thomas could toss him about like a raggedy doll.

"Not today, Thomas. Just ... go home."

Bad choice of words. Thomas went for the predictable snark.

"Sorry, my master. I'll swing around, grand sir. Wouldn't want to defy the little Chancellor lord."

Trevor heard knuckles crack. Thomas balled his fists.

OK. Be smart. It's what Mum says: Truth first.

The nearest lift approached from Level 25.

"Please, Thomas. I know we're not supposed to be out, but it's my brother. He ran off. I need to find him before ..."

Trevor felt a hot breath which smelled of garlic.

Typical.

"Connor's loose?" Thomas laughed. "And we're worried about the Swarm. You need to put shackles on that little freak."

The door opened. Trevor raced inside, praying Thomas did not

4

follow. He swiveled around to find the mountain with his nose stuck to within an inch of the threshold.

"I-I'm sorry, Thomas. I have to go now."

Thomas bared his teeth as the door slipped shut.

"I'll be waiting, Trev. I always wait for you."

Unlike many Solomon bullies, Thomas backed up his threats. Trevor brushed it off for the moment. One crisis at a time.

The amp tracker showed Connor exiting through the lobby. Why didn't security stop him? Or maybe they tried, but the brat slipped through their grasp like an eel.

The answer became apparent when he reached the lobby: It was empty save a pair of cleaning drones. Something else chilled Trevor.

Horns. Outside.

He hadn't heard them since the civil war.

"Cudfrucker."

As he exited Obersson Tower 17, Trevor passed panicked residents rushing inside. No one tried to stop him, although a secure drone hovered in the grand plaza, instructing all citizens to take shelter.

Was this it? The real thing? Were they running the blockade?

Trevor crossed the plaza on the pedestrian bridge into Templar Park, where ornate gardens, tall oaks, and water fountains betrayed the urgency of the day. Connor was two hundred meters ahead, making for his usual haunt. Not even the city's defense horns deterred him.

"Please let it be a drill," Trevor muttered.

He found Connor alone at the children's playground, yet he wasn't playing. The boy was shouting through his tears.

"Fritz! Fritz! Here, boy."

Trevor grabbed his brother by the shoulders and swung him around.

"What are you doing out here? We're in dang ..."

Connor squished his lips.

5

"F-Fritz. He ran away. Over there."

He pointed toward thick botanical gardens surrounding a pond.

"Shit, Connor. Where?"

"I don't know, Trevor. You have to find him. He won't come."

"He probably can't hear you over the horns."

Trevor feared making the tough decision. If they left the dog, Connor would scream and kick all the way home. Trevor gave it his best and shouted for Fritz to the top of his lungs.

"Again," Connor insisted. "He can't hear you."

Trevor complied, but how long to wait? The glass city rose around them in giant columns stretching for several kilometers. Were they the only two fools standing outside in this canyon?

"C'mon, brother. We have to start back. Fritz will catch up."

Connor pushed him away.

"No, Trev-*or*. He's my dog. We ..."

Something caught the boy's eye. A second later, he ballooned a churlish smile through his tears.

"Fritz!"

The dachshund leaped out of a thicket of shrubbery and dodged playground obstacles. Connor fell to his knees and welcomed Fritz into his arms.

"You brought him outside without a leash?"

Connor cuddled the dog in his lap.

"He hates the leash."

"Fine. We'll talk about it inside. We have to go now."

"No. I want to play."

One thought entered Trevor's mind:

I'm not going to have kids when I grow up.

"Connor, look around. There's no one else. It's not safe out here. I promise ... as soon as we get the all-clear, we'll spend a whole day at the park. Whatever you want to do. Just ... please don't be a monster about it. We have to go."

Connor relented, but they hadn't walked twenty meters before the brat pointed west of the city, through the great canyon.

"Wow. Trev, look! What's that?"

Trevor saw a cluster of suns burst into life and fade as quickly.

Wormholes. Oh, no.

Seconds later, the apertures gave birth.

Though the wormholes opened several kilometers from the city, Trevor did not mistake the objects that exited.

"Warships. Connor, we need to hurry."

"But it's so pretty. Can't we watch?"

Trevor didn't answer. The horns blared across the city at a higher pitch. No, this was definitely not a drill. A second burst of apertures inside the original few hypnotized the boy.

He saw scattered, pinpoint flashes of yellow and green intersecting the many clustered warships. Then the sky turned pink, blotting out the combatants.

"Oh!"

They said it together.

"What happened?" Connor asked.

"Don't know. Explosion of some kind. C'mon. Inside. Now."

Instead of running, Trevor pulled the awestruck little brat, who almost fumbled Fritz while insisting he wanted to see the whole show.

The battle burst through the wide, pink fog.

Three warships. The lead drew fire from its pursuers and returned blasts from its aft turrets. Trevor didn't recognize its configuration.

The enemy was here. They were coming.

"Please, Connor. That's enough. We have to go faster."

"But it's getting closer. See."

The enemy ship carried a plume of black smoke from its aft as it descended but wasn't spinning out of control. The city's defense perimeter launched missiles from the ground. They smashed against the warship's belly without effect.

It was bigger now. Almost to the city. Too close.

Trevor had enough of this. He scooped up his brother and pressed on. How many more wormholes were about to open? Thousands of citizens had evacuated Redux; they assumed the largest city would be the first target. Yet Mum never proposed they leave. Too much work to do.

He kept his eyes laser-focused on Obersson Tower 17. Its lobby, its safety, was maybe two minutes away at this pace. If he didn't obsess on the danger, it would pass. The defense shield or the UNF warships would finish the job.

It would be a great story to tell someday.

The strategy might have worked had he not felt the city tremble around him. A thunder rolled between the glass towers as the sound of cannon fire intensified.

"Fritz!"

Connor dropped him meters shy of the pedestrian bridge into the plaza. The dog barked at the approaching goliath.

We won't make it.

The Swarm war cruiser filled the canyon as it tilted side to side. It was too big. Too wide.

It clipped Obersson Tower 10. An explosion near the top sent glass and debris raining down. Its engines screamed and its bow dipped. It was coming down on top of ...

Trevor didn't think. He lugged Connor down a green slope until they found refuge beneath the bridge.

"Fritz. You forgot Fritz. Trevor, he ..."

"Shut up. Please. Just shut up."

Trevor held his brother tight as the enemy blotted out the sun. When it passed over them, Trevor caught a glimpse of the red scorpion on its belly. So the reports were true.

Up close, the cruiser was so much bigger. Even worse: Longer. It didn't seem to end. And it was about to crash. Would it bury them alive? Had his carelessness killed them both?

More explosions. Debris smashed onto and around the bridge in fiery chunks. The earth fractured and vibrated at the crash.

Small detonations followed and then a few hopeful seconds of bliss. They were alive. They made it.

Two more warships approached, both flying well above the glass towers. Trevor recognized them: UNF warships like the one Father served on.

The warships delivered pinpoint green blasts that splintered the brief midday peace.

"Where's Fritz?" Connor asked, snaking out of Trevor's grasp.

"I hear him. He's OK."

Indeed, the dog never stopped barking. He competed against the roar of the UNF's aerial barrage.

"Give me your hand, Connor."

"No. Got to find Fritz."

The boy tried to escape but lost his balance and slid into the edge of the stream. Trevor raised his legs and pushed off. He joined Connor in the water before the brat sank.

"Help me, Trevor. I can't swim."

"Hold tight. I'm here."

This time Connor obeyed without hesitation. Had the dire nature of the moment finally hit him? He burrowed his way inside big brother's arms as Trevor righted himself and found the bottom. The water reached his rib cage, but the current was weak.

"What now, Trevor?"

"Don't move. We'll stay right here. It's safest."

He hoped.

To the west, two-man fighter craft descended from the warships. To the east, Trevor saw smoke, fire, and a mountainous beast lying prone on the plaza. Its massive engine array glowed yellow.

"I'm sorry I ran away, Trevor. I'm sorry. I don't hate you."

"Never thought you did, Connor. Just hang tight. OK?"

Soldiers in full body armor approached from both directions. Energy weapons as big as arms fired wide strips of laser bolts.

Debris continued to fall in flaming ribbons. Glass, metal, fixtures, wood furniture. Fritz stopped barking.

Trevor ordered himself not to cry. If they somehow survived this battle, he dreaded seeing what remained of their little world.

2

23 years later
Amity Station, Collectorate Unified System
208 light-years from Earth

T HE VOICE FROM BEHIND needed to go away. Trevor had nothing against the woman; she was following orders. Her timing, however, was shit.

Trevor stared at his pom's M-chain. Why didn't Ana respond from her tablet? Even in her most brittle state, she loved to play around with glyphs and symbols in lieu of a coherent message. She knew Daddy wouldn't mind.

The girl didn't come out of her room before he left. Trevor thought she'd have calmed down by now — at the very least, Effie would set their daughter straight.

"First Deputy, sir," the annoying voice continued from behind. "Ready when you are."

Trevor cursed under his breath. He closed the pom and tucked it in his uniform's jacket. *Give her time.* That's what Effie said after last night's blowout. What choice did he have?

"Apologies," he swung about. "Family matters."

The Hokki woman — a full foot shorter, hair in a tight ball, eyes black as the space between stars – crimped a polite smile.

"We're all cursed with one, sir. It can be a struggle." She extended her hand. "Sec Deputy Hoshi Oda."

"First Deputy Trevor Stallion. If we're going to be partners, I'd prefer Trev. I hear people aren't quite as formal in Haven."

Hoshi tucked her hands behind her back.

"We try to keep it casual here. It's not like Harmony Sector. We don't engage with diplomats and IC reps all day."

Did he detect a hint of jealousy? If only she knew ...

"Right. Just ordinary folks here. The backbone of Amity."

He didn't think the line was funny, but Hoshi laughed all the same.

"I've been doing this job for a year, Trev. Trust me, there's nothing ordinary about the people of Haven."

He saw her point.

"True. Ordinary people don't choose to spend years inside a giant canister fifty light-years from the nearest planet. I've been here so long, I tend to forget. Shall we?"

Trevor allowed his escort and new partner to lead the way from Haven Security Administration toward the rifter docks. She didn't condescend by pointing out who occupied what office or any routines that matched his years of experience in Harmony.

Good, he thought. One less embarrassing moment.

"I heard you've been at this for some time, Trev."

"Oh, yes. A lot of life poured into this station. I understand you're coming up on your second year."

"Tomorrow, actually. Three hundred standard days."

"Two-year rotation?"

She nodded with a sharp, military assent.

"UNF deferment. I also applied for an IC grant, but the UNF came through first. Plus, it sets me up for a nice career."

Oh, yes. She'd fit in well with the United Naval Forces. No doubt she developed that disciplined gait after a monthlong stint in Basic Training School.

"Good timing. This is their first expansion since the war. Heard last week they're recommissioning three warships."

They exited the office complex near the bow of Haven Sector and approached the docks.

"I'm surprised it took them so long," she said. "What with the way things have been going out there."

Trevor didn't want to get into the weeds on this issue, but his previous assignment gave him insight most people outside Harmony Sector lacked.

"Nobody expected Black Star to become such a menace. But money and politics delayed the response. Usual."

"I try to steer clear of those conflicts."

"Smart, Hoshi. Ever heard of the Marshall Group?"

"Don't think so."

"Hardliners. They believe UNF expansion is a slippery slope toward killing their Rights of Sovereignty. They tried to hold up the appropriations bill."

As they reached the docks, where twenty dual-frame rifters hovered, Hoshi pointed to the one they'd use for today's tour.

"We have people like that back home on Hokkaido. They're cudfrucking morons." She caught herself. "Excuse my bite."

"Excused."

Hoshi revealed a bit of an edge. He liked it. His superiors in Harmony Sector never appreciated colorful language while on duty. Though that was only part of what did him in.

"And what truly spins me up, Trev? After all the UNF did for my people, and all we contributed to the Collectorate – the heroes of the war, and then President Aleksanyan – you'd expect them to show nothing but gratitude."

Hoshi broke into a sheepish grin.

"Oh. So sorry, Trev. How did we get from introductions to politics in less than two minutes?"

"Blame me. I used to spend my days around people who talked of little else. It's second nature."

They hopped aboard the open-air rifter. Each pressed a thumb against the Nav bank. The AI verified their Amity LinkPass through their gene stamp; the bank's green display unlocked their vital data.

"ALP confirmed," the AI announced in a tone-neutral voice. *"Level Five certified operators."*

He pointed to her steering arm.

"You have the honors, Hoshi."

"You're the senior officer."

Trevor tried not to sound annoyed.

"True, and I'll pull rank when it's warranted. But you're officially my tour guide, so I defer to your expertise."

She mumbled her thanks and grabbed the wheel. The rifter's safety cascade flickered around them in a blink. Hoshi set her course deep into Haven Sector, but not without a little snark.

"Chief Dorrit said you might not cooperate today. He said your nose might be a touch on the high side for Havenites."

Trevor never had much use for that overstuffed bastard. Chief of Security Hannibal Dorrit didn't disguise his indignation at Trevor being appointed his First Deputy without consultation. Trevor was already devising ways to avoid the man. No sense pissing off another superior — at least not in the short term.

"One thing to know about me, Hoshi. I'm the model of cooperative until I'm not."

She chuckled. "What happens then?"

"Desk work and regrets, mostly."

Hoshi nodded. She had yet to accelerate the rifter.

"Ah. Yes. I heard a little something about the incident. Sorry."

"A *little*? No need for apologies. Everyone in Sec Admin knows at least a little. If you don't mind, I'd rather not discuss details."

"Of course. Before we head out, can I ask one tiny question?"

OK. Here it comes.

"Tiny? As in what? Two words? Three?"

14

"Chief Dorrit let slip you've served several rotations. Most deputies move to Central or rotate out of Amity in two years. What holds you here?"

He kept his irritation bottled but slipped her the side-eye.

"That's what you call *tiny*? Oh, well. I can see you didn't inspect my profile. It's all there."

"Dorrit gave me ten minutes heads-up."

"Sounds about right. Hoshi, I don't serve terms. I've lived more than half my life on Amity. Grandfathered in, so to speak."

Her eyes grew in sudden revelation.

"Oh, it's you! The Lifetime Deputy."

That label again? He really needed to make a change.

"I dearly hope not, Hoshi. I'm only thirty-five and free to book passage on a transport today." Under his breath added: "Maybe I should." Effie warned Trevor: His reputation would precede him. "I was deputized fifteen years ago. I moved here with my brother when I was sixteen. What can I say? I got used to the place."

More to the point, had nowhere else to go and was damn lucky to be anywhere after the war.

"Nineteen years," she gushed. "That means the station wasn't finished when you arrived. You must have a million stories."

"Only four worth telling. Maybe someday after we've settled into a nice routine, I'll bore you with them."

"You have a deal, Trev. Ready for the tour?"

He oozed in sarcasm: "Can't wait."

Hoshi would point out nothing he didn't already know, but the tour would give him a couple hours downtime. He needed it to think through his next strategy – how to repair the shit he'd made of his family.

Visualize sitting down with Ana to help her through the confusion. She thought he didn't love her anymore.

It was a great plan. Naturally, it went straight to hell.

15

3

HAVEN SECTOR IN SOME WAYS reminded Trevor of his childhood home, Philadelphia Redux. The residential towers and wide avenues – in this case, moving walkways called Swiftraks – clustered together in tight formations along a grid pattern. They formed canyons, at the bottom of which green areas created the illusion of nature. That's where the similarities ended.

The parks lacked trees, and the manufactured streams ran on recycled water. The sun and moon were nonexistent inside this cylinder, which extended two kilometers bow to stern. In its place, stationary glowdrones dotted Haven like the brightest evening stars. Collectively, they generated enough light to mimic the effect of a far-north city where the sun hovered for months above the horizon.

Neither cold nor warm. No wind, no fragrance, a perfectly unnatural balance of aesthetics. Haven, like companion sectors Harmony and Episteme, simply *was*.

The shift to sterile and cloistered both fascinated and unsettled Trevor when he arrived as a boy. Now, he'd long forgotten what it felt like to shiver on a January morning or sweat on a July afternoon. If he ever returned to Earth, natural sunlight would damage his eyes unless he wore dark glasses for a few days.

The gravitational transition would be more stressful.

"The longer we stay, the more likely we'll never leave," he once conceded to Effie. "Planet life is so messy."

Was he building a case to remain the Lifetime Deputy? Or had the continuity of Amity Station softened him? Trevor didn't want to believe he was afraid of reassimilating to terrestrial life.

Effie had resided here almost as long, building a career in the Diplomatic Resolution Corps. Yet duty called his wife off-station a few times every year, just enough to keep her firmly planted in both worlds. She had no plans to leave the DRC, but bureau postings occasionally opened on Collectorate member planets.

The future seemed simple in the first years of their marriage. Effie made a smart, practical case.

"It won't be as difficult as you think," she once said, cuddled in his arms after making love. "We'll live in a city with a great transit system. We'll have a comfortable high-rise flat with the best blackout curtains. You'll find an executive job in corporate security. Could be worse."

"How?"

She blew in his ear.

"We could buy a farm. Raise animals. Plant things."

"In the dirt, you mean?"

"That's usually where they go, last I checked."

He imagined himself wielding a hoe to break up soil.

The horror.

"I walked in mud once when I was a kid," he told her. "My parents took us on an excursion outside Redux. I forget exactly where, but I recall having the best time."

"And now?"

"Oh, I'd be disgusted."

Effie wasn't surprised. She sniffed under his arms.

"Not even a slight musk. We could make love for another hour, and you'd still be odor-free. You're unnatural."

"Or maybe," he said with a wry grin, "I'm the *only* natural one."

"I blame the showers. You take too many."

They'd gone down this verbal riff often.

"I cut back."

"Only after they threatened to slice our water ration."

"Fine. You win the point. But I'm down to one water and one steam per day, three minutes max."

"You," Effie said between a long, deep kiss, "have a problem. There should be a support group for people like you."

"The sanitary?"

"A more accurate term is obsessive-compulsive."

"I wasn't aware wanting to be clean was a disorder. OK. Fine. I'll start a support group myself. Our motto will be 'happily odor-free.'"

Trevor enjoyed that banter. The rigid formality of life inside Harmony Sector was a heavy load to bear. He loved those moments when they could set free their private faces.

He missed Effie. She hadn't touched him in weeks. These days, she found pleasure in another bed.

Trevor lost track of what Hoshi was telling him as they ventured into the heart of Haven. Assuming she said anything worth hearing.

"Swiftraks?" He asked.

His guide steered the rifter toward the main walkway between the mid-level residential towers.

"Yes. Um. The leapers. You've heard about them, I assume?"

He decided not to sound ignorant to the issue.

"*Leapers.* What sort of problem are they causing?"

"Most of the time, it's no more than a nuisance." She pointed to the crowded Swiftrak, on which pedestrians moved at three times standard walking speed. "When they come out and leap off-shift, they pose less of a danger. But they prefer the challenge of leaping over a crowd."

Oh. That.

They never had such an issue in Harmony, but he heard about the

18

practice in Haven, where ninety percent of Amity's children resided. The lighter gravity meant anyone who got a good running start on a Swiftrak could push off and leap forward in ten-meter bounds. The thrill made sense; who didn't want to feel superhuman? But gravity had its limits. The leaper often did not stick the landing. Bruises and broken bones, along with the occasional tussle, caused considerable consternation.

"How many incidents on average?" He asked.

"Four to five calls a day. Half are after-the-fact, disgruntled eyewitnesses. They wonder why we don't coffin the practice."

"The others?"

She settled the rifter into the transit lane between walkways.

"Sprains, minor phasic triage, a few bruised egos."

Trevor saw no one in either direction misbehaving. Good. He'd caught a quiet moment.

"To be fair, I understand why people are disgruntled. They shouldn't have to put up with it. HVSA can stamp it out. Why hasn't that happened?"

Hoshi said something under her breath. Trevor didn't catch it.

"We could, but we'd have to patrol the Swiftraks constantly. We don't have enough bodies to cover off-shift. Frankly, it's all we'd ever do, Trev."

"In theory, yes. What about punishment? The regs allow for fair penalties."

Her frown spoke loudly: No, it said, you don't understand how life works here.

"Ninety-nine percent of the violators are kids. Four out of five of those are Natives. They're hands-off. Chief Dorrit's orders."

The haze cleared away. Trevor wasn't surprised.

"He's afraid of them, isn't he? More specifically, their parents."

"Them and the paperwork. We send them on their way with a stern warning."

"An empty threat. Yes?"

Her sigh confirmed his suspicion.

The population of children born to Amity Station had grown in recent years. Seven hundred fifty as of a week ago; an engineer in Episteme Sector expected twins in a few days. Natives – which included his seven-year-old Ana Marie – represented a shift from Amity's original mission concept.

At first, the Amity Charter ruled out anyone making a permanent home here. It assumed diplomats and Interstellar Congress reps, as well as scientific, engineering, and support workers would rotate through the station. Even elected positions were term-limited, ensuring a steady turnover that allowed new opportunities from applicants across the forty Collectorate worlds.

Five percent of the population had lived here more than a decade. Only seven others surpassed the Stallion brothers for longevity. Most parents of Natives were influential or knew the proper contacts to run interference should their children get into trouble.

"Chief Dorrit doesn't like confrontation," Hoshi said.

"Huh. Especially when it comes barging into his office."

"You understand, Trev."

"What I understand is that he's begging for trouble. There's going to be a serious accident someday. The kind you can't look past. Will it take someone's death to change policy?"

She held up a hand as if to stop his protest cold.

"You're not wrong, but we do things differently here. Dorrit says punishing children is a bad look for the HVSA."

He had to chuckle.

"Bad look? I thought wanton law-breaking was a bad look. Perhaps I'm too anal."

"They're kids, Trev. They're searching for an outlet to have fun in a place where there isn't much, if we're being honest."

Hoshi pointed toward the far end of Haven, where the sector's energy plant loomed beyond a mile of additional housing, restaurants, shops, and clubs.

"I once saw a Native enter the Swiftrak right about here and leap in ten-meter bounds nonstop. It was incredible. He reached the Crossway lifts in under a minute. I'm actually surprised more people don't do it."

Trevor's eyes followed the fabled course to those lifts, which rose fifty meters in white columns up to transit stations inside the Crossway, one of two enclosed ribs that linked the three sectors. The double-layered Blue Line provided dedicated tubes for passengers and cargo. In one direction, Harmony Sector. In the opposite, Episteme.

"Perhaps it's my age talking, Hoshi, but this problem needs to be managed. If it's sport they want, then let's set aside dates for Swiftrak races off-shift. Cordon sections and establish rules."

"Could be a reasonable compromise, Trev, but I doubt these leapers will be mollified."

Lovely. Less than an hour on the new job, and he was already proposing change. Old habits …

"I should take a proposal to Dorrit."

Hoshi shook her head.

"As First, that's your prerogative, but I'd recommend you hold off a few weeks. Give the Chief time to accept you."

"Oh. What qualifies as acceptance? Will I have to pass an unspoken test?"

"Dunno," she snickered. "It's unspoken. What do you say we continue on? I want to show you through some of the trickier neighborhoods. There's a lot to learn, Trev."

He very much doubted that. The residential blocs were largely indistinctive by design. No one here lived in luxury penthouses while looking down upon hardscrabble unfortunates. The Amity Charter mandated equity in housing, even among the Harmony elites and the command staffs of the three sectors. The President of the Collectorate enjoyed only a few more square meters than the lowest-tier maintenance technician. Turnover through two- and three-year rotations ensured the neighborhoods remained diverse and unable to form insular traditions.

Or so Trevor had assumed.

"Some changes are subtle," Hoshi explained as she piloted the rifter into the Justinia bloc. "Took me a few months to notice."

"Such as?"

"Take Justinia. There are eight hundred residents in these five buildings. Forty percent came from the Dark Quadrant."

Hoshi used a common slur that referred to Boer, Mauritania, Zwahili Kingdom, and Moroccan Prime, whose populations descended from Africans on pre-colonial Earth.

"How can that be? The charter mandated no ethnic clusters. Amity is a counterpoint to the Chancellors' forced migration."

Even as he said the words, Trevor understood the irony. His descendants were Chancellors – he traced his lineage back nine hundred years to men and women who happily cleansed Earth of those they considered "lesser." And Effie? She hailed from Mauritania.

A mocha-skinned ethnic married to a Chancellor was a sight to behold.

"It sounds nice, Trev. In principle. But people are tribal by nature. They want to be surrounded by similar values and customs."

"I thought we were beyond that."

He remembered the homogeneity of Philadelphia Redux before the Chancellors lost the civil war. Even afterward, he encountered few of what his caste long referred to as "indigos." Nineteen years in Harmony surrounded by reps from all forty worlds shifted his mindset.

"You've lived here too long," Hoshi said. "Most residents are short-timers, but they're dozens to hundreds of light-years from home. Living near one's own kind eases the transition."

"Fair enough. But that doesn't explain how they're able to cluster. The residential assignments are beyond their control."

"Not exactly. They've learned how to manipulate the Housing

Authority. They keep track of the applicant rolls from their home worlds plus who's about to leave Amity. When people back home win the lottery, they already know what bloc to request. Sometimes, to the specific flat."

"The Authority assigns at random. It's the law."

She smiled with that figure-it-out-already vibe.

"Ah." Trevor's idealism about Amity dropped a notch. "Bribery."

"Nobody cares if an engineering student from Boer ends up in Justinia bloc or Haldeman bloc. Happy citizens are peaceful."

Trevor thought of all he'd learned as a student to history.

"My ancestors used to say the same about the colonies. Easy for them. They had all the guns and the ships. They could make peace happen real fast."

"That's our goal in Haven. Peace today, peace tomorrow."

Trevor studied Hoshi with a skeptical eye.

"Dorrit's mantra?"

She nodded. "Told me not ten minutes on the job."

"I'm all for peace, but not at the expense of tossing trouble into an airlock. How does clustering affect neighborhood behavior?"

"Varies. In Justinia, they're quiet. Even evasive."

"To us?"

"To any outsider. They'll smile and shake your hand. But they're not much help in an investigation, unless they feel they've been wronged by assholes down the Swiftrak."

"I'll keep it in mind."

"Every bloc's different. Speaking of, we have nineteen more."

"I assume Dorrit told you not to skip even one."

Hoshi smirked. "His exact instruction, with tongue firmly in cheek: 'Stallion is pedantic. Drown him in the details.' I don't think he's an admirer, Trev."

"I won't apologize for having standards." Trevor felt the hairs on the back of his neck stand up. Bastards like Dorrit never failed to set him off. "The details matter, Hoshi. They solve problems and save

23

lives. We're not uniformed babysitters and glad-handers."

"You don't need to convince me."

Maybe he did.

"These are dangerous times, Hoshi. It might seem like we're protected out here. Three warships guarding the station, and the toughest Customs inspectors anywhere. It creates an illusion. I've seen too many people fall for it."

She hid her emotional cues well. Did she think him as paranoid as some of his ex-colleagues on Harmony?

"We're not blind to the threats. And you're right. This uniform stands for something. But we're also not stormtroopers and technocrats. These are regular people in Haven making the most of a great opportunity. We keep them happy, stay out of their way. Live and let live. That's our charge, Trev. It works."

She grabbed his hand and added: "Trust me. I'm on your side."

Trevor heard sincerity in her tone, but he also spent years dealing with the best practitioners of verbal gymnastics. They knew how to telegraph sincerity yet mean not a whit.

"I'll remember your words the first time we're at odds. And we will be. Trust me."

He had no idea just how soon.

4

S IX NEIGHBORHOODS LATER, Hoshi's holobank sprang to life with a notification. She opened the InComm on her wrist plate to review the report. Trevor focused on the headshot of a man in his early twenties. Blond, tiny nose, rigid jaw, emerald green eyes.

"Ulbrecht Hann," he read, as Hoshi spoke the particulars.

"Engineering student at the Maynor School on Episteme. Reported overdue by his mentor. They say he hasn't responded to his personal comm." She sighed with clear annoyance. "They request HVSA to check it out."

"Lives in Andromeda, Flat 529. Looks like we're the closest."

Hoshi rolled her eyes.

"I'm sure it's nothing. Probably partied at the Raison Club, and now he's sleeping it off. Likely disabled his comm. He wouldn't be the first student to take that route."

Apparently, Hoshi took the "live and let live" motto seriously. The blasé approach didn't shock Trevor anymore.

"We're on shift, Hoshi. Let's do our job. The tour can wait."

She reset the rifter's course.

"I thought you said we weren't babysitters."

"He's a grown man who has other grown men worried. That

means we should worry."

Hoshi moaned. "As you wish, First Deputy."

Her tone wasn't called for. Was he imagining things? The woman lost her edge when called upon to check on a resident's health.

No. You're being paranoid. They're not all apathetic drones.

En route to the next housing bloc, Trevor reviewed the man's biography. Arrived from Yaniff seven months ago on an Interstellar Congress grant to study trans-wormhole shielding tech.

"Huh. Interesting."

"What's that?" She asked.

"Trans-wormhole. Ever heard that term before?"

"No. I'm not wired for the things they teach in Episteme."

Amity's third sector, which focused on scientific research and engineering, regularly broke new ground on matters of interstellar concern. Less than one percent of applicants to its many divisions made the annual cut. That placed Ulbrecht Hann in rarefied company.

"It's not my forte either, Hoshi, but it's a strange term, don't you think? We mastered safe, mobile wormhole travel twenty-five years ago. Perhaps they're developing a new generation of worm drives. I'll look into it later."

"Suit yourself."

When they arrived at Andromeda bloc, Hoshi settled the rifter to a hover position outside the Level 5 Emergency Vehicle Mount. She voiced her ID Code toward the EVM's AI interface. A platform jutted out beneath the rifter, and a portal into Level 5 pixelated open.

"OK," she said. "Let's go knock on a drunk man's door."

"And hope that's all it is."

When Trevor hopped out onto the platform, he triggered his standard-issue wrist plate. A hologram displayed the HVSA LinkPass data spool.

"Gradient F7. Stallion. Full access report with trend waves. Resident: Ulbrecht Hann. Haven. Andromeda bloc."

They rounded a corner on approach to Flat 529.

"What are you doing, Trev?"

"Preparing."

Hoshi glared at his holo with jaw agape. They passed two residents in the corridor. She didn't speak until clear of them.

"That's his full LinkPass history. We're not allowed to view it except in emergencies or suspicion of criminal ..."

"I know the regs. I'm not violating the man's rights."

"You're being intrusive. It's not how we do ..."

"Please don't say, 'It's not how we do things here.'"

She grabbed Trevor by the arm and stopped him at 525.

"Dorrit will go on a rampage. He forbids us from viewing LinkPass history without his explicit instruction."

Trevor found a quick end-run.

"The Chief hasn't said ten words to me since I arrived. And you warned me after the fact. I'll know better next time. Right?"

He grinned; Hoshi did not.

"If you stow it quickly, he might not receive a system alert."

"Oh, I think it's far too late for that. We're here."

Hoshi didn't wait for Trevor's approval to press the door chime. Trevor studied the data rather than wait for a verbal reply. He reached a conclusion after Hoshi triggered the chime a second time to no effect.

"Take a look," he told her, flipping the holo in her direction. "Mr. Hann has not engaged with an access point in 9.2 hours."

"That's all? I sleep longer than that on my days off."

Trevor couldn't remember sleeping longer than five hours a day in the past seven years. His rest cycle altered forever when Ana Marie came into his life.

"Here's the problem."

He showed Hoshi trend waves derived from Hann's daily regimen. Like all residents, the man used his gene stamp everywhere he ventured in Amity: Clubs, restaurants, other flats, the Crossway, public rifter checkout, Maynor School, even his personal kiosk for home-cooked meals.

A life constantly tracked. The price for living in Amity.

"With few exceptions, Ulbrecht Hann has followed the same routine for a hundred standard days. See here? His usual sleep cycle. A consistent window from H17 through 23. Last night, he entered the flat at H15. He never used his stamp after that. He's inside."

She raised a brow, but Trevor knew she wasn't sold.

"So, he partied earlier than usual, shut off his comm, and didn't set an alarm. A smart kid made a stupid mistake."

"Maybe. But I'm curious."

"What do you ...?"

"Let's check on the man."

"We have no probable cause to enter his flat, Trev. He's been off the LinkPass Grid for less than ten hours."

Hoshi was right on one count: The law bent over backward to preserve residential privacy. So much so that obtaining a search warrant often proved a legal nightmare.

"I intend to do this by the law, Hoshi. The Amity Charter reserves the right of security and health personnel to breach private quarters when there's adequate suspicion of residential distress. Call me adequately suspicious."

He ignited his G7 credentials to access Flat 529's entry code.

"Worst case: He overslept. He'll be so embarrassed at causing a stir, he'll thank us from saving him further embarrassment."

She rubbed the back of her neck.

"Unless he reports us for Improper Invasion."

Trevor studied everyone in his orbit to catalog their body language. He had memorized three of Hoshi's tics.

"Not you, Sec Deputy. Me."

Trevor overrode the entry sequence. The door slipped aside. Before crossing the threshold, he followed the regs:

"Ulbrecht Hann, this is First Deputy Trevor Stallion of the Haven Security Administration. We are here to investigate a report of your absence from an intended engagement. Please verbally confirm your presence and that you understand my words."

It was a script, of course, and Trevor damn well knew better than to deviate from it. He made that mistake once only. When no one responded, he continued:

"Under Statute 42-C of the Amity Charter, I hereby invoke the right to investigate residential distress. I am entering your home."

Someday, that Charter is going to get one of us killed.

He didn't intend to grab his standard-issue pistol, holstered beneath his red and silver jacket. Famously, pistols had only been fired inside Amity five times since it opened. Two were accidents. One death. Not bad considering how many millions had passed through the station. Like the warships outside, it created the illusion of a world shielded from danger.

The front room was small and efficient, like ninety-nine percent of flats across Amity. It was also tidy. A loveseat, two chairs, vidscreen, dimmed lights on a softly padded floor. Pair of slipshoes at the loveseat's base. Walls barren. Opposite the living space, a kitchenette with two cabinets and countertop kiosk. Didn't appear to have been used recently.

It spoke of a quiet, disciplined man leading an orderly life.

Too orderly for Trevor's taste. He steeled himself for the bedroom, at present shrouded in darkness.

He glanced over his shoulder.

"Feel free to join me," he told Hoshi, who had not crossed the threshold. "Launch a snapdrone to run a BluScan."

"What? Why?"

"Hedging my bets. Do it, please."

He didn't wait for her objection and proceeded inward.

The bedroom auto lit as he entered. It seemed to be owned by a different human altogether. Lunatic, more like.

The bed linens lay disheveled everywhere but on the bed. The air mattress had deflated. A melon-sized red stain painted the wall above the headboard. The standup wardrobe lay on its side, one door unhinged, clothes strewn on the floor.

Another red stain, similar size, plastered to the wall where the wardrobe once stood. Trevor stepped closer. He saw a crease in the wall and recognized human blood.

Trevor knew what he was about to find, either on the other side of the deflated bed or in the water room. He'd studied the literature and crime-scene scans from every world where these things occurred. The pattern was unmistakable.

He stepped gingerly through the evolving crime scene. When the water room's light flickered on, his eyes caught two things: Shattered glass and a disjointed arm on the floor.

Only when he stepped into the threshold did Trevor see what was left of Ulbrecht Hann. The former engineering student lay in a pool of his own blood, but that wasn't the interesting bit.

"I warned them this would happen," he whispered. "Cudfrucker."

The dead man's eyes were wide open with joy, his smile frozen in unbridled ecstasy. However, his jaw was broken – the bone visible near the base of his left ear. His forehead was battered and caked in a red soup that filled his hair like an off-brand gel.

He was naked and twisted. His arms and legs contorted at the joints in manners not allowed by nature. His penis was hard and purple, and his right scrotum had burst.

"What happened in here?" Hoshi asked at the bedroom door.

"Call it in. Better for Dorrit to hear from you."

"Call in what?"

"MOD."

Trevor pointed into the bathroom. Hoshi shook her head.

"You can't be serious, Trev. There's no way he could ..."

She slapped a hand over her mouth upon seeing the remains and turned away.

"OK, fine," Trevor said. "I'll notify Dorrit."

Hoshi squeezed his arm.

"No. You can't report an MOD. W-we don't have proof."

"Sure we do. Should I show you the case scans from thirty-two planets? This is Motif."

"No. He could have lost his mind on any number of drugs. Maybe something they developed in Episteme. We ..."

"Have to report this for what it is. I understand the implications, Hoshi. But we can't hide it: There's Motif on Amity."

She backed away and begged Trevor to hold off.

"Yes. We have to report it. Of course. But not as an MOD. We call it a Case 10."

She couldn't be serious.

"Unexplained death? Hoshi, the man broke every limb and smashed his head into the wall in at least three locations. Yet, he was laughing to his final breath. This is a Motif overdose."

He pointed out the snapdrone now flying through the bedroom.

"I guarantee the BluScan will pick up K3 residue."

Kerasunehyde Trilucin (K3) was the unique active ingredient inside the drug, making it susceptible to calibrated sensors.

"Trev, you're getting ahead of yourself. There's not one reported case of Motif passing through Customs."

"*Reported.* The sensors aren't foolproof, and certain metals are known to camouflage it. Smugglers are good at what they do. There are ninety-two thousand potential customers on Amity. I doubt Ulbrecht Hann was the only one who wanted to fly."

Trevor opened InComm on his wrist plate and made the call. First day on the job, and it was about to get worse.

Much worse.

5

EFFIE OFFERED SOUND ADVICE before Trevor left Harmony Sector for his new job. "If you do make a stink, at least wait until you've built trust equity." Fine for her to say; she was a diplomat. She doled out her opinions in measured doses.

Trevor knew everyone she worked with in the DRC; couldn't stand the lot of them. He smiled at social events, shook hands, engaged in pleasantries, and sedated himself with multiple trips to the bar.

"Nice concept," he told his wife while packing. "I'd prefer they earn *my trust* first."

She lingered in the bedroom doorway.

"You weren't a cynic when we married, Trevor."

"Back then, you called me an old soul. It's more or less the same."

Effie frowned at the assessment.

"You never fail to make my case. Trevor, you'll be threading a needle over there. Avoid any incidents, and I think another door will open in six months, give or take. Memories are short."

That was her go-to line, but Trevor didn't buy it. Memories and grudges lingered in the political world.

"Six months with my head down and my mouth shut will not turn me into a new man. I'm well past the point of no return."

32

Her cheery outlook dissipated.

"What am I to do with you?"

He chuckled. "I gave you seven years to plot a solution. Me? I got nothing."

She glanced into the common room, where Ana napped on the sofa. Effie closed the door.

"It's not quantum algorithmics, Trevor. You pour every ounce of affection into our little girl and leave nothing for the rest of us."

He zipped up the satchel.

"Not true. Fell mad in love with you the first day we met. It's all still there. You just don't want it anymore."

The words fell off his lips with reckless disregard. Yet he said them at last. He wanted her to confront their divide.

Effie kept her distance and shaded her eyes.

"You're right, Trevor. I don't."

The literal opposite of what he dreamed of hearing.

"How long?" He asked.

"It doesn't matter. I still love you. I'm just not *interested*."

"Strategic word choice. Just like a diplomat." He grabbed the satchel and slung it over his shoulder. "No worries. I won't beg."

Effie grabbed him before he reached the door.

"You're not going to leave without talking to her."

He shook off his wife.

"Of course not. But she won't understand."

"Because she's learned from her Papa: Every truth hides a lie."

She wasn't being fair, so Trevor searched for a cruel reply.

"Like every time you tell me, 'I love you,' when what you mean is, 'I need a quick fuck to remind me of Reginald Endowi.'"

He regretted the words when they passed his lips. Standard operating procedure. It was also the first time he mentioned the DRC colleague she'd been cuddling for months.

She didn't deny it, which made sense. Effie never shied away from the hard bits.

33

"Whatever our issues, we're still her parents. That won't change. Before the situation goes any further south, I ask you to be on your best behavior over there. Don't ruin it. This may be your last chance."

Those words continued to gnaw at Trevor even as he contemplated the gruesome scene in Ulbrecht Hann's flat.

Best behavior. Don't ruin it. Last chance.

Somehow, he'd been anointed as the villain.

The lifetechs would arrive soon to recover the body. Dorrit might also haul his considerable ass over here. Hoshi warned him the Chief would rampage at a reported MOD.

Let him try.

"Hoshi, redirect the snapdrone. I want it to scan for K3. Start with the wardrobe and the nightstand."

"You think there's more?"

Trevor glared at the twisted body and sighed.

"Oh, yes."

She entered new orders into her wrist plate, and the hornet-sized device unleashed a red scan, beginning at the fallen wardrobe.

"How much?"

"We'll find one lonely pad or an entire stash. I doubt he supplies, but we can't rule it out."

"Why only one?"

The question surprised him. Had she not been briefed?

"Most users – especially new ones – buy two pads."

"Why?"

She wasn't up to speed. Trevor was shocked but not surprised.

"Motif is expensive, and the deaths are common knowledge. So, Black Star suppliers make the drug more appealing. Buy one, get the second ninety percent off. It's a loss leader with a special pitch: The first pad will give you a great ride, but it's the second go that provides the total experience."

She nodded in a moment of clarity.

"Sounds like a two-for-one drink deal at the Raison Club."

"Same principle. They get you inside. The rest is pure profit."

Hoshi had settled into a more professional demeanor the past few minutes as reality set in.

"How do you know all this, Trev?"

He constructed an answer that didn't sound condescending.

"I read. And I have a contact in SI. I see the field reports."

Her lips puckered.

"I think everyone in Sec Admin should see those."

"Best idea I've heard all day, Hoshi."

Trevor hoped she would take the cue and confront Dorrit, but he dared not bet good credits on it.

The snapdrone reached the bedstand, where the red lines from the scanner morphed to green. Hoshi studied her wrist plate.

"K3."

"OK then. Let's see what Mr. Hann was hiding."

He opened the two drawers, both of which were empty. Trevor ran his hand against the underside until he felt a bump. He tugged at the object, but it resisted before finally giving way. The prize was black and coin-shaped.

"Is that a lodestone?" She asked.

"It is. Huh. He must have thought the metal would shield K3."

Lodestones were magnetic components to gravstraps, built into the in-soles of every resident's shoes and easily activated in the event of sudden gravity loss.

"I don't understand," she said. "Lodestones are registered in the inventory spools. Why would he remove one?"

"Gravstraps only require two of their lodestones. The third is a backup." He saw the surprise in her eyes, a trait becoming far too frequent. "Hann was an engineering student. I'm sure he knew."

Trevor rotated each side of the object in counter directions until the lock slits matched. He pulled apart the lodestone to reveal a small white pad no bigger than a fingernail.

"Motif in the wild. Place the glossy side on your tongue, give it about thirty seconds to melt, and enjoy the ride."

She leaned in for a closer look.

"How can something so small destroy so many lives?"

"That's not the question we need to ask."

She backed away and recalled the snapdrone.

"How did it pass through Customs?"

If that was how it arrived. Trevor held back his evolving theory. He decided to test Hoshi's instinct.

"One more question even more important."

She nodded before softening her voice.

"How much more is on the station?"

He studied the life-altering pad that had seduced more than a billion humans in the past three years.

"Far more than anyone is willing to admit."

A third voice entered the fray.

"Now that is an assumption with no supporting evidence."

Chief Hannibal Dorrit consumed the doorway, hands on hips. He filled out better upright, but his girth was unique on Amity and, by Trevor's standards, downright obscene. How long since he last reported for a mandatory fit room session?

Dorrit glanced away from Trevor and focused instead on Hoshi, who saluted. Trevor had never seen military deference applied in Sec Admin. If Dorrit expected the same from his new First Deputy, he'd have a long cudfrucking wait.

"Show me the body."

Hoshi led him to the water room, where he studied the scene for a moment and let out a prodigious groan from his considerable gut.

"A promising life undone too soon. Pity."

The coverup began straightaway.

6

DORRIT PAID TREVOR NO MIND when he asked Hoshi, "Have you scanned the premises?"

She cleared her throat.

"All but the water room, Chief."

"Hand me the snapdrone and transfer the data report to the Executive Partition."

Did he hear Dorrit right? Was the bastard really doing this in front of his second in command? Adjusting the scene before the lifetechs arrived? Was he about to take possession of the Motif pad and make it disappear?

Trevor asked, "What's happening here, Chief?"

Dorrit acknowledged Trevor with a wispy smile between large, overindulgent cheeks.

"Doing my job, Mr. Stallion. Protecting Haven Sector."

"How's that, sir?"

Trevor heard a faint, dismissive chuckle. Dorrit stared with the smugness of a card shark who knew he couldn't lose.

"Before you called in the MOD, I'm sure Hoshi warned you against it. Yes?"

"She did. As senior officer on site, I had final word. And this *was* an MOD."

His eyes latched onto the lodestone and its content.

"Apparently. But as you will soon learn, Mr. Stallion, we in Haven handle sensitive matters with discretion. We're not so heavy-handed or ... I don't know, let's say *verbally tactless* ... as some of you in Harmony might be."

Trevor ignored the obvious broadside to the incident that got him tossed from Harmony Sec Admin.

"Chief Dorrit, I'm the appointed First Deputy, which means I am the senior investigating officer for HVSA. According to Amity regs, I took charge of this case the moment we discovered Mr. Hann."

Dorrit retrieved a cloth from his chest pocket and wiped his nose.

"Day one, and you're quoting regs to me. Apparently, you learned nothing in your prior position."

Modulate your tone, Trevor. Don't give him a reason ...

"I am the longest serving security officer on Amity, and I'm merely stating the law. All data from this investigation falls under my direct supervision, with your wise consult, of course."

Wise. Trevor carefully slipped in a small deference.

"He's right, Chief."

Hoshi showed a backbone. OK, so she wasn't hopeless.

Her support gave Dorrit pause. Even led to a begrudging nod.

"You know the law, Mr. Stallion. But the power you reference is not absolute. Any investigation will be conducted at my discretion."

Not the first time he'd been talked down to by a technocrat who'd grown too comfortable with his alleged power.

"No worries, Chief. I'll be discreet while I investigate."

Dorrit stared at the lodestone.

"We'll discuss the particulars in my office, Mr. Stallion."

"Trev, if you don't mind, Chief."

The big man's flexing brows suggested otherwise.

"How do you suppose the victim extracted the magnetic core?"

Dorrit was testing him, so Trevor played along.

"As an engineer, he would have access to a phasic wrench in Episteme. Then again, so would any maintenance tech in Amity."

"What are you suggesting?"

"The pads may have been planted in the lodestone before he bought them."

"I see. You imply there's a Motif operation on the station?"

So that was the test. Dorrit wanted to label Trevor an alarmist.

"I stated nothing of the kind, Chief. I'll need to track the man's history and interview his associates. We can't rule it out."

Dorrit reached for the lodestone.

"May I?"

Trevor complied. If Dorrit intended to end-run an investigation, at least Trevor had a witness.

"Are you aware, Trev ... I may call you that, yes? Are you aware of the scandal that will arise if the public learns of this?"

"It would unnerve people. Yes."

Dorrit resealed the lodestone.

"We're one of only two places in the Collectorate to avoid this scourge, Trev. Do you know the other?"

"Aeterna."

He nodded. "And even if the immortals fell victim, they'd consider it a minor inconvenience. Die horribly only to regenerate ten minutes later." Trevor heard disdain in his tone; the usual mask for immortal-envy. "However, all but ten current residents of Amity are mortal. They value the safe harbor we provide. Any suspicion that Motif is passing Customs and being sold on this station would undermine our authority and their trust."

Rather than challenge Dorrit's obvious design at silencing an investigation, Trevor took the gentle road.

"I agree, Chief. Amity was built to bring together humans of all persuasions in common cause."

"Correct. You and your brother have lived here longer than almost everyone. You've seen the great work firsthand."

"I have, Chief. I'm proud of it."

"You'd hate to have a role in corrupting that progress."

"I would. As a senior officer of Sec Admin, what I'd hate more would be allowing a problem to fester until it compromises everything Amity stands for."

To Trevor's great surprise, his boss laid a hefty hand on his shoulder and sighed with what sounded like relief.

"Excellent. We share the same interest. Which is why you will lead an investigation into illicit drug use in Haven, but not Motif."

Same interest, my ass.

"Excuse me, Chief?"

"Your report, which you will co-author with Hoshi, will avoid any reference to Motif. Rather, you will report that the victim appears to have died from a massive overdose of a toxic compound not yet identified, pending a phasic analysis by lifetechs."

"Chief, this is ..."

Dorrit removed that friendly hand and waved Trevor silent.

"You will insist you found no additional evidence of this compound in Mr. Hann's flat, and your initial conjecture is that he crafted it on his own. Now, now," he told both deputies, "before you express your exasperation, allow me to explain.

"This report will permit you to investigate Mr. Hann's activities since he arrived. You'll have lease to interview anyone you desire. But you will never mention Motif. If anyone suspects your true purpose, you will disavow any link to Motif."

Cudfrucker. These people are all alike.

"What about the physical evidence on the snapdrone?" He pointed to the lodestone. "Or that?"

Dorrit lock-sealed the tiny device.

"I studied your jacket, Trev. Your service record is exemplary in spite of the obvious handicap. Can't say the same for your brother."

"Don't bring Connor into this, please."

Dorrit's features softened.

"You're right. He's not one of us. I overstepped. My point is this: You have devoted most of your life to Amity's betterment. Aspire to that standard in this investigation, within my stated parameters."

Coverup parameters.

These were the moments when Trevor often initiated a game of self-sabotage. He took a deep breath and thought of Ana; she was a good salve.

"Chief, did you know my grandfather?"

Dorrit shrugged, no doubt wondering about relevance.

"After a fashion. I spoke with Maximillian on occasion, but I never had a chance to befriend the man before he died."

Five years felt like yesterday.

"My grandfather loved this place. He wanted Amity to be perfect, but he knew it would only be as great as the people inside it. He taught me vigilance above all else. Seal the cracks before they expand. He would be appalled by what we're discussing."

Dorrit did not shift into offended-authoritarian mode. He eyed his deputies in equal measure.

"Maximillian Vanover was a product of a different era. Peace is simple when threats to it can be easily eradicated. Such is not the case in the age of Motif and Black Star. Our best hope at cleansing Amity of the scourge is to fight a quiet war."

"Half measures, you mean. One hand tied."

"At times, it will feel that way. Progress will seem slow. But it *will be* progress, I assure you. So long as you follow the parameters."

Trevor heard the lifetechs enter the flat. Dorrit ordered Hoshi to show them back. She complied but winced her displeasure. At least, Trevor thought that's what he detected.

Then he saw something else, this time in Dorrit: Uncertainty.

The fat man's eyes betrayed the weightiness of his proposed plan. Truth slapped Trevor upside the head like a blast rifle.

This isn't the first time. Cudfrucker!

Trevor refused to let the opportunity slip away.

"How many others have there been, Chief?"

Dorrit avoided Trevor's eyes.

41

"Other what?" He said.

"MODs."

"None." Then Dorrit muttered, "Officially."

Dorrit must've known he couldn't contain the truth any longer.

"Unofficially?" Trevor asked.

"Four."

"How long?"

"Nine months."

"Findings?"

"No connection between the deceased."

Keep your cool, Trevor. Earn some of that trust equity.

"So, Chief, either we have a problem in Customs or an active distribution network on the station. Or both."

Dorrit watched the lifetechs enter the water room.

"Welcome to Haven, First Deputy. If you have further questions, address them to me directly. Keep the paranoia to yourself."

Trev heard that line before. Central transferred him a day later.

"I'll try to contain my comments to the facts in front of me, Chief."

Dorrit grunted as he glanced back at Trevor. Yeah, his bullshit detector rose to Status Red.

"See that you do, Trev."

Dorrit wandered into the midst of the lifetechs and whispered instructions as they took charge of body retrieval. The cylindrical trauma carriage hovered outside the water room.

Trevor developed an action plan while pacing in the outer room. Hoshi soon joined him.

"The Chief has everything under control," she said. "He wants us to clear the corridor."

"Sure. No sense scaring the wits out of the neighbors."

"He says we're to direct any inquiries to HVSA."

Of course they were.

"And anyone who happens to follow through will find our official response to be lacking. Right?"

42

Hoshi bowed her head as they departed the flat.

"Chief says the deceased was a nobody. People won't care."

"Disagree. Bio said he has a mother on Yaniff. She'll be more than a little interested to know why this happened."

Hoshi said nothing, which Trevor understood. Deaths were rare on Amity – natural or otherwise. The DRC handled all notifications of kin, meaning no one in Sec Admin ever faced the awkward task.

"He left behind both parents and three younger sisters, Hoshi. Two hundred ninety light-years away. So yeah, it will seem like he's nobody. If they seek legal recourse, they'll be paid for pain and suffering. Enough credits to move on from their grief."

She held up. "You make it seem so ... cold."

"No, it's practical. Just like the way Flat 529 will be sterilized and prepared for a new occupant. Perhaps another engineering student. Who knows?"

"Life goes on. Residential space is at a premium, Trev."

He saw her fighting off the emotions.

"Don't I know. My point is, they'll turn over the matter quickly and quietly. Amity's reputation as a safe harbor will remain intact."

"That's the goal."

"The political goal. Yes. What if it's in danger? And what if we're too efficient for our own good?"

She moaned like someone who sorely regretted working today's shift. Why couldn't Dorrit have assigned someone else to escort Trevor about Haven?

"You're going to disregard the Chief's parameters. Aren't you?"

Trevor hated leading questions – unless he was asking them.

"He charged me with investigating a drug overdose. I intend to pursue the answers wherever they lead. It's why they pay me."

"I'll be trapped in the middle."

"Yep. You'll have to confront your conscience, but I'm sure you'll come down on the side of justice."

He wasn't sure. Not even close. But Trevor was stuck with Hoshi unless Dorrit said otherwise.

They smiled at passersby and asked the curious to move along. Thankfully, the neighborhood was thin mid-shift. At a quiet moment, with the corridor clear in both directions, Hoshi said:

"I assume you'll want to start questioning his contacts right away."

"Best when fresh."

"Where do we start?"

"Episteme."

"If you don't mind, I like to work on a full stomach. It's almost time for luncheon. If you'd like, we can get a quick bite at Hamish Bistro. We passed it back at L3. Remember?"

He didn't feel peckish until she brought up the subject. However, she suggested a so-called 'garden fresh' restaurant. Not a kiosk in sight. Hoshi had an exotic budget for a Second Deputy.

"I'll pass, thank you. I have noodles waiting for me at home."

Trevor thought to add, "I'm a cheap bastard," but he preferred to hold that in reserve.

"All moved in?"

"More or less. Living with my brother for now."

"Is that Connor? The one the Chief was talking about?"

They'd known each other for a few hours, and already she dove into family matters.

"It is. He's seven years younger. And to answer your inevitable question: No, we're nothing alike."

He used to celebrate that difference. Now, it worried him.

7

E FFIE DIDN'T UNDERSTAND why Trevor resisted moving into Sec Admin's executive housing. She predicted the brothers would be at each other's throats within a day.

"You don't understand C," he told her. "You never did."

She rolled her eyes with the ease of a polished curtsy.

"I love Connor. But you are order; he is chaos."

"We always find a way to meet in the middle."

Effie laughed as they stood outside their flat, Trevor having flung a bag over his shoulder.

"Sure. After a little bloodshed."

She had a point.

"That was a long time ago. I put too much pressure on him. C's a grown man now. He knows I meant well."

They weren't twenty minutes removed from Trevor's broadside about her lover, but Effie displayed a short memory. She brushed at his uniform with the attention given during better times.

"I don't want his antics to become a distraction. He'll draw out the worst in you. I've seen it before."

"That *is* his superpower. Fortunately, I know all his tricks. And frankly, being alone is a bigger distraction. Plus, he only lives two minutes from Sec Admin."

"Good. The moment he goes off his nut, pack your things and move to exec housing."

He pulled away from Effie. She'd only go on about reasons to push his brother aside. She never appreciated their bond.

"Enough, OK? Talk to Ana for me. Tell her I'll be back around in a few days."

The girl had sat on her bed, staring at her father in tears and clutching a doll. She said nothing and resisted his plea for a hug. He left her alone before falling into tears himself.

I have to get the hell out of here.

"She'll come to her senses, Trevor. I'll make sure she calls your pom when you're off-shift."

"Yeah. Thanks. That would mean the world."

One less weight among many.

He took the Crossway train to Haven and checked out a rifter at the station docks. Connor lived in Demeter, a twenty-two level high-rise within earshot of the Crossway. He had given Trevor the LinkPass sequence and told his older brother to make himself at home. The quiet flat was a cluttered mess but for the bed, which Connor had made with military efficiency – like Trevor taught him growing up together in Harmony.

Trevor smiled, tossed his bag on the bed, and reported for duty.

Hours later, he returned to his new home for a quick lunch of noodles and veg before starting the investigation. This time, the flat was occupied.

The front room had been converted to a holographic sea. Its clear blue water rose to Trevor's knees. He heard the slow rise and fall of ocean waves, the call of a seabird, and detected the hint of a salty spray. Those surprises paled against what floated atop the water.

Connor sat nude in the lotus position, eyes closed, arms extended like a bird's wings folded upward. His golden hair, which he usually tied into a ponytail to meet employment regs, fell over his shoulders and onto his well-sculpted chest. Connor's penis, long a source of pride, extended upward like a missile launcher.

I can't wish that one away.

Trevor didn't bother asking what his brother was into this time.

"That's a fine welcome," he said en route to the kitchenette.

Connor neither flinched nor opened his eyes.

"Oh. Hi, bruv."

Trevor spun up the kiosk directory and tapped the condensed lunch he knew Connor kept in healthy supply. He selected a pellet from the inventory cabinet and slipped it into the processor.

OK, fine. Time to deal with this.

"How can you afford an antigrav bubble, C?"

"Can't. It's a twenty-day lease."

The kiosk hummed. Lunch was eighty seconds away.

"I trust you went through a legitimate dealer this time."

"Yes, bruv. Auto-signed my life away for six hundred creds."

"Pricey. Does it meet your lofty standards?"

Connor peeked with one eye.

"Curious men don't set standards. It's all about opening doors."

Trevor chuckled.

"Insight into what lies beyond and beneath. Heard it before."

"Don't throw dirt, bruv. It's perfection. You should try it."

"Sure, C. Remind me the day before your lease is up. Apologies for interrupting. Must've forgotten when your shift ended."

Connor opened his other eye and snapped his fingers. The ocean vanished. He unwrapped his legs and leaped off the bubble.

"All good. I been hovering for an hour. Nothing like it."

Trevor leaned against the counter and begrudgingly admired his brother. Connor built a body worthy of sculptured immortality. Every muscle that could rip did.

"I have an open mind. Tell me."

Connor smirked as he stretched. More like an exhibition, really. A show to demonstrate the reward of spending more hours per annum in a fitroom than anyone for the past ten standard years.

"It's not in the telling, bruv. It's experiential art."

A non-answer. Typical.

"OK, throw me a nugget. Where did you learn this technique?"

"A mate in EngSec 9. Jeon. He's Shailin. That's a tribe on Indonesia Prime. They call the technique Loutah. He says they've been practicing it for five hundred years."

The kiosk dinged, expelling a slender dish with steaming lunch. Trevor grabbed a fork and shuffled the noodles.

"They use an antigrav bubble and a hologram, too?"

Connor winked. "You know me. I like to shift up the recipe."

"It's original. Very ... *you.*"

"Thanks. Hey, while you got the kiosk, can you pop in one of those for me? And add a pellet of red cabbage."

"You gave up half your space for me. Least I could do." Trevor hesitated before ordering the pellets. "Should give you enough time to dress. Then we can sit down and have a little lunch together."

Connor held his ground, forming a sheepish grin that always preceded something Trevor didn't want to hear.

"So, yeah. It's like this. I ain't big on clothes when I'm at home."

Well, Effie did warn me.

"What? You traipse around here in the nude all day?"

"This is my private space. I live as I was born."

"Huh. Is that more of the Shailin philosophy?"

Connor got a kick out of his older brother. He grabbed those ripped abs for a full-on belly laugh.

"You still got the same droll sense of humor. Trev-*or.* You gonna order up my pellets or what?"

"Sure. But would it be so difficult to slip on ... something? At this point, even a pelvic strap would be an improvement."

Connor threw up his arms in mock indignance.

"What? You don't like staring at my cock? Do you know how many partners have enjoyed my miracle?"

"Connor, if you'll ..."

"Men hundreds of light-years away still speak of my artistry."

"Ah. Deepstream with them, do you?"

He shrugged. "Once in a while."

"And when you bring a boyfriend home, is he good with fulltime exposure?"

Connor pushed past Trevor and ordered the pellets.

"I hate that term, bruv. My lovers are full grown."

Trevor wondered where he went wrong in this conversation. Oh, yes. Now he remembered: The instant he entered the flat and didn't turn around.

"I apologize on all counts. That whole *display* ... it threw me."

"No worries. We ain't lived together in nine years. And truth is, I'm in a dry spell. Haven't laid anyone in seven months."

Trevor risked a bit of snark.

"Run out of fresh inventory?"

Connor pretended to take a dagger to the heart.

"Sharp, bruv. Sharp. But nah. I took a break. Truth is, I'm tired of getting my heart broke. Every time I fall in love, the prick finishes up his rotation and he's off-station."

Connor said it in a light-hearted vein, but Trevor sensed genuine pain. His little brother adopted the defensive style soon after the war, when they faced an uncertain future.

"Did anyone ever ask you to leave the station with him?"

"Just one. Kofi Amonesh."

"I remember him. I think. About three years ago?"

"Yeah. Never had anybody love me that hard. We even talked about marriage. Scared the shit out of me."

OK. This was new. Connor had often confided about his affairs, but Trevor assumed they were limited by sexual appetite.

"What happened?"

"Moroccan Prime."

"Oh. That."

"Kofi actually thought he could bring a Chancellor home to his family and nobody would be killed."

"It would've been a risk. But times are changing. Attitudes about our caste aren't as rigid as they used to be."

Connor winced.

"I love you, Trevor. I do. Really. Best brother I could ask for. But sometimes ... you don't see through the veil."

"Which means what?"

The kiosk produced Connor's steaming lunch. He threw a pinch of pepper on the dish and grabbed a fork.

"Let's eat."

Connor plopped on the loveseat and wrapped his legs lotus style. He sniffed the meal's aroma and sighed.

"I remember the day you introduced me to KNV," he said. "It was the first really good meal we had on Amity."

Changing the subject. Another Connor tactic. Trevor sat in a chair across from his brother.

"About the veil. What did you mean, C?"

He slurped noodles and wiped his lips.

"Simple, bruv. Look at us. We're at least six inches taller than just about anybody in the crowd. They see it in our eyes, our jawbones ..." Connor set down his fork. "Don't get me wrong. I love my body. It's my opening sales pitch. And I don't give a fuck about the genetic engineering ... we're as human as any men. Better even. But nobody has to ask ... straightaway they know we're Chancellors."

They indulged in this topic before. Trevor always suspected Effie took grief from her family when they married, but her relatives never raised an objection in his presence. Every Deepstream with the in-laws went well.

"They know we're not responsible for the past, C. Yes, there's bias. But they recognize what we've given to the station. And most ... well, *some* ... still remember Grandfather Max." Trevor didn't have the time to rehash their lingering 'handicap,' as Chief Dorrit called it.

"Still, I'm sorry about Kofi. You two had something special. Have you heard from him since?"

Connor grabbed his fork and slurped noodles. He talked with his mouth full.

"Not a word. When I refused to leave Amity, he called me a Chancellor cunt and stormed out. Just as well. Who the hell wants to live on Moroccan Prime?"

"Sounds like that marriage would not have worked."

Connor snickered. "You think, bruv?"

Amid his own chuckling, Trevor said:

"You're a piece of work, Connor."

"Correction. Work in progress. That's what the Loutah is about. Digging down to see how much more work I have to do."

"Oh? And what have you learned?"

"Not sure yet. I was actually hoping ..."

Connor cut himself short and lapped his tongue against his top lip, an old tic signifying regret at having spoken too soon.

"Hoping what? Tell me, C."

"Maybe save it for later. You just moved in. I don't want to overstep my bounds."

"C'mon, now. What was my first commandment after we were left on our own?"

He grew a nostalgic smile.

"No secrets. We share everything."

"Yep. Got us through the worst days."

"Sure did. But we were kids then."

"Now we're men. What of it? Men can't share?"

"It's not that easy, bruv. You probably can't tell, but I'm thrilled you're here. I knew you and Effie were going through a tough stretch, and then with what happened on Harmony ... well, I was really touched when you asked about crashing here."

Trevor thought that call had been awkward. Connor seemed hesitant at the time, as if backed into a corner out of obligation.

"I was surprised you agreed, C. I know you've loved being on your own all these years."

"Sure. It's been ... fun. But I kind of liked those years when it was you and me. I missed the Stallion brothers."

"Me, too. So, what is it you hope?"

Connor finished his luncheon and set the dish aside.

"I know everyone thinks I'm rootless. I've been bouncing around the station for ten years. After all this time, the best I can say is I'm cleaning washer fans in the air recycling system."

"No need to explain. You haven't found your niche. The search is harder for some."

Connor shaded his eyes and cracked his considerable knuckles.

"Yeah. That. I think I'm close to something big. It's always been right there in front of me, but I couldn't see it. The Loutah is helping me understand."

"Good for you."

"I'm scared, to tell the truth. That's why I'm so happy you're here. I was hoping you could help me make sense of it. Like you always used to do."

Trevor thought his little brother had grown past accepting counsel from anyone – let alone the man who all but raised him. Yet today, he reached out. His indomitable confidence wavered.

"I've always been here for you, C. You might not have felt that way after Effie and Ana came along, but you were my whole world before them. Anything you need ..."

"Thanks, bruv. Means the world."

Trevor wasn't so blind as to believe each encounter with his unpredictable brother would settle into the old, familiar rhythm, but today's opening exchange encouraged him.

"We'll talk later. I should run. An overly long luncheon on my first day won't sit well with the new boss."

"Sure, Trev. Oh, and the same promise goes for me. Anything you want to share ... I'll give a good listen."

Was he hinting at something? Connor frowned as he added:

"Effie left a message on my pom while I was at work. Asked me to go easy on you."

"Ah. She say why?"

"Didn't have to."

He would've been shocked if Effie spilled any news. She avoided loose lips and hated people who thrived on verbal theatrics.

Trevor took both empty dishes to the kitchenette and left them there for Connor to sterilize.

"We'll compare schedules. Find time for an evening out. Yes?"

"Love it, bruv. Already got ideas."

"Never had a doubt." Trevor couldn't leave without nipping one tiny issue in the bud. "So, about your fulltime exposure ..."

"Living as I was born."

"Yeah. That. I'm not terribly comfortable with it. You have an amazing body. You're proud. I understand. But I'd appreciate a small gesture. A compromise, for when I'm around."

Connor's shoulders sagged.

"Bruv. I hear you. Solution is real simple."

"Oh?"

"Follow my lead. The only reason you're uncomfortable is because you're clothed. If we're both nude, it'll seem natural."

Trevor stifled a laugh. What did Effie say? "He draws out the worst in you."

Nope. Not this time.

"C, I can say with confidence that within seconds after you were born, a nurse wrapped you in a cloth. Your first excursion au naturel was brief. I'm sure you don't climb inside the washer fans nude. Look, I don't want to disrupt your life, but if I'm going to live here, I can't stare at you like this all day."

Connor smirked. "You're jealous of my cock. Fine. I have thongs. But that's as far as I go."

"It's a start."

"But when you're on shift ..."

"Yes. I'll call ahead if you're not expecting me."

"Excellent, bruv. I think this is going to work out nice. Stallion brothers ride again."

It felt like the right way to leave things, but as Trevor approached the door and reset his mind toward the job that lay ahead, he fell upon an interesting notion.

"You work in EngSec 9. Yes?" Connor nodded. "What are your maintenance zones?"

"Blue, mostly. Z40 to 50."

"Huh. That's near the Halifax R&D complex."

"Why? You looking to learn the ins and outs of washer fans?"

He recalled Ulbrecht Hann's employment jacket and specifically the division where the dead man studied trans-wormhole shielding tech. Trevor's first interrogations would take him to Episteme.

"Amity maintenance teams go about their business largely invisible, but I'd wager they see and hear damn near everything. Sound right?"

Connor shrugged. "We got eyes and ears, too. They just don't allow us to talk out of turn."

"Of course not."

Within certain parameters, Trevor thought.

"I'll share later, C. And you're right. This feels nice."

Trevor returned to the job recharged. He had an investigation to run and many answers to uncover. The real trick was doing it without pissing off the wrong people this time.

8

TREVOR WANTED TO FILE his incident report at Sec Admin HQ like he wanted a phasic drill inside his skull. Instead, he flew his rifter to the public docks and took a lift to the Crossway. He found a comfortable chair on the platform of Mogandi Station and opened his wrist plate.

A thin crowd of Havenites inched forward as a tubular train approached. A disinterested voice filled the platform.

"Attention. Blue Line approaching. Destinations: Haven Kimba, Harmony Midvale, Harmony Aleksanyan. Please stand clear until full stop. Allow all passengers to disembark."

This wasn't his train – he'd be heading in the opposite direction. Yet the scene reminded him of the early days, when he brought Connor to the Crossway. After they spent time watching folks from all over the Collectorate come and go, the brothers used their unlimited LinkPass to ride between sectors, check out rifters, and wander Amity with no set destination.

People-watching used to be great fun. Amity featured a diverse collection of humanity, in stark contrast to the homogeneity of each member planet. The brothers guessed who came from what home world and passionately debated the merits of their case.

They pointed out the smallest features that might suggest ethnic or racial differences. Over time, Trevor thought they lost sight of the central tie: All were human.

"Feels like a lifetime ago," he mused.

Now, he studied passengers for body language. What did they give away about their lives? Their state of mind? Most Havenites worked in either Harmony or Episteme, fulfilling roles in the apparatus of government or supporting the station's goal of advancing worlds through scientific vision.

For the most part, they were the unseen but essential workers like Connor. The ones who kept the lights on, the water running, and the air flowing. Purposeful drones leading ordinary lives while making twice what they would back home.

How did Ulbrecht Hann feel about life on Amity? Would his travel history across the station reveal any interesting trends? Trevor intended to jump on that after the first batch of interviews. Now, to that tricky incident report.

He expanded the holo and dictated, his voice steady but low to avoid drawing attention. He described Ulbrecht's corpse in purely clinical terms. The rest was another matter.

Dorrit told him to investigate the death as a drug overdose, to never mention Motif during said pursuit. However, he didn't explicitly order Trevor to scrape the word from his incident report.

Trevor reflected. *Yes.* His memory was perfect on that score.

"I diagnosed the presence of Motif based upon my understanding of extensive studies on the subject as well as my discovery of a lick pad which I found among the deceased's possessions. He hid the object in a modified gravstrap lodestone. A simple BluScan found the pad, suggesting the deceased incorrectly believed the magnetic shielding would allow K3 to evade detection.

"I do not believe the deceased brought Motif onboard Amity when he arrived seven months ago. This does not preclude that the drug initially evaded detection at Customs. However, it raises questions of how the deceased procured the drug and whether Motif is being sold on Amity Station. My investigation will examine these concerns."

Trevor thought better of his wording. No sense in letting Dorrit pursue a case for insubordination. He continued:

"However, per HVSA directive, I will attempt to refrain from openly discussing Motif during this investigation."

'Attempt to refrain.' Yes, that will work.

Bullshit, but doable.

He reviewed the full report and submitted it into the record. Nothing Dorrit could do now to alter the wording, though he'd no doubt drag it behind the Executive Partition for as long as legally allowed. Even then, the Chief might improvise. He admitted to other Motif cases not being reported as such. How did he achieve the coverup? The Sec Admin central data spool, by design, could not be manipulated at any pay stamp.

Effie would tell Trevor not to assume the worst. Her motto: 'Trust but verify.' Precisely the advice he'd expect from a diplomat.

He didn't know Dorrit well; saw the man quarterly at Unified Sec Admin confabs but never engaged the blustering buffoon. Damn well never expected to report to him, either.

"Where have you been?"

A voice rose from his wrist plate. He clicked the holo to expand Hoshi, who spoke in a hushed tone.

"Luncheon ended an hour ago," she continued.

Had it been that long? Yes. Perhaps. At least six trains stopped at Mogandi since he arrived.

"I submitted my report, Hoshi. I assume you did as well?"

"Dorrit just read yours. He's raging."

"I'm at Mogandi Station. Join me."

"Avoiding him won't help your position, Trev."

"We have business in Episteme. Coming?"

Hoshi rolled her eyes.

"Soon as I can."

"Next train should be here in about four minutes. Hurry."

Trevor disconnected the call. Earlier, she committed to the investigation. Now, she hesitated.

Trevor blamed himself. If he'd joined her for luncheon, he also might have talked her into avoiding the office. He hadn't forgotten how she saluted the Chief earlier. Was she more afraid of Dorrit or of losing her shot at a promotion before her rotation ended?

He'd seen it before. A two-year officer arrives on a UNF deferment, plays the game, looks for an edge, moves up the ranks. The higher pay stamp translates into higher UNF officer posting.

If this was Hoshi's game, he'd need to keep a watchful eye. 'Trust but verify' took on a new meaning.

Four minutes later, seconds before a train emerged, Hoshi raced onto the platform.

"Announcement. Blue Line approaching. Destinations: Episteme Hanimoto, Episteme Kallcunik. Please stand clear until full stop. Allow all passengers to disembark."

He greeted her with a smile, to which she responded:

"How about a heads-up next time?"

"I try to be flexible with my schedule. Nice lunch, I trust?"

The doors opened to a smattering of departing Havenites.

"It was filling, as my mother would say."

"Huh. Mine used to say the same. How about that?"

Their wrist plates activated upon entry, asking for them to confirm a destination into their LinkPass. Hoshi waited for Trevor's lead.

"Hanimoto."

They took the nearest cushioned seats.

"How about you, Trev? Good lunch?"

"Can't go wrong with KNV. Ate with my brother. He was nude. Ever heard of the Loutah?"

"Yes, but ... I'm sorry, what? Nude?"

"He's not built like the rest of us. Where we tend to turn left, he goes right. I admire him. Also worry about him."

"OK. I'm sure that's a long story. I've heard of the Loutah, but I'm not into spiritualism."

"Neither am I. In less than a minute, we have two things in common. A good sign, Hoshi."

The doors closed. Seconds later, the train built momentum. On the far track, the Green Line express flew past in the opposite direction. It raced between the terminal stations in Harmony and Episteme, usually moving a higher class of clientele.

"Did Dorrit offer a parting shot?" Trevor asked.

"He reminded me of the parameters for our investigation."

"And insisted you make me comply. Yes?"

"In so many words."

"Sorry, Hoshi. As you said earlier, you're trapped in the middle. You know, he could just as easily as have contacted *my* plate."

She shook her head.

"That's not how he works. The Chief wants you close enough to smell his breath. He hates holo interfaces."

Now the morning made more sense.

"That's why he joined us on site."

"The tenor changes when he enters a room, and he knows it. He can't control the moment if he's not present."

"Noted."

The train entered the three-hundred-meter gap between Harmony and Episteme sectors. The Crossway offered no external view of the spectacular Ark Carriers turned space stations, but the overhead tracking guide showed progress through the tube. They were ninety seconds from Hanimoto Station.

"So, Trev, I reviewed your jacket over lunch. I felt embarrassed because I didn't before we met. And the Chief mentioned your grandfather like someone important. Bottom line, I had no idea about your family."

"Surprise. We all have one."

She spoke with a tinge of reverence.

"Maximillian Vanover. The man who made all this happen! My jaw was on the floor reading about him."

Trevor didn't want to go there, but Hoshi had obviously found a propaganda piece about the man. This would not be his first time clarifying history.

"He was important to Amity. Yes. Prevented three Ark Carriers from being dismantled, and designed the Crossway. Maybe you're too young to know. It took tens of thousands of people and two wars to make this place a reality. My grandfather was a great engineer, but he had a personal agenda."

"What do you mean?"

"Grandfather Max did right by Connor and me, but he was an old-guard Chancellor looking to save his legacy. He was on the losing side during the Earth Civil War. Our family lost almost everything. He sold most of what we did have to call in his last markers. When the People's Collectorate formed and discussed ideas for housing the interstellar government in a neutral system, he stepped forward."

Trevor expected Hoshi to temper her admiration. He was wrong.

"Sounds to me like a man who put bitterness aside to do the right thing for the most people."

"That's how history generally sees him."

"But not you?"

Almost to Hanimoto. How to put this conversation to bed?

"I'm a student of history. I read everything I can get my hands on. The measure of a man is often far more complicated than what you'll find on most public data spools. I know more about Grandfather than most. He was many things, but Max Vanover was not a hero."

She shaded her eyes in a moment of reflection.

"Regardless, I'm sorry about your loss. It must've been difficult."

"It was expected. He prepared us."

"But at least you had him. After what happened to your parents … I can't imagine how you and Connor endured."

The train slowed. Good timing.

"We weren't the first kids to survive a tough childhood. Won't be the last."

"Announcement. Now arriving: Episteme Hanimoto. Please stand clear until the doors have opened in full."

Trevor hoped she heard enough to let the subject rest. The truth he knew ran up against years of countless platitudes. He hadn't found the time or courage to show Connor the damning bits, so he wasn't about to lean on them for a stranger.

They confirmed Transit Exit to their LinkPass upon departing the train.

"Where first?" She asked.

"Maynor School. He would've been assigned a mentor. We also need to speak with the headmaster and his classmates. Did he have a friendship circle? I want to build a strong profile of his activities, beyond what I can find in his LinkPass history."

Hoshi nodded. "Lot of legwork, Trev."

"Which is why we'll likely need to split up. Mr. Hann's death won't be announced until kin are notified. We have twelve to fourteen hours at best. I want to learn everything we can before the news hits. Assuming we find anything worth pursuing, there's still Halifax R&D. Bigger operation, very delicate."

"Interacted with them before?"

He chuckled while leading her to the public docks.

"Worn this bar for fifteen years. Amity is only six kilometers long lined up end to end. You see?"

"I do. No place here you haven't been."

He chose a rifter, grabbed the steering arms, and laid in his course.

"More or less, Hoshi. More or less."

His dislike for Episteme Sector grew with each visit.

By day's end, Trevor had his fill of the cudfrucking place.

9

U NLIKE THE OTHER SECTORS, Episteme was an industrial city. Factories with huge assembly floors, arenas for testing engine designs, laboratory complexes for dozens of scientific disciplines, and the Collectorate's largest indoor test farm. Residential housing snaked through this maze, a far cry from the uniform high-rise grid in Haven.

Vital work took place here; these people constructed the future. Yet the place turned Trevor cold for reasons he long struggled to decipher. As they approached the Maynor School, Hoshi said:

"I'm always struck by how noisy Episteme is."

Hundreds of whizzing rifters – not all controlled by disciplined pilots – compensated for less Swiftrak lanes. Auto-haulers moving between the city and its spaceport added a steady hum overhead.

"Are your ears ringing?"

"A little, now that you mention it."

"Been here much, Hoshi?"

"Fourth visit."

"Sounds about right. If you come a few times a week, the ringing will disappear. My grandfather called it the 'rhythm of progress.' He wanted Episteme to be loud."

"He succeeded."

"It was worse years ago. Then the chieftains at Halifax, Mullen, and Atumwa used their influence with the President to push through a noise ordinance and pay for sound dampeners."

Hoshi grimaced.

"Wait. The President and IC have no legislative jurisdiction over internal Amity matters. How could they ...?"

"The usual trick: Smoke and mirrors. The Amity Interior Board didn't have a half billion credits for a quality dampening system. The chieftains, President Aleksanyan, and their IC cronies deemed the noise a threat to 'Collectorate environmental security.'"

She stifled a laugh.

"Never heard that one before."

"Nor had anyone else. They reallocated funds meant for atmospheric cleanup projects on two planets."

"Cud. That couldn't have gone over well."

Trevor remembered the tension inside the halls of government during those days. Being First Deputy meant organizing a security phalanx to hold back protestors.

"It was a shitstorm, especially when the Big Three released their quarterly profit stacks. Those bastards could have paid for the dampeners twice over."

He guided the rifter around a bend toward the docks outside Maynor's front entrance.

"Wow. I didn't pay much attention to Amity back then, Trev. Did they rescind the legislation?"

He wanted to burst into laughter, but Hoshi needed to learn how things really worked without being patronized.

"No. They followed the politicians creed: In time of trouble, create a distraction."

"Which was what?"

Trevor settled the rifter into a nice slot hovering inches above the docking platform.

"Something to do with the shipping unions. Bottom line: the Amity

Board got their credits, and the dampeners went online a few months later."

They hopped off, and Trevor braced for what awaited inside.

"That's the way it is here, Hoshi. Two castes: The seen and the unseen."

"I don't follow."

He didn't blame her. She hadn't been around long enough.

"Think about it. Harmony is the center of government and diplomacy. Episteme houses the most important scientific minds. The elites in both sectors live a short walk from work. Yet their support staffs, their interns, students, and the service and maintenance teams commute from Haven."

Hoshi stared at Trevor with a quizzical "so what?" demeanor.

"You find this troubling, Trev?"

He chuckled. Someone else who didn't know much history.

"Before the Civil War, my ancestors ruled Earth. Centuries of absolute control even though they were outnumbered ten to one by the service class. A blend of ethnics they called Solomons."

"Oh, yes. I remember. It was the Solomons that rebelled."

"They won. Afterward, my people lived with them as equals. No choice. Humbling but inevitable. When men like my grandfather retrofitted these Carriers, they were intentional about how they designed housing."

Hoshi gasped with the sure sign of revelation.

"You're saying they built this place to create social strata."

Trevor nodded.

"On Earth, the Solomons lived in the outer stretches of the cities, segregated from Chancellors. They came to work, quietly did their bit, and returned home. They weren't poor by any means, but they weren't allowed to inhabit the same stratosphere as my caste. It's not as obvious here, I'll grant you."

"So, it's nuanced?"

"Good word."

"Even if it is, Trev, it's far more equitable than most planets. Don't get me started about Hokkaido. I could go on for hours about the seamasters."

She made a valid point. Almost every member world divided its people into the privileged, the downtrodden, and the masses in between. Amity's subtle distinction shouldn't have bothered him.

They passed students en route to the front portico. Trevor lowered his voice.

"Let's put it this way, Hoshi. When my brother took his first job in maintenance, he was told to vacate his flat in Harmony because he no longer qualified for residency. The Housing Authority assigned it to an ambassador's chief of staff. Connor didn't care. He's fine so long as he has a bed."

"But you were pissed?"

"Still am."

"OK. Fine. I see your position, but I respectfully disagree, Trev. And I don't see how it's relevant to our investigation."

He snapped back.

"Everything's relevant. A man is dead. A student. Not one of the elites. Pay attention to how the headmaster, the mentor, and his classmates respond to our questions. You'll see the difference."

Trevor didn't regret falling down the rabbit hole of Amity social dynamics; they fascinated him to no end. The day he and Connor arrived, the station felt like a pioneer boomtown bursting at the seams. It morphed into something he no longer recognized, run by people who lacked the pioneer spirit.

Maybe his critics in Central were right. Maybe the 'Lifetime Deputy' needed a change of scenery.

Trevor and Hoshi flashed their wrist plates at the door-mounted LinkPass Reader and entered the lobby, upon which a young woman in a pink flowered sari greeted them.

"Good day, officers. I am Deena. How might I assist you?"

"Headmaster Thet," Trevor said.

Deena the greeter responded with what Trevor called a permanent smile. She reminded him of folks he encountered daily in the diplomatic corps. Perhaps they trained her.

"Headmaster Bien Thet is currently engaged in private consults. I'd be delighted to add you to his schedule."

The lobby acted as an echo chamber, amplifying the conversation.

"We have urgent business on behalf of Security Administration. Please inform Headmaster Thet to suspend his consults."

If Trevor's request threw the greeter, she showed no hint.

"The Headmaster has a full schedule, as you might imagine, but he supports the hard work of the ESA. I'll happily inform him of your visit and encourage him to contact you at his earliest convenience."

That sounded about right. A drone would've done just as well.

"We are not Episteme Sec Admin." Trevor pointed to the color code atop his chest bar. "We're from Haven. And I have legal claim to forcibly excuse Mr. Thet from his duties. I'm sure he's in your ear. Contact him now. We'll meet him in his office."

The mention of Haven raised an eyebrow. Deena glared at the bars but never lost her pleasant demeanor.

"I'll see what I might arrange, deputies." She pointed across the way to empty sofas. "We have a lovely waiting area. Please."

Trevor nodded Hoshi in that direction and waited until the greeter retreated. As expected, she tapped an ear bead and spoke, her back turned to the deputies.

"Follow me," he told Hoshi. "He's not far."

"Shouldn't we wait for ..."

"Not enough time in the day." They entered the nearest corridor leading deep into the school's administrative offices. Trevor mapped everything while waiting at Mogandi Station. "Did you notice how she reacted when I mentioned Haven?"

"Not especially. Perhaps she was embarrassed by the error. She might not be familiar with our colors."

"You're not going to give an inch on this, are you?"

"On what? Your theory about Haven being a home for second-class citizens? The unseen?"

He brushed off her challenge.

"Expand your worldview. Drop into Harmony and Episteme more often. You'd be surprised what you find."

She chuckled under her breath.

"Says the man who hasn't left the station in nineteen years."

The reply hurt for almost a second. It was not original.

Trevor pointed to the office approaching on their left.

"I'll take lead."

"Ah. I'm to remain silent then."

"Not if you have something important to add. Don't take offense, Hoshi. I earned the right to pull rank."

"As you say, First Deputy."

Her tone confirmed: She took offense.

"It's not personal. You don't know these people like I do. They jump at the first sign of weakness or hesitation. Oh, and don't be fooled by their platitudes."

Trevor entered the headmaster's office complex and zeroed in on the next obstacle. A short, rail-thin black man in a white business robe released a finger from his ear bead. Trevor didn't need to guess who spoke on the other end.

He looked like a first cousin to the man Effie had been sleeping with the past few months. Not a pleasant first impression.

"All the best to you, deputies. I am Iber Faciendo, Executive Assistant to the Headmaster. As you were told in reception, Mr. Thet is occupied at this time."

He pointed through a glass divide into a larger office, where a crowd of perhaps two dozen sat in a semi-circle facing Thet, who relaxed in a tall, cushioned chair with huge arms.

"Tell the Headmaster to say his goodbyes and meet with us, or he can make an excuse and join us out here. Although I can't guarantee how much time we'll require."

Iber also mastered the permanent smile, but Trevor detected a wiser creature hid behind it. For one, a man well-versed in Amity law.

"I see," Iber said, nodding to both deputies. "Determination is a trait the Headmaster values in his students. He will no doubt respect yours as well. Please. Follow me."

A section of glass pixelated to become an open door. The assistant motioned for the officers to stand beside him behind the audience, all of whom appeared to be in their twenties. A couple, Trevor reasoned, were likely teen prodigies. He estimated at least fifteen member planets were represented.

One student, who Trevor reckoned was a Damascene from the planet Euphrates, spoke to Thet with head bowed.

"My dilemma remains bent toward the question of how far might we allow these excesses of progress to take us? We dare not repeat the mistakes which opened the gates to the Swarm War, yet the advances made because of that war are undeniable. I find the mere idea of reengagement with the other universes more terrifying than compelling. What say you, Headmaster?"

Trevor didn't expect this. The kid spoke well but with undeniable subservience in his tone. Was Thet an administrator or a religious leader? The man in charge motioned for the student to take a seat. Thet caught his Exec's eye and nodded.

"You speak of a natural conflict, Nyad. I hear it voiced in every rotation. It goes to the heart of being a scientist. We are often torn between possibility and pragmatism. Episteme was designed as a place where we can weigh both in equal measure. I encourage you and your classmates to engage in this rich and open-ended debate."

Thet, wearing a tan business robe with intricate red embroidery on the sleeves, lifted both hands, palms facing the students.

"Business requires my attention at this time. I implore you to reflect deeply and, as always, set your mind to the infinite."

The students rose as one and bowed to Thet. They filed through the pixelated door in reverential silence. When the last of them passed, Thet retreated to a small desk in the far corner of his office and waved the deputies forward.

"Thank you, Iber," he told the assistant. "Silence the door on your way out."

Trevor led Hoshi through the bowl in which Thet's audience sat. Only as he approached the headmaster did Trevor pay attention to the office décor: Hanging plants, a panoramic screen displaying nature views from the Collectorate worlds, and antiques from those worlds on stands. Not what he expected from the leader of an engineering school.

He decided to keep their exchange formal as long as possible.

"Bien Thet, I am First Deputy Trevor Stallion. My Second is Hoshi Oda. We're here to ..."

"Ask questions?" Thet betrayed a cheeky grin. "You're certainly not here to audit classes. Please. Sit." He turned to Hoshi. "Hokkaido, yes?" After she confirmed her home world, Thet pointed to the tall ceramic pot on his desk. "Pearl tea. Would you care for a cup?"

Hoshi waited for Trevor's approval. Formality ended quickly.

"I grew up on pearl tea, Headmaster. You'll be hard-pressed to match the quality. We're renowned for our blend in New Seoul."

"So you are," he said, pouring. "We take a slightly different approach in the Wai-Chiang Province on Indonesia Prime. The leaf is less mature and a touch bitter at first taste. But the finale enriches mind and body." He handed Hoshi a cup. "You, Trevor?"

"No. Thank you. Never been much of a tea drinker."

Out of annoyed courtesy, Trevor waited for Hoshi to sip and react. Thet leaned forward as if desperate for her review.

"It's lovely," she said in a muted tone. "I can't help but miss the sweetness. Very pleasant, though."

Fine, Trevor thought. If a little cultural exchange made Thet feel more comfortable, all the better.

"Mr. Thet, we're here in regard to one of your students."

"Bien. Did Iber explain what was happening when you arrived?"

Trevor glanced back at the empty bowl.

"Your students?"

He nodded. "First years. The one you heard – Nyad – arrived last month. A promising young man who is struggling to adapt to life in Episteme. I make a point of consulting with all my students each quarter. They are under immense pressure to succeed. In here, we never discuss coursework or apprenticeships. I give them voice. I want them to know they are seen and supported as human beings. Out there, the Collectorate knows them only for their skillsets."

"You have over a thousand students. That's a lot of consults."

He sipped pearl tea and wiggled his tongue between his lips.

"This batch is a touch off," he told Hoshi. "My apologies. I'll need to have Iber brew a fresh pot." He set down the cup. "Ah. Trevor. If I'm not mistaken, you still haven't recognized me."

"What? I know you?"

"Seven years ago. Your wedding reception."

He drew a blank. Was this guy playing games?

"You have me at a disadvantage."

Thet tilted his chin upward to a condescending angle.

"The receiving line. We said perhaps ten words. Your grandfather invited many of his colleagues. Maximillian always put on a show where family was concerned."

That much Trevor remembered. The reception was twenty-five percent larger than the guest list. Yet Max ensured ample food, drink, and tables for the add-ons.

"Yes. He did. But sorry, I don't remember you. Don't take it personally. Now, to business please. We need to know everything you can tell us about Ulbrecht Hann."

Thet dropped his cheeks. He didn't try to hide behind a mask, as Trevor anticipated.

OK. This just got interesting.

10

THET REACHED FOR THE TEA, hesitated, and sighed. "What has Ulbrecht done this time?"

Trevor had planned to delay the news, but Thet's reaction suggested now was a good time to spring it.

"He died last night. Drug overdose."

The headmaster leaned back and stared above the deputies.

"Dear. So much promise, lost too soon."

"Excuse the assumption, Bien, but you don't seem shocked."

This time he sipped his cup dry.

"Surprised but not shocked. Ulbrecht has been troubled of late. What drug?"

Trevor squirmed. "It's not important. Tell me about Ulbrecht's behavior. It will help us understand why he did this."

Thet switched his focus between the deputies.

"Deputy Oda, how many competitors did you overcome to secure a rotation on Amity?"

"A few dozen, as I recall. I came here on UNF deferment."

He nodded. "Then you had it easy. Maynor receives millions of applicants per year. In the last term, we reviewed seventy-four thousand candidates from Yaniff and selected three. Ulbrecht was our first choice."

"That's impressive," Hoshi said. "He doesn't seem like the type to fall in with drugs."

Trevor quickly recaptured control of the conversation.

"Anyone is susceptible to temptation. What would lead a promising student down that road? And what specific troubles have you had with him?"

Thet said, "The pressure on these students is staggering. They defied enormous odds to find their way here, and they rightly assume a ticket to Maynor assures success in the field of their choosing. In fact, many of our graduates are hired by Halifax, Atumwa, and the other major engineering interests.

"Those who return home as free agents are expected to become powerhouses in their fields. Here, we work at the leading edge of technology and design. First years are often overwhelmed by the curriculum and the demands of their concurrent apprenticeship. A few reach a breaking point."

"Ulbrecht?"

"Yes. His behavior has been erratic for the past month. His mentor reported inconsistencies in work ethic and temperament. I counseled him myself last week. It did not go well."

"How so?"

"Consults are confidential. I was concerned we might have to initiate expulsion proceedings."

"On what grounds?"

"Academic impropriety. Another student accused Ulbrecht of data-fixing, a difficult charge to prove. In addition, criminal malfeasance. Ulbrecht allegedly threatened the life of a fellow student from Yaniff."

Trevor winced. He saw nothing of the latter on Ulbrecht's jacket.

"Did anyone report the threat to ESA?"

Thet sighed.

"No. The eyewitness statements did not align. As the matter was inconclusive, we chose to keep it in-house. I had hoped — incorrectly, as it now seems — to catch Ulbrecht before he fell."

"We'll need to speak with his mentor, the student he supposedly threatened, and others in his peer group."

"Of course. Iber will provide that information as well as his curriculum plan."

"What else should we know about Ulbrecht?"

Thet relaxed and smiled like a doting father.

"Just a brilliant mind. Someone capable of being remembered through history. Dear, the difference he could have made."

"I gather he was studying wormhole technology."

Thet's jaws tightened as the smile vanished.

"No. How did you ...?"

"It's on his jacket. Trans-wormhole shielding tech. I never heard of it."

Trevor always looked for tics. In this case, Thet rubbed his palms together in steady circles. He suspected the headmaster of holding something back, but the man's response stunned him.

Thet broke into raucous laughter.

"Dear, that Ulbrecht. If you saw it on his jacket, he must have added it to his biography as an inside joke. And a good one."

"How so?"

"Very simply, trans-wormhole theory is relegated to the lunatic fringe. These are the same people who believe we can reestablish gateways to the other universes. It's a needlessly complicated and ridiculous pseudoscience."

"Is it? I recall that student, Nyad, mentioned reengagement with the other universes. He seemed very concerned, like it was something people were actually considering. You did not exactly dissuade him."

Trevor watched those circling palms and Thet's eyes.

"At Maynor, we do not censor or denigrate anyone for an opinion. I simply encouraged Nyad to keep an open mind, knowing it would lead him away from the reckless voices."

Or straight to them.

Trevor didn't say it aloud. He had enough information for now.

"Unless there's anything else, Deputy Oda and I will leave you to your space. However, I do caution you not to make any sort of public statement until Sec Admin has cleared protocol."

"Of course," he said. "You'll forgive me if I don't stand. I'm still struggling to process it all."

"Certainly. We'll speak to your Exec about those names. Thank you again. We're sorry for your loss."

He motioned Hoshi to follow, and they were halfway across the bowl before Thet said:

"Was it Motif?"

Shit.

Hoshi raised a brow as Trevor debated how to respond.

"Why do you ask?"

"Sec Admin would not send two deputies to my office if Ulbrecht died of a simple overdose. You're conducting a criminal investigation. Tell me I'm wrong."

Trevor hated threading a needle. He preferred a direct approach.

"The toxical report is pending. Do you have any reason to suspect Ulbrecht of using Motif?"

That felt like a good way of skirting around the Chief's order.

"Maynor students know better than to risk their lives in such needless fashion."

"Of course. Too much on the line. Thank you again. If we have more questions, we'll be in touch."

After they collected names and locations for their next interviews, Trevor escorted Hoshi to a quiet spot at the center of campus. They stared over a balcony down to a Zen garden. The school wrapped around it, rising six levels.

"OK, Hoshi. Any conclusions?"

She stiffened her shoulders.

"Now I'm allowed to contribute? Thank you, Trev."

"Didn't ask for snark."

"Of course. My apologies. I think we know what happened to

Ulbrecht. He had an emotional break. He was desperate. He thought Motif would bring him relief."

"Could be. Anything else?"

"Headmaster took the news well, considering. I'm sure this will be an embarrassment for the school."

That's it? Can't she see the obvious, or is she that damn lazy?

Trevor didn't want to piss her off when he needed Hoshi for important legwork.

"Thet assumed Motif the instant I mentioned overdose. Yes, he took the news well – *too well*. Notice his hands? He was nervous. The laugh was forced and out of character."

"How can you say that? We only just met him."

"He was deflecting. It's a hallmark of insecurity."

Hoshi crinkled her lips.

"Or maybe you're trying to make something of nothing, Trev."

"I prefer it to the opposite. If I'm wrong, I'll apologize later and move on. But if I'm right ..."

"Understood. And we still don't know how he acquired Motif."

"Correct. Which brings us back to Thet. He would not have zeroed in on Motif without cause."

"You think it's been a problem with other students."

Good. She's coming around.

"There could be a history. He didn't report Ulbrecht's threat to ESA. He doesn't like to see stains on the school's reputation go into the official record."

"Makes perfect sense."

"Which is why we have to move fast. He's huddling with his Exec even now to plot a strategy for containment. Thet is Amity old guard. He knows everyone who matters."

She frowned. "You think he'd go over us?"

"This morning, the Chief admitted there were other MODs before today, but none on the official record. It's a stretch, but what if we found a link between those cases and this one?"

Hoshi stepped back. Trevor saw her head spinning.

"Slow down, Trev. We're barely into it, and you're implying some sort of conspiracy. Are you always this paranoid?"

"Prove me wrong, and dinner's on me. Best restaurant in Haven."

He made such an offer before but in Harmony. Knew he'd lose. But that was with Effie, and Trevor needed a backhanded way to rope her into a date. Five months later, they married.

Now, he just wanted to motivate his Second Deputy.

"Where to?" She said.

Trevor called up a holo from his wrist plate. It threw open a map of Maynor School.

"Level 4, Room 17."

"Why?"

"According to Ulbrecht's class schedule, his Mentee Group has been in session for twenty minutes. If we're lucky, we can corner the students who knew him well before anyone gets in their ear."

Hoshi studied the list of names the Exec transferred to their plates.

"They're all first years."

"Anyone from Yaniff?"

She scanned five jacket briefs and shook her head.

"Perhaps the student he threatened was in a different group."

"Could be. We'll find him. First, to 417. We'll break them up and interview separately."

Like so many clever gameplans, that one fell apart as soon as they arrived.

11

THE BEACON FLASHING ABOVE 417 set clear terms: *QUIET. STUDY IN PROGRESS.* Trevor took a gander at Ulbrecht's schedule. The session would last another forty minutes. Nope, he thought. Too dangerously long to wait.

He pressed the door pad, which turned green. The door slid open whisper-soft.

At first, no one noticed the deputies in the threshold, which gave Trevor time to digest the unexpected design. Dark wood panels with a glossy sheen surrounded the octagonal room. Blue light cast from above a central workstation softened the effect.

Three students stood at separate workstation portals, racing their hands over digital projections while data scrolled past them in lightning-fast waves. Two others huddled against the far right wall, interacting with a hologram. They whispered while pulling and prodding at what appeared to be the guts of a starship engine.

An older man, hands behind his back, patrolled the room. He looked over their shoulders and nodded silent approval.

Until he saw Trevor and Hoshi.

His eyes ballooned into silent rage as he rushed the deputies.

"Out," he said through gritted teeth. "These students are not to be disturbed. Can you not read a simple ..."

Trevor pointed to his bar.

"I love nothing better than to read, but our visit can't be helped. You are Mustafa Chait?"

The mentor leveled a hand against each deputy's chest and tried without success to push them back.

"We will talk outside. Now. Please."

Trevor caught the fleeting eyes of the students, who picked up on the disturbance but quickly returned to their studies. Chait was twice their age, with a steeled jaw and piercing black eyes. A far cry from the diplomatic headmaster. Trevor muffled his voice.

"Sec Admin business, Mr. Chait."

"I don't care. No one will disrupt my students' routine. Clear?"

OK. Fine. Then let's have at it.

"You contacted HVSA about Ulbrecht Hann's absence. Yes?"

Chait's rock-solid demeanor cracked.

"This is about Ulbrecht? Where is he?"

"Dead. Overdose."

The mentor dropped his hands and shaded his eyes.

"I ... ah ... I don't believe it."

"Sorry to bear this news. You reported him as overdue. For a class or an apprenticeship?"

The man lost his bearings, as if in a fog.

"What? Oh. Cud! He ... Ulbrecht apprenticed for Halifax in stellar cartography."

Trevor thought that seemed a bit underwhelming for someone Thet had said might one day make history.

"Mapmaking?"

Chait sneered. "It's more advanced than it sounds."

"Fine. That's not why we're here. We need to interview these students. I understand mentee groups are asked to spend a great deal of time together."

"What are you implying, Deputy ...?"

"First Deputy Trevor Stallion. Only that they might know his frame of mind and why he'd do something like this. But let's start with you, Mr. Chait. Did Ulbrecht have a habit of reporting late for work or class?"

Chait glanced over his shoulder. The students remained dutiful to their studies.

"No. Never late. Ulbrecht was a brilliant student on track for a remarkable career. In fact, I've never seen anyone master the curriculum so quickly and with such artfulness."

Huh. Interesting.

Trevor caught Hoshi's frown. She too heard the inconsistency.

"No problems with his behavior toward other students?"

Chait paused for a beat, eyeing each deputy with care.

"None. Are you trying to imply something?"

"Headmaster Thet said Ulbrecht was accused of data-fixing and threatening another student's life."

He crimped his lips, as if caught in a lie.

"Ah. That. Nonsense. The charges were overblown and quickly forgotten."

"Then you might want to have an aside with the headmaster. He doesn't share your perspective."

If Chait knew anything of consequence, he wasn't about to reveal it in this setting. Trevor knew the signs of people retreating into a defensive cocoon.

"We will. And ... I apologize for putting my hands on you both. Mentee work is vital for my students. Please respect it and save your questions for later."

"Sorry. Can't oblige."

"If you tell them about Ulbrecht, you will disrupt their lives."

Hoshi beat Trevor to the reply.

"That's what happens when friends die, Mr. Chait. Whether they learn now or by day's end doesn't matter."

"If you'd prefer to wait outside ..." Trevor added.

Chait straightened his jacket.

"No. I'll stay right here to make sure you don't harass them."

"Wasn't on the agenda, Mr. Chait."

The mentor called the five students to attention.

"Everyone, please set a pause on your work. These deputies wish to speak with you on a matter of grave concern."

Trevor used his long-hewn skill to identify them as an Earther, plus one each from Boer, Hansen's Landing, Indonesia Prime, and New Bangkok. He often confused the final two and couldn't be certain. Four men, one woman.

At first blush, he thought they all looked exhausted — not a surprise if they endured the level of pressure Thet claimed. Working under Mustafa Chait's omnipresent eyes might have contributed, too.

Trevor introduced himself and Hoshi.

"I have the sad duty to inform you that we are here to investigate the death of a fellow student. We will ask each of you ..."

The woman from Hansen's Landing, a smaller member world with descendants of Australians and New Zealanders, stepped forward.

"Ulbrecht. Are you talking about Ulbrecht? Is he dead?"

Her left hand shook.

"Yes. He died last night. We're investigating the circumstances."

The woman clasped her hands against her chest. The five men held their ground, their eyes wandering. Chait did not move to comfort the woman, who shed a rush of tears.

Among the men, a dark-skinned native of Boer stepped forward.

"How did it happen?"

"An overdose."

The man crossed his arms and shook his head.

"Unbelievable. What an idiot. What a waste."

"Your name?"

"Jor Kerrindos."

"How well did you know him? The question goes to everyone."

Jor divided his attention with the starship engine hologram he'd been working on.

"Very little," Jor said, waving off Trevor. "He was my lab partner for a short time. We were not compatible."

Trevor asked the curly-haired student from Earth for his name.

"Freddie Lighthorne, sir. I guess you could say Ulbrecht and I were fair friends, as much as you can be around here."

"Explain."

Freddie eyed the mentor, who had yet to interfere, much to Trevor's pleasant surprise.

"It's no secret. Every day's long around here, sir. Don't have much room for extra life. Some of us aren't as fast as Ulbrecht."

"As smart, you mean?"

The Earther nodded.

"Most of us work day and night to keep on top of the mill. Ulbrecht, he got out. Entertained himself."

"Invited you along?"

"All of us." Freddie looked around the group to make sure they agreed. "Can't speak for these fellas, but one night at a club with Ulbrecht was enough for me. Nice fella, but intense, you see."

"I do. Which club?"

"Raison. It was always Raison for Ulbrecht."

On that point, the men nodded in firm agreement.

Trevor returned to Jor.

"When I said he died by overdose, you called him an idiot. Did you believe he had a problem?"

Jor focused on Chait before answering.

"We all have a problem around here. It's like Freddie said. Our studies take up most of our lives."

"Nice try, but you didn't answer the question."

"He did," Chait finally interrupted. "I warned you not to harass."

"I'm not, Mr. Chait. Jor, you know what I meant. Did Ulbrecht have a problem with drugs?"

"I don't know about his business, but he was into some kind of magic. Walked around here with enough energy for three, and the rest of us dragging on our heels."

A student who might have passed for Bien Thet thirty years ago slapped Jor on the shoulder.

"That was Ulbrecht. Boundless energy, like a drone with an endless power source."

"And you are?"

"Ashraf Diep."

"Close to Ulbrecht, were you?"

The man from Indonesia Prime smiled.

"Not per se. We had little in common, but I admired him. He had a brilliant mind."

"That seems to be the consensus. And what of you?" He faced the last male, from New Bangkok. "Your name?"

The man cleared his throat.

"Sil Mariputti. I agree with what the others have said. For my part, Ulbrecht was very curious and ambitious. He would have gone far."

"Did you ever engage with him socially?"

Sil nodded. "I drank with him at Raison a few times. But only drinks. I never stayed long."

"But Ulbrecht did?" Trevor addressed everyone; they agreed. "Did he talk about his extracurricular activities at Raison or otherwise?"

The men did not respond, but the woman wiping her tears did.

"He was a good man and smart. He would never take a risk like that. Not with drugs."

"Last night, he did. You are?"

"Eliza. Eliza Hutton."

She glanced at her peers before she faced Trevor. They avoided her eyes.

Interesting.

"How well did you know Ulbrecht?"

Her complexion turned pale. She leaned against the workstation and took rapid breaths. Hoshi stepped in to help.

"I'm sorry," Eliza said. "I feel dizzy."

"You see, Deputy?" Chait said. "I said this would be disruptive. Look at her."

Trevor might have suggested she take a seat, but there were none to be found, a detail he only now recognized. He thought it a fascinating approach to 'thinking on one's feet.'

Eliza thanked Hoshi for the attention but brushed her off.

"No. I'll be fine. Just give me a moment. This comes and goes."

Of course. He should've recognized the symptom right off.

"Bucher's Syndrome?"

She nodded.

One percent of residents suffered from the thyroid disorder created by the light artificial gravity. Usually it affected visitors from the higher-gravity worlds; Hansen's Landing qualified.

"It's better than it used to be," Eliza said. "Only happens when I get emotional like this."

Chait didn't let it rest.

"I'm going to insist the interviews end now. If you want to schedule times more convenient for my students, feel free. But Eliza is clearly in no condition."

Not quite yet. Eliza was the only one who appeared visibly shaken. Perhaps the others were so wrapped up in their scientific pursuits that they lacked empathy. Or maybe they were just garden-variety assholes. Either way, Trevor wasn't about to leave Eliza. Hoshi intervened.

"Mr. Chait, is there a room nearby with chairs?" She said. "Miss Hutton needs time to recover properly. I promise we won't push her too hard."

Their eyes locked. *Good job, Second Deputy.*

Chait sighed with surprising reluctance.

"There's a break room next to 426. The dispensary includes an option for synchwater. It will help reestablish her equilibrium."

I know what it does, Trevor thought. *I didn't step off the liner yesterday, smartass.*

Trevor silenced his indignation, a new strategy. Effie warned him for years to take care of what crossed his lips. He wouldn't be dealing with this mess had he listened.

He told Hoshi to escort Eliza to the break room.

"As for the rest of you, please be advised that until Ulbrecht's death is made public, your silence is mandated." To Chait, he added: "Our apologies for interrupting their studies."

Chait tucked his hands behind his back.

"See to it Eliza is returned without delay."

Trevor caught up to Hoshi and Eliza en route to the break room. His mind whirred about the possibilities. Except for the woman, no one reacted to the news like he expected. He imagined Chait quickly shutting down any further conversation and insisting the students return to their studies. Would any object?

If Maynor School was the reward for an extraordinary scientific mind, Trevor considered himself blessed to be somewhat ordinary.

They found the break room empty – a fortunate turn. Eliza thanked Hoshi for holding her arm all the way there. Hoshi, in turn, triggered the dispensary for a glass of synchwater. Trevor sat across from Eliza and waited for her to consume the beverage.

"OK, Eliza. Based on your reaction, you know more about Ulbrecht than the others. Am I wrong?"

She shook her head.

"You were close friends? Or more perhaps?"

Eliza clasped her hands against her chest again and shifted between the deputies.

"It was Motif. Wasn't it?"

Shit. Here we go again.

"I'm sorry. We can't discuss those details."

"You don't have to." She leaned forward. "Whatever you found wasn't his doing. They murdered him. Ulbrecht was murdered."

12

TREVOR NEVER SAW THAT COMING. He also had no reason to assign her claim to anything more than grief. The least he could do was show respect by hearing her out.

"Strong accusation, Eliza. What do you base it on?"

"A feeling."

He resisted rolling his eyes.

"That's not much."

"No. Not *my* feeling. Ulbrecht's."

"Explain."

She drew circles on the table with her forefinger.

"He thought he was in serious danger."

"Told you this, did he?"

"Brought it up every time I met him in private the past two weeks. Ulbrecht said he was about to expose a group of people working against the Collectorate."

"What people?"

"He said if I knew, I'd be in danger, too."

Straight down Conspiracy Theory Alley. *Great.*

"Did he at least hint at their plans? 'Working against the Collectorate' can mean many things."

Eliza rubbed her hazel eyes, which were red and haggard – likely

85

exhausted by the demands of Maynor School.

"I know two things. The first is that he only mentioned it when we were in Haven. Two days ago, I brought it up on the way to our apprenticeships in Halifax. I suggested he speak to Headmaster Thet. He shushed me."

"And the second thing?"

"The last few times we were alone together, he talked endlessly about Black Star. He'd become obsessed with them."

OK, so that was a bit more grounded. Not to mention indirectly connected to the deceased's cause of death.

Hoshi joined the interrogation.

"Is that why you asked about Motif?"

Eliza nodded. "What I said before was true. Ulbrecht would never take any illicit drugs – and certainly not Motif. He was fanatical about his health."

"I hate to break it to you, Eliza, but that drug has screwed up a billion lives and counting. Many of those people were smart, healthy, and appeared to be responsible. Anyone can have a lapse in judgment. Perhaps Ulbrecht ..."

She spoke through steeled jaws.

"Never. He was the strongest man I knew. I loved ..." Eliza took a deep breath and gathered herself. "He wanted to make the future better for us all. Ulbrecht believed his mind was a gift intended for that single purpose."

Hoshi offered a supporting hand, while Trevor reset his strategy before his own paranoia kicked in.

"If I hear you correctly, Eliza, you're suggesting the drug we found in Ulbrecht entered his body against his will. Yes?"

She nodded, so Trevor threaded that needle.

"OK. Let's say for the moment that Motif was involved. I'm neither confirming nor denying. If someone wanted Ulbrecht dead, there are far more effective ways of killing him. Less than four percent of users die from an MOD."

Hoshi nodded, but Eliza shrugged.

"I can't explain it, Deputy. Will there be a toxical report?"

"Certainly. If his cause of death was more complicated, our lifetechs will find out. What else can you tell us, Eliza? The others in your group talked about the Raison Club."

She rolled her eyes.

"Be careful what you take from those cudfruckers. Pardon my bite. They were all jealous of Ulbrecht. Everyone who knew him was. But yes, he loved the club scene. It was a release."

"Did you spend much time with him there?"

"No. I needed sleep. Ulbrecht ... he had more energy than he knew what to do with."

"Did he ever mention any specific people he met at Raison?"

"No. He invited me many times. Said I needed what the club offered, but nothing specific. I don't cater to that lifestyle."

Hmm. What it offered. Motif, perhaps?

"OK. You've given us enough to move forward. Hoshi, anything you'd like to ask?"

The Second Deputy surprised Trevor.

"Eliza, did you know Ulbrecht threatened another student's life? Someone also from Yaniff."

Shit. How did Trevor let that nugget slide past?

"Oh. Yes. That was weeks ago. He had an argument with a friend from back home. It wasn't a serious threat."

"So, you were there?"

"No. He mentioned it to me later. He actually felt bad about it."

"What was the student's name?"

Eliza tapped her forehead.

"Oh. It's ... he's on a different track. Oh. Yes. Orval. I don't know his last name. Sorry."

Hoshi smiled. "Erdogan. We already know."

"I'm sorry. I'm not thinking clearly. There's probably more I can tell you. After I go home, I'll meditate on everything."

"Thank you, Eliza." Trevor regained the lead. "You can contact us at Haven Sec Admin whenever you feel comfortable. We'll make ourselves available. In the meantime, I recommend you don't mention what we discussed. Think you can do that?"

"I give you my word. Please, find who did this to Ulbrecht."

He wasn't about to make promises he couldn't keep. A pair of students entered the break room; time to shut this down.

"We'll pursue every angle, Eliza. Now, if you're up to it, why don't you return to 417. Your mentor seemed insistent."

She bowed her head.

"You have no idea. Thank you both."

Trevor and Hoshi said nothing after Eliza left, but their presence drew whispers from the other visitors.

"Perhaps some place less public," Trevor mumbled.

After they entered the nearest lift without company, Hoshi said:

"I was wrong, Trev. I thought this trip would be a waste of time."

"And now?"

"If there's even a chance she's right about Ulbrecht ... what have we walked into?"

"Damned if I know. But I intend to find out. You'll have my back on this when we report in to Dorrit. Yes?"

She winced at the sound of his name.

"He'll say it's mad conjecture. A grief-stricken lover. Jealous rivals. A headmaster trying to protect the school from scandal."

Trevor heard the Chief raging already.

"Ah, yes." The lift opened to the administrative level. "Good men and women who represent the best of the human race. Hard workers under great stress, trying to deal with a shocking loss. We must protect the institution from scandal."

"A coverup?"

"He won't think of it that way. They never do."

They muffled the conversation while approaching the headmaster's office. Thet's answers appeared to be filled with misdirection, but

88

Trevor needed to be sure.

"For now, we don't mention Eliza Hutton's accusation."

She yanked his arm.

"What? We can't do that. It's a direct violation of ..."

"I know the regs, Hoshi. It's not for long. I have some avenues I want to pursue. If she's credible, I'll know before day's end. Then we'll tell Dorrit."

He saw skepticism in those conservative eyes.

"What is it, Hoshi?"

"Holding back information got you booted from Harmony Sec Admin. Are you willing to take that risk again?"

OK. There it was. She was fishing.

"Did some heavy reading over lunch, I see. Look, it's more complicated than the HSA report. When I've known you long enough to trust you, I'll fill you in. You won't get a better offer."

She let go of his arm.

"It's your career, Trev."

He couldn't resist a chuckle.

"What's left of it."

Trevor made a beeline for the exit, a storm of tasks in need of sorting as soon as he returned to Haven. He began the day intent on steering clear of rough patches, focusing only on how to make right with Ana. Now the job wrapped its predictable tentacles around him. Like always, little would stand between Trevor and the answers he sought.

Which went to the core of the problem.

He kept his head down as they passed through the lobby but couldn't help notice the greeter stare at them like a woman forever offended.

Trevor might have brushed it off were the path out of Maynor clear. Instead, as he flashed his wrist plate against the LinkPass reader, another deputy entered.

"Shit," he muttered before flashing a phony grin.

13

"T REV." THE ESA DEPUTY held up a hand. "Why did I think it might be you?"

The man spoke with no obvious antagonism.

"Been a few weeks, Thomas."

The deputy winked at Trevor's partner.

"Hoshi Oda. Good seeing you again. Hooked you up with the Lifetime Deputy, did they?"

She extended a hand.

"Chief Dorrit wanted me to learn from a man of experience."

"You won't find more than in this guy. Don't know if experience equates to wisdom in Trev's case."

Hah, hah.

Enough with the banter, Trevor thought. He shook Second Deputy Thomas Quinlan's hand.

"I doubt you just happened to be in the neighborhood, Thomas."

The deputy consumed his smile.

"I was redirected from patrol. ESA received a call that Maynor students were being harassed by an off-sector deputy. No one from Haven or Harmony had checked in with our Admin today, so I suspected it might be someone who tends to be proactive, as they say. You came straight to mind."

Thomas' accusations of protocol violation were never subtle.

"I'm not side-stepping the regs. We're investigating a death that occurred in Haven. I'm lead."

"And there was no harassment, Thomas," Hoshi added. "We asked routine background questions."

Thomas had slimmed down considerably from the man of chiseled granite who arrived on Amity three years ago.

"Not what the complainant claims, but we'll see about ..."

"There, Deputy!"

A familiar voice interrupted the reunion. The greeter Deena neared, finger pointed at Trevor.

"They're the ones. They ignored me when I told them to wait for the headmaster. Then they barged into his office and demanded an audience. Then they refused to leave and disrupted a private mentee class."

Deena lost her permanent smile. That didn't bother Trevor so much as how she knew their activities. Appeared she was more than a sweet face to welcome visitors.

"Thank you," Thomas told her with a dismissive wave. "I'll take care of this. Feel free to return to your duties."

"Make sure they are barred from Maynor."

Thomas didn't reply. Rather, he escorted them to the public docks and tapped into his wrist plate.

"A death, you say? Maynor student?"

Trevor confirmed the basics without mentioning Motif.

"Lifetechs will finish their report in a few hours. Probably just a case of a fool who got carried away and lost his life. I wanted to make sure we covered the angles before the news goes public."

Thomas weighed the explanation with tongue in cheek – a tic that hadn't changed in decades. To Trevor's surprise, the ESA deputy shrugged.

"Sounds like a reasonable response. I doubt you harassed anyone. Ruffled a few egos, maybe. But that's your style, Trev." He stepped closer with a menacing glare. "Look. I don't want to mess with your investigation, but I'll have to add a note for the record. How about you check in with us next time? A courtesy."

"Sure, Thomas. I appreciate the soft touch."

A rap on the shoulder preceded a self-satisfied grin.

"Old friends have to look out for each other," Thomas said. "I'll let you two on your way and smooth the ruffles inside Maynor."

Trevor thanked the Second Deputy with just enough syrupy gratitude to pass muster then hopped on a rifter and plotted a course to the Crossway. Hoshi soon brought up the obvious.

"Old friends, he said. How long have you known Thomas?"

Yeah, well, he couldn't avoid it.

"Unfortunately, most of my life."

"So, he's an Earther?"

"Thomas Quinlan was my first-ever bully. The anti-Chancellor bigotry was more intense back then. I was twelve, he was sixteen."

Her jaw slipped in obvious fascination.

"Now he's here. What are the odds?"

"Not as long as you think. We were neighbors in Philadelphia Redux. Swarm attacked the city, destroyed part of our building. Connor and I lost everything. Our mother, the flat. His family survived. His parents weren't jackasses. They looked after us."

Memories. He never learned how to shut off the worst ones.

"They were very generous," Hoshi said.

He accelerated the rifter with the Crossway in clear view.

"They thought it would be temporary. Four days later, we got the news about Father. He was killed in the last battle of the war. A few days turned into two years. That's how long it took Grandfather Max to concern himself with us."

"I assume you and Thomas became friends?"

Trevor cleared his throat.

"We tolerated each other. Not long after Connor and I moved on, he joined the UNF. I lost track of him, which was for the best. He meant to make a career of it, but the UNF downsized. He spent a few years working various badges back home. Three years ago, he applied for an Amity rotation. Deepstreamed me. Asked for a personal recommendation."

"Did you?"

Connor once joked that marriage would make Trevor soft. The kid brother wasn't wrong.

"He was going through a rough patch. I reviewed his jacket ... and yeah. I vouched for him to Central with one caveat: That they station him in a different sector."

"You have a big heart, Trev."

"Not for Thomas. I did it to repay his parents."

"Good you did. No telling what sort of hard-ass might have taken us through the ringer if Thomas hadn't shown up."

Trevor wanted to put this matter to bed.

"Don't be deceived, Hoshi. I'd wager my pay stamp he's playing an angle. Thomas applied for a promotion not three months after he arrived. He's never risen past Second Deputy even though he was retained for a second rotation. I heard through the chain he thinks someone is blocking him."

"Ah, so he's as paranoid as you."

"Nope." He snuck in a wink. "He's been blocked at every turn."

Did he see confusion or disgust in her frown?

"Why, Trev?"

"I gave him a break in a moment of weakness. I keep hoping he'll resign and leave the station."

"Huh. He probably suspects you."

"If not, he's a moron. I'm sure he was pissed when I moved into this job. He wants that First bar." Trevor knew he gave away too much. "We never had this discussion, Second Deputy."

She looked away as they neared the lift.

"Never, First Deputy."

Trevor said little on the return train but assured Hoshi he'd try to play nice with Dorrit.

"I'll spend the next few hours in the office. We have research to do. If the Chief needs to spit fire, I'll be a willing target."

Haven Sec Admin's layout matched the other two offices, so Trevor found his private space and settled in without need for acclimation. Even the café kiosk was equidistant from the one he often used in Harmony.

He nodded to the other deputies, most of whom he knew in passing – especially those on second rotation. If they were curious about how he was adjusting or wanted the full scoop on what brought him to the "working class" sector of Amity, no one seemed willing to start the queue, which suited him just fine.

He laid out instructions for avenues he wanted Hoshi to pursue and began transcribing his notes from the interviews. That lasted all of ten minutes.

"A word," Chief Hannibal Dorrit said, casting a sudden shadow.

Trevor followed him into a double-sized glass office he once dreamed of occupying on Harmony. Dorrit kept a largely clean desk, apparently to leave room for the hologlyphs of family. Trevor counted at least ten kids, all of whom he assumed were grands.

"Please," Dorrit motioned to a chair which naturally sat low against the Chief's elevated lift. Trevor knew the routine.

"I'm sure you'll soon submit a report?"

"Putting it together. We made some interesting discoveries over there. Need to follow up."

Dorrit winced as his carcass fell into the big seat. He reached for his left knee, which he flexed.

"My ever faithful wife insists I spend more time in the fit room. What would you advise?"

OK. Another game-player. Trevor didn't have time to be set up.

"I never comment on personal health choices, Chief. Seems a bit ... I don't know ... *personal.*"

Dorrit massaged the knee, as if that would help.

"Come now, Trevor. You're not known for being apolitical."

95

Fair enough.

"I spend an hour a day in the fit room. You're more than welcome to join me, Chief. I'll share my wealth of advice."

Yeah, that wasn't about to happen. Dorrit released his hand and plopped it on the clear desk, upon which he leaned forward.

"I've spent ten uncomfortable minutes conversing with Sharif Al-Jani. He's concerned that you created a stir inside Maynor. Now, Sharif is by all accounts an unbearable prude who makes my moderate approach to the job seem downright unbridled. However, he is my equal and can choose to leap over me with Central. I'll not have it. Do you understand the implication?"

Trevor had never run afoul of ESA Chief Al-Jani, but the man was known to be territorial and a high-quality friend to the boards of Halifax, Atumwa, and Mullen.

"I might, Chief, but I'd prefer you speak plainly."

"Then I will. Trevor, I find myself deeply conflicted by your presence. So much so, that I recognize we got off on ill-mannered footing this morning. I'd like to square a few things before I send you back to your desk."

Trevor anticipated a dragon spitting fire; instead, he found a reasonably composed and even contemplative boss.

"I'm at your mercy, Chief."

"Perfect."

Dorrit pointed to the panoply of hologlyphs.

"You're a family man, Trevor. You appreciate having loved ones. Especially your daughter. Yes?"

"I do. Although my family is much more compact."

"Hmm. My parents were fruitful, as they say. Nine brothers and sisters. Four grandchildren of my own, and twenty-four nieces and nephews. One withering problem. All but my wife live on Catalan. I see them four times a year. Once a standard quarter. As I grow older, heavier, and less fond of risk, I find myself wishing those reunions were more frequent. Permanent, actually."

Here we go. Everyone always needed a story to back their way into an explanation of their worldview. Trevor played along.

"Sounds like a man who's planning to retire soon."

Dorrit snapped a finger and pointed at Trevor like firing a gun.

"My rotation ends in five months. Fulfilling the contract ensures a handsome pension. My wife and I have plans. I intend to make them reality. Which means I have no interest in anything other than a soft landing to this job.

"On my last day, I want Central to honor me with a cake and a trinket of their choice then a private ride to the spaceport. I intend to drink wine for the duration of the ninety-minute wormhole and never, not ever, set foot on Amity again. Now, this isn't to say I have no interest in the station's well-being. Of course, I do. Its success remains vital to the Collectorate's future. And I want my people to protect it against threats both interstellar and domestic.

"Doing that requires prudence, discipline, and balance. I cannot abide discord here or among the sectors. To answer the question bubbling behind your lips, Trevor: No, I don't intend to hold your hand or require you to ask permission each time you leave the office. You're the most experienced security officer on Amity. Also the most controversial. And to my mind, someone who should have been fired.

"However, you walk a carpet of roses in high places thanks to your grandfather's ghost and his surviving cronies. I expressed my strongest objection to Central regarding your reassignment. They reminded me of the end date to my rotation."

Dorrit's considerable cheeks turned bright red as he laughed. Trevor couldn't help but admire the oversized creature for a shocking display of honesty.

"Thank you for the clarity, Chief."

"I don't want you to lose your job, Trevor. You have a lovely wife and daughter. The shame they would feel ... no. Not something I want a family to experience. So, you may continue your investigation. If it requires a return trip to Episteme or Harmony, brief me first. If I order you to close the case, you will do so without comment. Do these conditions sit well with you, First Deputy?"

Trevor cleared his throat. As if he had any choice ...

"They do, Chief. You'll get no trouble from me."

"Lovely."

Dorrit motioned him out with a flick of the wrist.

"One request, Chief. The other four MODs. I'd like access to the data spools. We have to be sure these are not connected."

Dorrit huffed like a man in dire need of more exercise.

"Take what you have, Trevor. Show cause for expanding the investigation. Then – and only then – will I consider the request."

Trevor steamed but allowed the indignity to pass. Ten embarrassed minutes later, he cleared his mind and found resolve.

Something was off. Way off.

Instinct took control, and it told Trevor one thing:

He had a murder to solve.

14

T REVOR'S OFFICE OVERFLOWED with visual data. He turned his back on the bank of monitors that broadcast from fifty of Haven's public secure cams. He concentrated on the other two-thirds of his space, where he had filled a holospread with dozens of annotations.

These dataflicks – transcribed notes embedded on white popups – hovered against the spread like unstable decorations on flimsy tree branches. Interview texts, analyses, hypotheticals, and biographies intermingled, some connected to each other by hand-drawn lines.

Amid the convolution rested everything Trevor had gathered on Ulbrecht Hann – including trend waves based on seven months of LinkPass history. Three hours into creating a jigsaw with no fixed image, Trevor added dataflicks on Raison Club.

He heard a knock followed by:

"I don't know whether to be impressed or concerned," Hoshi said. She didn't wait for permission to enter, not that Trevor would have refused. "Is this how your mind always works?"

He grinned at her reasonable assessment.

"Paranoia in the wild. Pull up a chair."

She grabbed a swivel and joined him.

"What are you looking for, Trev?"

"Patterns. Links. Inconsistencies. Confirmation."

"Of what?"

"That my instinct hasn't betrayed me."

"You're convinced it was murder."

"I want to be. That's what confirmation bias is all about."

"I checked in with the lifetechs. We should have the toxical in two hours. But even that might be inconclusive. If all they find is Motif, they'll book it as an accidental overdose. And if we can't show the Chief it warrants further investigation ..."

Trevor sighed.

"We close the case without comment. Exactly what his killer expected us to do."

"You sound like Eliza Hutton."

He heard a growing skepticism.

"You think she's overwrought. Even a liar?"

Hoshi grabbed Eliza's dataflick and expanded it.

"Not what I said. At all. But she loved Ulbrecht. Love is ..."

"Trust me, Hoshi. I know what it does to a person. And yes, it's possible Ulbrecht thought he was in danger but exaggerated the threat. He might have been more paranoid than anyone."

She pointed to dataflicks clustered together, each containing a headshot of a student in Ulbrecht's mentee group.

"Their profiles? Trev, you aren't pulling from their ..."

"Just their public bios. I'm not violating the Charter. I'll stay away from the LinkPass history ... for now. But the moment they become material witnesses, I'll be running trend waves on the lot of them. By the way, good work on the backgrounding for Bien Thet and Mustafa Chait."

Hoshi thanked him with hesitation.

"I did as you asked, Trev, but I really don't see how it helps."

He gave Hoshi the side-eye. Was she serious? Trevor pushed his swivel toward those two profiles, around which he had posted dataflicks with their contradictory stories and a series of what-ifs.

"Thet and Chait have incredible resumes. Thet was part of the team that built Maynor from nothing. He led two colleges on Indonesia Prime before and after the war. Chait is serving his fourth rotation, with praise galore from the student reflection boards. He was a mechanical engineering professor at the top school on Marianas. Before that, supervised the redesign of their largest lunar mining facility. Tripled their output inside a year.

"These men are some of the best in their fields. They're supposed to be on the same page about Maynor's students. Agree?"

Hoshi shrugged. "I would hope so."

"Yet when we asked about Ulbrecht, they contradicted each other. Thet said he was on the verge of expulsion. Chait praised Ulbrecht and said the so-called threat on Orval Erdogan's life was nothing. How does that happen?"

Hoshi stared at the info she compiled and shook her head.

"Chait was Ulbrecht's mentor. He was naturally more protective. Maybe even in denial."

It wasn't a bad theory, but Trevor laughed anyway.

"Mustafa Chait? That guy? I was surprised he didn't walk around those students holding a whip. They didn't answer our questions without looking at him first. He knew everything about his mentees."

"Perhaps the headmaster withheld information from Chait."

"Why? Thet said he consulted with all one thousand students every quarter. You saw how reverential they were toward him, like they knew their lives were in his hands. I'm sure he meets with the mentors on a regular basis."

Hoshi didn't respond to his point. She switched into reverse.

"Hold on a minute, Trev. Did I hear you right? You expect those students to become material witnesses? As in, suspects?"

"I'm not saying anyone in that room is a killer, but the four men didn't exactly shed a tear at the news. Not so much as a quiver. Eliza said they were jealous of Ulbrecht. And they shared a consensus: No one could match his mind or his energy. Thet said Ulbrecht would've made a huge mark in history. The loss should have hit them where it hurt. Aside from Eliza, they were empty vessels."

He pointed to Jor Kerrindos' dataflick.

"This one stands out. Insulted the guy not thirty seconds after learning he was dead. Said they were incompatible lab partners. Made a point of putting distance between him and Ulbrecht."

Hoshi said, "OK, so he's a jackass. Maybe he saw Ulbrecht as a competitor. One less obstacle in his path."

"People have killed for less."

She stifled a laugh.

"Paranoid *and* cynical."

Trevor slapped his bar.

"That's why they pay me the big creds."

"When was the last time you investigated a murder?"

"Never. Not even trained as a detective. But I pay attention, Hoshi. It's all about the details. My wife says I would be great in SI." Trevor admired the incoherent product he threw together in short order. "There's an answer here. I feel it take shape every time I move around a few flicks."

"Sure you aren't kidding yourself?"

He dared not take that bet, especially on the off chance that he was, in fact, delusional. This wouldn't be the first time he saw a tempest in a teacup. Trevor ignored Hoshi's challenge, but she wouldn't let up.

"Trev, if we're going to talk about details, then let's revisit the most problematic. You already established that Ulbrecht had no visitors last night. No one accessed his door after he returned home. We can't get around a simple but inconvenient fact: No one forced him to take Motif."

He couldn't square that truth with Eliza's claim, which had to mean he wasn't thinking far enough afield.

"Physically? No. Ulbrecht was alone. A given. But if you were staging a murder to look like a simple overdose, you'd have to be extra clever. Yes?"

OK, so maybe I'm reaching. Maybe. Shit.

Trevor ignored Hoshi's grimace and shifted his focus.

"I need to speak with Orval Erdogan. He and Ulbrecht knew each other before they left Yaniff. See here."

He pointed out biographical data predating their rotation.

"Twice they competed in transnational engineering contests. Orval finished third in both. Ulbrecht took first in one, second in the other. These young gents were rivals from the start."

Hoshi grabbed the relevant dataflick and read the details.

"That might explain the threat. These men hated each other."

"Or maybe not. Take a look at this."

He pointed out Orval's address. Hoshi raised an intrigued brow.

"Andromeda 557. OK, that's interesting."

"Ulbrecht's floor. You told me this morning that people beat the Housing Authority's assignment process so they can be clustered with their own ethnic groups. Orval and Ulbrecht arrived two days apart and became instant neighbors. Either they knew how to play the game and wanted to be close by, or that's a hell of a coincidence."

Hoshi nodded. "I see where you're going, but it's also possible their relationship changed afterward. Seven months is a long time."

"It is. Which is why I need to speak with Orval."

"And since he lives in Haven ..."

Trevor snapped his fingers.

"I won't have to clear it with the Chief."

"I assume you'd like to do it before the toxical report."

"Fresh is best."

"OK. I'm good whenever you're ready, Trev."

"Appreciate the flexibility, but Orval won't be home for another hour. He's in apprenticeship at Atumwa, and you're scheduled for solo patrol. Aft grid."

She groaned, of course. He knew the feeling.

Solo patrols, most of which involved walking neighborhoods and checking in with local businesses, rarely amounted to anything but an opportunity to present the colors and allow residents to know Sec Admin was keeping tabs. Good exercise, but little more.

"I'll switch with Sinjun," she said. "He owes me for last week."

"Wouldn't hear of it. I can handle the interview myself. Orval is going to be tricky. He and Ulbrecht were both Turks. They've known each other for a while. Two badges might intimidate him."

Trevor heard the objection before it crossed her lips.

"If this does turn out to be a murder investigation, I intend to be your partner. Frankly, you need someone to act as a check. I acquitted myself well today when you allowed me to contribute."

An eventful day in her young career. No doubt. Still ...

"Yes, Hoshi. You added some valuable touches. Don't worry. I'll keep you in the loop."

"I could go over your head."

She wasn't serious; Trevor heard mockery in her tone.

"I see." He replied with a playful grin. "A little insubordination on the first day? Nice."

"Not at all. I think the Chief would want us to be thorough."

"Hah. Dorrit wants all this to go away. Look, Hoshi. We were thrown together into this ... whatever it is ... by happenstance. He could've assigned anyone to me this morning. You did well, all things considered. I'll handle the interview. After the toxical report returns, we'll evaluate the next step, assuming there is one."

Trevor didn't intend to sound patronizing, but her disappointed Hokki eyes told a different story. He never meant to hurt her feelings, but the same could be said a hundred times over since he first wore the bar. Effie once claimed her husband introduced a new verb into Engleshe:

"*Trevored,*" she said. "Feeling smaller and less worthy after an encounter with Trevor Stallion."

"That's not fair. I never go into a conversation looking to beat someone down."

"Yet you succeed more often than not."

Effie offered to teach skills she developed in the DRC. He vowed to use them, but lack of patience with other humans got in the way.

Hoshi insisted she didn't take it personally, but her tone suggested otherwise. Trevor tried his usual reassurance:

"I'm no linguistic master. Each day with me gets easier. Trust me."

"You're sure I can't switch with Sinjun? I'd really love to ..."

"No. Follow the routine. Right now, I'd say there's even odds we won't have a case after today. If we do, you're on my team."

She looked around, as if someone was missing.

"What team? You have a roster?"

Fair point.

"For me, two is enough. A third voice is a nasty ringing in the ear."

"So, you could never do a job like, say, headmaster?"

His personal pom chimed inside his jacket.

"Thet scares me. I don't trust anyone who accepts bows."

Trevor grabbed the gold-lined comms device, which flipped open like an ancient pocket watch.

Life stopped when Effie's tear-soaked face rose into a holo.

He knew that helpless, empty stare.

Please, no. Not again.

"Talk to me," he said.

"It's Ana. She's seizing."

"How bad?"

"It's violent. Worst in years. Trevor, I ..."

"No need. I'm there."

"Hurry."

In a flash, life simplified. A man might have been murdered, and Trevor walked a tightrope with his new boss. So what? His little girl was going through hell, and her father was to blame.

Life. Real simple.

15

"WHAT DO I TELL THE CHIEF?" Hoshi asked as Trevor bolted for the door, unsure when he'd return.

"My daughter's sick," Trevor yelled back, glancing toward the glass office where Dorrit sat amid his family hologlyphs, oblivious to the disturbance. "Nothing else matters."

He grabbed a rifter and made a mad dash for the Crossway. There, he'd be stuck for … how long?

Trevor checked the train schedule. Next one to Harmony was eight minutes out. Might as well have been eighty.

C'mon, Trev. Get a handle on yourself. She needs you at your best. No sobbing. Not this time.

He waited on the platform, tapping his fingers on the bench in a calming rhythm.

They had almost talked themselves into believing the shudders were behind Ana. She hadn't seized in four months, and even that one was mild compared to the previous. Lasted less than an hour, and she was cogent most of the time.

Of course, the doctor gave them fair warning:

"The earliest we've ever seen this condition phase out is ten years old. At some point, we expect the age minimum to decrease. Ana's most recent shudder is a positive sign. Perhaps she'll set the new standard."

Doc Edina Forster was the leading expert on neurofascitis. She smiled, laughed, and engaged like an old friend. So much so, Effie and Trevor inferred something close to a promise in her forecast.

A hundred ten standard days later, the nightmare returned with a vengeance. *Violent,* Effie said. *Worst in years.*

Each episode triggered memories of the day they first received the news. Ana Marie was a week from her first birthday when the twitching began. Her little arms jerked, and she kicked uncontrollably. Her fingers played an invisible piano. Her cries turned to shrieks as the shudder continued, the condition attacking her joints.

"I'm so sorry," Trevor told Effie after the diagnosis. "Look what I did to her."

Effie rejected his apologies. He doubted their love would survive the revelation, but his wife insisted nothing could break them.

"We knew there was a risk, Trev. I wanted her anyway. I'm as much to blame."

Disruptive neurofascitis, they called it. One of many legacies of the Chancellors' long genetic collapse. Thousands of cases arose across the Collectorate in the decades after the last supplies of brontinium extract dried up.

For centuries, Trevor's ancestors modified their biology to enhance growth both physical and intellectual. Their pursuit of supremacy over the human race knew no limitations. The extract, drawn from the hardest known mineral on the forty worlds, proved pivotal.

Then every vein of brontinium disintegrated on the only planet where it was found. When Hiebimini died in 5311, the Chancellory faced a slow, inexorable death of its own. Insiders hid the truth: Without extract, Chancellors would lose the ability to bear children. Their progeny would be diminished, and illnesses they avoided for centuries would return en masse. The caste would die out in five or six generations.

Trevor and Effie first consulted Doc Forster two months into the pregnancy. Trevor assumed Effie would do the practical thing. Then

Forster presented hope.

"Two percent. Your genetic profile," she told Trevor, "rates the likelihood of genetic defects in your child at two percent. If you were both Chancellors, the risk would increase tenfold."

He thought the number was too high and also contradicted a promise Grandfather Max made him and Connor when they were teenagers. Max insisted they take the new drug that promised to halt the Chancellors' demise.

"Doc, I've been receiving regular shots of Verita 460 since I was eighteen. I was told it would prevent anything like this from being passed down if I had children."

She nodded in that I've-heard-it-all-before style.

"VT 460 is a miracle. Unfortunately, many Chancellors don't understand what it actually does. You were born before the drug was released. That means you inherited your parents' genetic collapse. VT 460 smooths out the rough edges, so to speak, but it's not a cure. Your children and their children will have to take it every year so long as they live. In time, it will reverse engineer centuries of biological modifications."

That night, after they went back and forth until agreeing to continue the pregnancy, Trevor said:

"The irony is I never wanted children before you. Connor wore me out when we were kids. I couldn't imagine doing it again."

"You'll change your mind the first time you hold her."

She was right, of course. Like in most things.

He said a silent prayer when the nurse handed over Ana Marie.

"You'll be perfect, my sweet girl. You'll have everything your mother gave you and fight off the rest."

If only.

Effie never voiced regret, never assigned blame, never admitted that she turned to another man because of it. Trevor assumed.

Those years whizzed past as he waited for the train, raced onboard, and began another countdown. 'Wit's end' described Trevor as he reentered Harmony Sector.

"Announcement. Now arriving: Harmony Midvale. Please stand clear until the doors have opened in full."

He did not wait that long. Observers must have feared a station-wide emergency given Trevor's panic. He broke speed regs on the public rifter, traveling two-thirds the length of Harmony.

The sector seemed brighter, cleaner, more energetic than Haven. The gardens were bigger and more lush and the Swiftraks wider. Facilities for the Interstellar Congress and Office of the President rose like pyramidal beacons. The spaceport spread out above it all, the largest of its kind in the Collectorate.

Yet Trevor focused solely on the tiny, oblong structure between the IC complex and the Amity Housing Authority. They brought Ana here for every seizure; his grandfather's ghost welcomed him.

Vanover Medical Center and Research Institute.

It wasn't the only place where Maximillian Vanover ensured his immortality, but it was the most prominent. The old man died a week after the renaming ceremony. *Got his glory*, Trevor thought at the time. *That's all he ever wanted.*

Trevor met his wife in Orange Wing: Neurology. Effans Labroque waited outside their daughter's room. She wore a casual one-piece tunic, far from the business formal that Trevor might have expected this time of day.

"What's happening?"

Effie blocked the door.

"They're finishing a phasic scan."

"What? They're still running it? Forster's usually done in five ..."

"It's not Forster. She's off-station. It's Beryl Sim."

"The hell? That guy shouldn't be anywhere near our daughter."

He grabbed Effie and prepared to push her aside.

"Trevor, I know how you feel about him. He misspoke that one time. You need to let it go."

"Not where Ana Marie is concerned. Please, Eff. I'm the only one who can soothe her pain."

Effie did not resist.

"That's why I called you, Trev." She pressed the entry pad. "Please, be respectful. He's doing his job."

So he claimed. They all did, even when they added a simple caveat: We can't do anything but let this play out and keep her comfortable during seizures.

Not good enough!

Trevor checked his frustration at the door, but it quickly reemerged when he saw the phasic stabilizer surrounding Ana's bed. The metallic hologram was barely translucent enough to see a human inside. A crawler arm hovered above the stabilizer field, emitting a blue beam that crept over his daughter.

"That's enough," he said, modulating his tone. No sense pissing off the doctor straightaway. "Drop the field."

Sim, whose burnt red hair and ample freckles never sat right with Trevor, raised his hands in a double stop sign.

"Deputy Stallion, we won't be much longer, I promise. We need all the data possible for Ana's long-term prospects. For others like her, also."

"I don't care about the long term. She's in pain now. She needs me now."

Trevor moved toward the phasic control box, but Sim's nurse blocked him. Trevor, eight inches taller than either man, swerved around to confront Sim just as the door closed behind Effie. Show respect, her eyes begged. Another word for restraint.

OK. I'll give him one chance.

"Have the shudders lessened?"

"Not yet. I fear it may be another two to three hours." Sim pointed to the holographic data spread along the stabilizer shield. "I have her on three hundred milligrams of Seraphed. The usual dose. Any more and ..."

"I know the risk. You're going to shut this down and allow me to do it my way. Doctor."

Sim did not possess Forster's sunny bedside manner. He was a technocrat, and Trevor knew how to deal with such people. When Sim said he needed the data stream, Trevor laid his ample right hand on the man's shoulder and tempered his tone.

"If I let go, I'm going to ball those fingers together. Three seconds later, you will be asleep on the floor. Tell the nurse to shut it down, or both of you are going to take a nap. Clear?"

"Trev, please don't ..." Effie stepped in.

"I got this, Eff. Make a decision, Doc."

Trevor knew Sim had every right to contact Harmony Sec Admin and report the threat. He also knew Sim had his own needle to thread, having built a checkered reputation during his rotation.

"Henri," Sim said. "Shut it down."

"Yes, Doctor."

Trevor backed away.

"Thank you."

"You're making a mistake, Deputy. This thing you do has no impact on the larger problem. Forster said ..."

"Forster isn't here. I know how to help my daughter better than any of you."

Effie backed away but offered Trevor a supportive nod. He took a deep breath and braced himself for the sight that tore at his heart.

Ana lay flat on her back, limbs jerking and twitching, held down by straps. Her eyes rolled back in her head; her tongue poked in and out as if lapping up invisible water; sweat rolled down the sides of her mocha face. Ana's deep brown curls, similar to her mother's, were wet and tangled. She moaned like a wounded animal.

Trevor unfastened the straps.

"I'm here, sweetheart. Papa's here."

He climbed onto the bed and gently pushed his left arm under her back while holding her knees close to each other with his right. Trevor ordered the nurse to raise the head of the bed to forty-five degrees. When the man hesitated, Sim gave him the green light.

Trevor maneuvered the little girl's body until she rested on top of him. He brought his knees forward and shifted carefully to his side until he wrapped Ana in an awkward sort of shelter. All the while, her elbows poked him in the gut.

"OK, sweetheart. Listen to Papa. Can you hear me?"

He didn't expect an answer at the beginning but knew it would be yes, if she could speak. Every doctor had tried to stop him – even Forster didn't believe Trevor's strategy would work. Nor could they explain his success.

"I read," he once told Forster in a condescending tone. He took that knowledge – specifically, that disruptive neurofascitis began its assault on the body at the intersection between the brain stem and the spinal cord – and applied it to his daughter.

Trevor pushed her hair out of the way and arrayed three left fingers to land at the precise location he believed the shudders could be controlled. He pressed his forefinger and middle finger inward as hard as he could to either side of cervical vertebrae 1C and his thumb on top of vertebrae 3C.

His right hand wrapped beneath and around her belly, and his legs acted as a new set of restraints to her kicking limbs. He'd have a few small bruises later.

"Sweetheart, listen to Papa. You want to sing along with me? It's your favorite song. OK? Join me whenever you're ready."

Trevor closed his eyes and gave all of himself to his life's most beautiful gift. What choice did he have? Her nightmare was his fault, after all. He'd never forgive himself for doing less.

"Have you seen the stars tonight?" He sang off-key. "They're so big and ever bright. Have you seen the stars tonight?"

He repeated both verses ten times. It was her favorite, the first song she learned. He sang it at bedtime by request, which was more often than not in the first years. After she turned four, Ana varied her musical tastes. Sometimes, she asked him to read. Other times, to tell her stories of growing up on a planet.

You don't deserve this.

Those words never crossed his lips – not in her presence. But the guilt lingered and consumed. Yes, the VT 460 would ensure an end to the seizures in a few years, but at what cost? Already, the doctors expressed concerns about her long-term joint stability. They worried how she would fare in a terrestrial environment with a higher gravity. Studies done on earlier victims of DF were not promising.

After he finished the first song, Trevor rocked Ana until her moans faded to be replaced by calm, steady respiration. The shudders slowed but only by a negligible pace.

Forster said from the beginning that the seizures could not be predicted, and studies showed no link to a child's emotional state. Yet Trevor couldn't help but remember last night. The wild, desperate look in her eyes when he tried to explain how the rules of his job forced him to move to Haven Sector. How the transfer was only temporary and that they'd see each other every day, even if on holo.

Her rage caught both him and Effie off-guard. In a practical sense, little would change in their schedules or time together, but Ana wouldn't hear it.

"She doesn't know change," Effie said. "Her world has always been small and safe and consistent. Give her time, Trevor. Perhaps she needs to go through this to see it isn't so terrible after all."

Wise words. Now, Trevor thought they were premature. Reckless, even. Yet he'd bought into them.

He rocked Ana, never lessening his three-fingered offensive.

"I'm sorry I had to go away, sweetheart. But I'm here now. I won't leave. I'll never leave. Do you hear me?"

In time, the shudders subsided. Trevor opened his eyes. Effie sat on the edge of the bed massaging Ana's hands. For a moment there, he felt love like they shared in the beginning.

Trevor wasn't naïve. Whatever they shared eroded long ago. Maybe Effie still didn't blame him, but now he was a salve for their daughter. Little more.

"Thirsty."

Ana's first word came as no surprise.

Trevor didn't let go, but Effie's smile said enough: The eyes had stabilized. The tremors in her joints lessened to a manageable tenor. The seizure was nearing an end, less than an hour after he arrived. The damage done couldn't be quantified yet, but the pain would end. Nothing else mattered.

"You're here, Papa."

"For my sweetheart? Always. Just lay still a few more minutes, and this will pass. OK?"

"OK. Can I get water, Mama?"

The nurse provided a cup with a straw.

"Here you go," he said. "Drink slowly. There's plenty more."

Doc Sim observed from the foot of the bed. His stoic features gave away nothing. Trevor didn't blame the man for not lavishing praise or suggesting Trevor's technique should be used on other such patients. In fact, there was no hard evidence Ana's condition lessened any faster in her father's arms, or that he reduced the potential for long-term physical issues.

Trevor knew only that his daughter's pain was fading for now. What the hell else mattered?

After Ana drank the cup dry, she asked the only question he dreaded:

"Papa, are you coming back home today?"

He saw terror in Effie's eyes. Just when all was well again ...

Trevor learned from his wife the diplomat.

"We are going to spend so much time together, sweetheart. When I'm not at work, you won't be able to get rid of me. Sound good to you?"

Ana forced her smile through what had to be numbing pain.

"Sounds great, Papa."

After the seizure ended, Sim gave Ana an elevated dose of

Seraphed to induce a necessary sleep and help the body recover. She'd be out for nine to ten hours.

Exhausted, Trevor met the doctor outside Ana's room.

"Look, I'm sorry about the way I entered. The threat. I hope you'll look past it. I'm not rational where my daughter is concerned."

Sim's features softened.

"You're not the first irrational father I've encountered. Nor will you be the last. For the record, Deputy, I acceded to you because Forster left instructions to that effect if there was an episode. You may not believe your method put Ana Marie's health in danger, but I do."

Sim did not threaten to go over Forster or report him to HSA. Rather, Sim walked away without further comment. Trevor accepted the small victory and reentered the room, where he stood beside Effie and watched their daughter sleep.

"They don't believe I make a difference."

"I do, Trevor. You've always gotten through to her in ways I couldn't. I will always love you for that."

He almost thanked her for the consolation. If only he knew for sure where it all went wrong.

"I'm going to ask for an exemption, Eff."

"We've been through this. They won't grant it. They'll say if they make an exception for you, then the Charter itself is worthless."

"Yep. That's what they'll say. So, I'll do every damn thing I can to pull at their heartstrings. This isn't about me. It's about her."

Effie sighed. "Or we could move into your Admin flat with you. It would be a little tight. You wouldn't be able to live with Connor anymore, but that was always a strange choice. Trevor, I ..."

"That's not a serious plan. You'll be miserable."

Her reply hit him like another dagger.

16

YOU'RE RIGHT, TREV. I'M NOT going to leave Harmony. And I'm not going to share a bed with you again. You will always be her father, but ..."

"Go ahead, Eff. Say it."

She stared into his eyes like the first time. Or so he thought.

"I used to imagine us growing old together. Now, the very idea turns me cold. I can't explain why. Trevor, I still love you, but only as the man who gave me Ana Marie."

Trevor wouldn't have felt worse if a wall tumbled on top of him.

"Which means ... what?"

"Nothing for now. But Ana needs to know things are changing. She needs to be prepared to hear the worst someday. If you move back in with us and try to act like we're a normal family again, she'll retreat into the same fantasy that led to today."

Now she'd gone too far.

"You're blaming this episode on me? For leaving?"

"She was fine for four months. If you had acquiesced to the ambassador's demands like I pleaded, Central never would have forced you out."

No. He wasn't going to do this again. Damn sure not at his daughter's bedside.

"Sure. Lay it all at my feet. I probably deserve it."

"Trevor, I'm sorry. I didn't ..."

"Leave, Effie. Just go home and freshen up. Get a bite to eat. I'll stay with Ana for a while in case she wakes up."

"Doc Sim says she'll be out for hours."

He replied with a you-think-I-give-a-shit glare. It did the trick. She wiped away the water congesting in her eyes.

"One hour, Trev. I'll be back in one hour."

"Give me five minutes notice, and I won't be here."

She made no promises. Trevor didn't care; he pulled up a chair and shifted his gaze to the most beautiful girl on Amity.

His plan, like so many, didn't succeed for long.

"She needs to be prepared to hear the worst someday."

Effie's words. He knew the implication, but his paranoia took it one step further. How much longer before his wife moved on from the DRC? Decided to resettle on Mauritania? Took their daughter to start a new life with Reginald Endowi?

He said it a hundred times over the next hour:

"I will never leave you, sweetheart."

The voice in the deep of his conscience, the one often telling him to slow down and take a deep breath, now warned him against rash behavior. He already compromised his job. What if he had hit Sim?

She was right. All you had to do was make a public apology. That asshole wouldn't have called for your job. You are going to stubborn your way off the station. They'll take Ana Marie. Slow down, Trevor. Slow the fuck down.

Two hours later, Effie gave him a heads-up. Trevor kissed Ana goodnight and all but stumbled toward the public docks. He was about to select a rifter when his wrist plate dinged.

He tapped the comm.

"Are you free to speak?" Hoshi asked.

"Yes, I'm good."

"Your daughter?"

117

"Better. What is it, Hoshi?"

He expanded her holo.

"I wasn't sure when you'd be available, but I thought you should know. The toxical came back."

Right. The case. He didn't think about it once.

"Ah. That. Has Dorrit ordered the case closed?"

She forced a smile.

"Actually, just the opposite."

That was unexpected.

"Talk to me."

"You were right: Motif was the cause of death. The lifetechs found nothing other than a high blood alcohol, which we expected. But there was a surprise with the Motif. Trev, his blood contained four times the normal level of K3."

"Compared to our other MODs?"

"Yes. They scanned the pad you found. Contained the same amount of elevated K3."

Hard to look the other way now.

"And we thought Motif was dangerous before. How did Dorrit react?"

"Like I've never seen. Trev, he's worried this time. He wants you back as soon as you're available. He won't slide this one behind the Executive Partition. What should I tell him?"

This day just kept on giving.

"I'm on my way."

He briefly considered hanging about the docks until Effie arrived. He didn't want to leave things in such a state, especially now that his job might have to take precedent.

No. Give her a day or two. Cooler heads.

By the time he stepped off the train at Mogandi Station, Trevor had rewired his focus. That same sense of urgency which gripped him hours earlier returned. Dorrit called in the ten deputies under his charge. The toxical summary floated above his desk.

He made a point of pulling Trevor aside.

"Your little girl. Is she better now?"

"Much. Thank you."

Dorrit pointed to the voluminous hologlyphs.

"My oldest spent half his first ten years in a phasic trauma ward. They said he wouldn't live to see twenty. Fortunately, they could not have been more wrong."

Trevor wasn't sure what surprised him more: That Dorrit wasn't the lazy, ill-gotten blowhard he had long perceived; or that Trevor felt a tinge of guilt for making that assumption. Either way, the simple exchange lightened Trevor's load.

Dorrit briefed his staff.

"Prior to today, there were four MODs in Haven over the past nine months. We found no connection between the cases and concluded that the pads accidentally slipped through Customs. I consulted with the other sector chiefs and Customs Enforcement. We agreed: Procedures at the spaceports would be tightened and no reference to Motif would be included in the permanent reports."

When the looks of astonishment subsided, Dorrit went on:

"Until today, we considered the problem contained. This morning, our new First Deputy and his Second discovered the body of Ulbrecht Hann in Andromeda bloc. You see here the results of Mr. Hann's toxical. I call your attention to the levels of Kerasunehyde Trilucin. The infamous K3. And this," he said, swiping through to another holo, "is the count from our other MODs. The difference is stark and, dare I add, troubling.

"The last thing we want to do is make assumptions. Nor will we go public about Motif until we know more. We will report Mr. Hann's death as a non-specific overdose. Whispers are sure to follow. For the time being, I am asking everyone to put your ears to the ground. Use the relationships you've built with your contacts. Every tip, every rumor. Dismiss nothing. Deputies Stallion and Oda will continue their investigation into Mr. Hann's death. Questions?"

Trevor had built a healthy list but gave his new colleagues a chance to jump in first. After three seconds of silence, he raised his hand.

"Have you consulted with Chiefs Al-Jani and Tasqur today?"

"Not as yet. I wanted my team to know first."

"Regarding the other MODs: Are you sure Al-Jani and Tasqur were forthcoming in your previous discussions?"

Dorrit narrowed his bushy brows into a defensive posture.

"Excuse me, Trevor. What is your implication?"

"You know what I mean, sir. Five MODs now, all in Haven. Statistically, that seems unlikely. Bad enough if word spreads it's happening here. But in Episteme or Harmony? The backlash would be out the airlock. They have a stronger motive to hide the truth."

Dorrit didn't respond with the predictable umbrage.

"We're all in this together."

"In some ways, yes. In others ..."

"Your point?"

"You said Customs agreed to tighten procedures. Great. But here's the problem. Motif with that potency of K3 would never get through Customs, no matter what techniques Black Star uses to hide it from our scanners. And Customs operates with support from the ESA and HSA."

Nods and whispers of affirmation followed. Dorrit noticed.

"Trevor, are you saying my fellow Chiefs are not trustworthy?"

"Not at all. But they're under political pressure, too. With all respect," Trevor said, using a phrase he hated, "you downplayed the previous MODs. Why wouldn't they do the same? Chief, we need to face a harsh truth. Either the pads Ulbrecht purchased were smuggled through Customs with inside help, or those pads were manufactured on the station."

The tenor shifted. Hoshi draped a hand over her mouth, Dorrit settled uncomfortably into his chair, and disgruntled whispers intensified. The bottom line was often inconvenient.

Hoshi said, "Trev's right. There's no good explanation. We have a problem, Chief."

Dorrit stared at his team, grumbled, and shook his head.

"Everyone out but Trevor and Hoshi. Return to your duties, and do not engage in unfounded conspiracy theories. Dismissed."

Trevor expected Dorrit to launch into him with a line of vitriol, halting the good vibes of empathy they had shared.

Wrong.

"Sit," Dorrit told them. "I'm quite educated in the realm of logical deduction. I considered both possibilities after viewing the toxical."

"You don't believe them?"

"Not what I said, Trevor. I have an open mind, so I don't rule them out."

Trevor realized he couldn't hide the third angle any longer.

"There's another direction we need to pursue. During our interviews, a fellow student – someone close to Ulbrecht – claimed he was murdered, ostensibly with Motif."

Dorrit slapped his desk.

"And you're only now telling me?"

"Because it seemed a longshot at the time. She had no evidence beyond Ulbrecht saying he felt in danger, and Motif is not a viable murder weapon. But at a much higher toxicity? We can't rule it out."

"The only problem," Hoshi added, "is that no one visited Ulbrecht's flat last night. He consumed the pad voluntarily."

"The obvious solution to that," Trevor countered, "is that he was specifically targeted. His dealer knew what would happen."

Dorrit puckered his considerable lips.

"So, we're now suggesting his murder was staged to look like an overdose."

"To be honest, Chief, that may be our best outcome."

Was Dorrit regretting his choice to allow the case forward?

"Best? Murder by Motif. I can't wait to hear your theory, Trevor."

Neither could he. Only now did his paranoia polish the theory into a usable narrative.

"According to Eliza Hutton, the student, Ulbrecht claimed he was about to 'expose people working against the Collectorate.' She knew none of the details. But let's say she heard right. More importantly, that Ulbrecht was right. If these people wanted to silence him without drawing attention, they'd try to put him down through unconventional means. Now, they could have tried to discredit his academic standing or manufacture a scandal that got him booted off-station.

"Problem is, those methods would have taken too long. Everyone we talked to agreed – Ulbrecht was brilliant. Really going places. So, if they needed him gone quickly, a clearcut murder would have drawn too much attention. We haven't had one in Amity in six years."

Dorrit nodded.

"I see the map you're drawing, but I question the premise. What you're alleging is that someone acquired – or manipulated – Motif with elevated K3 and talked Mr. Hann into having a taste."

"Yes. It would have to be someone he trusted. Eliza said he would never take Motif willingly. But brilliance and arrogance often go hand-in-hand. He was a curious man. He had a change of heart. He placed the pad on his tongue. Would he have done that if he suspected he was being poisoned?"

The Chief turned to Hoshi.

"Do you agree with this madness?"

Hoshi batted her eyes at both men before settling on Trevor.

"My partner is more experienced, Chief. I defer to him."

"That, Hoshi, is the definition of a non-answer. Trevor, you said murder was the best outcome. Why?"

He agreed with Dorrit. Hoshi was playing it safe. Still, it gave him slight leverage.

"The alternative is that we're seeing a new variation of Motif. If Black Star has reformulated the drug, increased its toxicity, then Ulbrecht was the first of many more victims to come. I recommend we send the toxical to SI. They have the most updated data. If they've seen these elevated levels before, we'll know what's happening. If not, we narrow the options."

Dorrit's long sigh told the story of a man whose dream of a soft landing before retirement had faded.

"I'm inclined to agree."

"If I may, Chief, we can skirt the usual channels and have this expedited. I have a contact in SI. An old friend. Oliver Jamison. He's been tracking Black Star for two years."

"He's stationed on Amity?"

"No. He's a field agent. Moves around. Last I heard, he was on Earth. I can deepstream him. He's discreet."

Dorrit pushed the holo of the toxical toward Trevor.

"Sync it into your personal pom. I don't want a record of it going out from your plate. In the meantime, I'll notify SI through standard protocol. A perspective from your contact can't hurt."

Trevor retrieved his pom, flipped it open, and dragged the holo over the tiny golden device. The holo flickered, cloned, and dropped into the pom.

"Whatever we learn," Trevor said, "won't eliminate the first two problems: There's a Black Star operative in Customs or a production facility somewhere in Amity."

"Or both. I understand, Trev. I'll speak with Al-Jani and Tasqur. You and Hoshi focus on the Ulbrecht Hann matter. I assume you'll have more interviews?"

"Orval Erdogan, another student from Yaniff. He knew Ulbrecht well. They were neighbors in Andromeda. We'll also expand our reach with other students. Chief, there's something else I need. The data from those other MODs."

Dorrit eyed the second holo with an awkward grimace.

"That information is still protected."

"I'll be careful. I need to be sure there's no connection."

Dorrit agreed. "Anything else?"

"Clearance to access the LinkPass history for everyone associated with Ulbrecht."

"Well, sure," Dorrit said with obvious snark. "Let's proceed with violating everyone's right to privacy."

"I don't see how we'll find the answers without it. Chief, I understand what I'm asking. If there's blowback, send it my way."

"Fair enough. But I won't put it in writing. I will not endanger my pension."

"Gotcha. I'll be careful. You have my word."

Dorrit chuckled.

"Your word. How many hours have we worked together?"

Trevor added the old MOD reports to his pom.

"Starting from the moment you barged into Ulbrecht's flat? I'd say about six. Will that be all, Chief?"

"It's far more than enough. You're dismissed."

Hoshi joined Trevor in his office, where his many dataflicks continued to hover.

"That went incredibly well, Trev, all things considered."

"Agreed. Dorrit surprised me."

"Where do we start?"

He tapped his noggin.

"I'm making a list. Up first: Orval Erdogan."

Among the many things on that emerging list was one topic that never arose in the meeting.

Raison Club. The place Ulbrecht claimed had exactly what his friend Eliza needed.

Trevor wasn't much of a partier, but he damn sure knew someone who loved that lifestyle.

Perhaps it was time for the Stallion brothers to ride again.

17

ORVAL ERDOGAN DID NOT RESPOND when Trevor announced himself. After an uncomfortable silence, the flat's door slid open. The young Turk, his complexion a darker tan than most Yaniff natives, stood in the center of the outer room, pulling hard on a digipipe. He exhaled smoke with his words.

"Been waiting for you, Deputy."

He retreated to a loveseat of the identical style found in most Haven flats. The outer room matched Ulbrecht's to the letter.

OK, then, Trevor thought. *He knows. That will save time.*

"I trust that's your permission to enter, Mr. Erdogan?"

Orval threw an arm onto the cushioned back and sighed.

"You badges play by every rule. Don't know what you're missing."

"*Every* rule? Debatable. Mind if I sit?"

"Unless you're not here to talk about Ulbrecht."

Trevor knew at once he made the right call in leaving Hoshi behind. He'd get more out of this character without a sidekick. Like the other students, Orval's eyes were as empty as they were weary. This fella was at wit's end, and not just because of the deceased.

"I'm investigating his death. May I call you Orval?"

"You're the badge. I offer no resistance."

"I assume everyone in Maynor knows?"

Orval tucked the cylindrical digipipe between this lips and pulled short puffs which the air recycling system quickly filtered. Trevor smelled bitter weed.

"About ten minutes after you finished with his mentee group."

"Now I see. Maynor students aren't big on rules. They were told to remain silent until the public announcement."

Orval's laugh carried a smugness Trevor often encountered from young, cutting edge know-it-alls.

"Then you should have detained them. Oh, wait. That would be against the rules."

Trevor crossed his legs. *This guy ...*

"You and Ulbrecht knew each other for quite some time. Were you good friends?"

"Ulbrecht didn't have friends. We were the competition."

"So, you two didn't manipulate the housing assignments? You just happened to find flats down the corridor from each other?"

"Oh. That. Ulbrecht's handiwork. He had connections. I went along with it because it was easier."

Trevor felt a fruitful interview coming on. Orval carried a weight he wanted to release.

"Did you socialize with each other outside school and job?"

"Explain *socialize*, Deputy."

"Visits to each other's flats. Recreation. Nightlife. Raison Club, for instance."

"Raison? Shit. That place was like his second home. We went there a few times, but only in the first month. I wasn't getting any sleep. Studies caught up with me. But not Ulbrecht. Not that cunt."

Orval stared at the smoke cloud spiraling to the camouflaged ceiling filters.

"You like the pipe, Deputy?"

"Not since I had a child."

"I was going to offer you one. Got plenty. It's called Stretch, from the Dinesh Vale. Goes down harsh, but it soothes what ails you. Sure you don't care for a puff?"

"Orval, your answer tracks what I heard at Maynor. The other students struggled to keep up with their obligations, while Ulbrecht exceeded without nearly the effort."

The student nodded.

"Yep, that was Ulbrecht. Half the effort, twice the results."

"Were they jealous?"

Orval shifted his body and leaned forward.

"Them? Sure. Me? Cud no!"

"Interesting. Records show he beat you in three major engineering contests on Yaniff. You weren't bothered at all?"

"I didn't lose, Deputy. I just didn't win. The key was getting noticed by the right people. I wanted a seat in Maynor."

"It worked. Congratulations. The headmaster said they selected three from seventy thousand Yaniff applicants. Has the seat met your expectations?"

Orval shifted in a blink between a frown and a forced grin. Trevor saw him looking for the right answer.

"Ask me in two years, Deputy. I smoke six of these a day. Helps me ride on an even keel. Declutters all the nasty thoughts."

"What about Ulbrecht? Did he have any dependencies you're aware of?"

"I never saw him with a pipe, or any other drugs. Man treated his body like it was a gift to the universe."

That tracked with Eliza's perspective.

"Were you shocked to hear he died of an overdose?"

"For about three, four seconds."

"Explain."

"Word is, he took Motif."

"I can't confirm that."

Orval grunted like someone who was in on the secret.

"Don't have to. Ulbrecht was obsessed with answering the big questions. People say Motif opens your mind to places humans aren't meant to go. Just what I've heard, you see."

"Of course. And yes, I've read testimonials. I also know how addictive and deadly it's become. How it's destroyed more lives than any drug in human history. So, you believe he might've sought out a Motif dealer, even knowing the risks?"

"Ulbrecht? Take a risk?" Orval massaged his eyes. "He built his whole life on risk. His reputation on risk. He would take any chance because every time he did, he won."

"What do you mean, Orval?"

"Deputy, he didn't win those contests on Yaniff. He cheated. Ulbrecht was a fraud. Yeah, he had a great mind. Maybe the best of us. But that wasn't good enough for him."

Trevor thought the bitterness proved jealousy. Mr. Runner-up had a chip on his shoulder after all. Yet Orval's tone had downshifted, like he was ready to dump the biggest weight.

"Cheating? Explain how."

Orval tapped off his digipipe.

"Ever heard the term 'phantom drill'?"

"No."

"It's a catch-all. I knew a few subcutes on Yaniff."

"Ah. Data spool hackers."

"Among other things. Apparently, these people have an ultimate goal. It's a fantasy, you might say. Build a program that can infiltrate every classified system in the Collectorate – government, military, or private – retrieve the data, and leave no trace."

"That's a dangerous goal."

"Yeah, well. Not for Ulbrecht. He built a phantom drill."

Never did a dead man interest Trevor more than right now.

"How do you know?"

"After those contests, I heard whispers that engineers had come forward saying parts of Ulrich's proposals derived from their own work. The scandal would've gotten out of hand, so the organizing

128

committees closed the book. But I didn't."

"Go on."

"I reviewed every detail of his proposals and compared them against what I could find through non-classified resources."

"What did you discover?"

"The underlying data was an amalgam of bits and pieces from everywhere and nowhere. No one piece was enough to prove theft. He synthetized the data into something new. The proposal was his, but it was built on the backs of people he stole from."

"Did you confront Ulbrecht?"

Orval chuckled.

"That's why I was expecting you. I heard you learned about his so-called threat on my life. Yes, Deputy. I accused him of fraud."

"You mentioned the phantom drill?"

"In private. I gave him a chance to come clean."

"Did he?"

"Not in a way that would hold up before a judge. Ulbrecht loved to talk in hypotheticals. He said, 'If I was the type of person who created a phantom drill and could access any data spool anywhere, why would I waste my time in school?' He almost sounded logical. Then he added a little something extra. I don't know, maybe he got feeling too smug. He said, 'If I was the type of person who could do all these things, I'm sure I could ruin lives. Especially people who make crazy accusations against my family's good name. It's a damn good thing I'm not that type of person.'"

Orval double-tapped the digipipe and inhaled.

"You had to be there, Deputy. I saw something in his eyes. A twinkle. A little madness. I don't know how else to explain it."

"I understand he threatened you in front of witnesses a few weeks ago." Orval nodded. "How did you respond?"

"He laughed afterward like he was joking. I walked away. Someone else complained to school admin. I couldn't prove what he'd done, and I knew Thet wasn't about to subject the school to a scandal. I wrote an anonymous complaint to Ulbrecht's supervisor at Halifax R&D."

"You accused him of data-fixing."

He exhaled a thin stream of purple smoke.

"I hoped somebody over there would have a spine and follow through. They're all gutless."

"Did you mention the phantom drill?"

"Not as such."

"Why not? If such a thing exists, it poses a threat to station security. For that matter, interstellar security."

Orval bowed his head as he smoked. He might have been releasing the weight, but it still dragged him down.

"I'm a coward, Deputy. I got my whole life waiting for me on Yaniff. I stepped about as close to the flame as I'm willing."

"OK. Let's take a breath. If Ulbrecht actually developed this phantom drill, where do you think we'd find it?"

"His pom, most likely. Everything on there's protected by his gene stamp, so he wouldn't have to worry about infiltration."

Trevor was afraid he'd say that. Poms were designed to be all but uncrackable. When owners died, their poms were usually disintegrated rather than anyone waste time trying to extract the internal data. Yet another product of the Collectorate's guarantee of personal privacy rights. It was not, however, helpful to anyone investigating criminal activity.

"Do you believe others knew about his program?"

"No idea."

"Think he used the data he collected against people?"

"Extortion? Wouldn't surprise me. Ulbrecht thought he was invincible. Why else would he have risked it all for Motif?"

Ideas upon ideas queued up inside Trevor, none of which he thought best to pursue with Orval.

"When was the last time you saw him?"

"Oh. Ah. Three days ago. He hopped off the lift and walked right past me without a word. I was more or less dead to him at that point. He figured I was no threat."

"Would you object if I reviewed your LinkPass history, just to confirm that your movements line up with your statements?"

The Turk straightened his shoulders into a defensive posture.

"You can check whatever you want. I have nothing to hide. But why do my movements matter? Am I being accused of something?"

"No, no. It's a standard part of verification." A little lie sometimes moved the needle forward. "Before I go, there's one odd topic I'd like to ask you about, especially given what you've told me. Ulbrecht's public biography says he was studying trans-wormhole shielding tech. Headmaster Thet laughed it off. He said it was meant to be ironic. That trans-wormhole theory is fringe science. Do you agree?"

Orval tugged at his collar. First time Trevor witnessed that tic.

"Ironic, how? Like a joke, Deputy?"

"Something along those lines. You're not laughing. Why?"

"I don't believe it's fringe science. Otherwise, I don't think they'd be working on it at Halifax. Did they mention his apprenticeship?"

"Interstellar cartography."

Orval sighed. "That's what they call it? Interesting. Back in the first month, when Ulbrecht thought we were friends, he told me about the job. His team is mapping black matter substrata."

"Why?"

"He said the aim was to improve safety of wormhole travel. I wasn't interested. It's not my specialty. But I remember he had that twinkle in his eye. He said, 'Wouldn't it be the ultimate if we could reopen the fissures?'"

Well, shit.

Trevor flashed back to the question a student asked of Thet.

"Fissures? As in, to the other universes?"

Orval nodded. "He and I were born less than a month after the fissures were closed. He took that as a sign. Ulbrecht took everything as a sign. He was going to be the first to cross over."

OK. Here we go down the black hole.

"What else did he say on that topic?"

"Never brought it up again. I work at Atumwa. It's possible he was spewing nonsense, but I don't think so. Like I said, brilliant mind. He didn't have to cheat."

Trevor heard enough. For now.

"Thank you, Orval. I appreciate your candor. If I have any more questions, I'll call ahead."

"Sure. Whatever works, Deputy. Just don't interrupt my sleep. I don't get enough as it is."

Trevor teemed with a strange excitement interlaced with equal bits of terror. If even half of what Orval claimed was true ...

"Cudfrucker," he muttered upon entering the lift.

He tapped his wrist plate and contacted Hoshi.

"What did you learn, Trev?"

"Fill you in soon. Did the lifetechs submit the effects list?"

After a short beat, she said:

"Oh, let's see. Here we go. Lifetechs logged it an hour ago."

"Check the inventory of personals."

"Sure. What are you looking for?"

"Ulbrecht's pom. Did they recover it?"

"Hmm. I'm scrolling through now."

He waited until she came back with the one answer he dreaded.

"Huh. No, actually. Strange. Everyone on Amity has a pom. Should we send the lifetechs back out to look for it?"

"No. I'm in his building. I'll do it myself. But I don't expect to find it."

She asked why.

"I hope I'm wrong, Hoshi. I might have just uncovered a motive for murder. Cud, I hope I'm wrong."

18

TWO HOURS AFTER TREVOR returned to Sec Admin HQ without a dead man's pom, he refreshed with a strong cup of café. Then he studied the collected puzzle pieces and reached a preliminary conclusion.

Ulbrecht Hann, equal parts genius and madman, developed a hunter-seeker program capable of entering any data spool unnoticed, capturing the information, and retreating in silence. Someone offered to buy the so-called 'phantom drill' if Ulbrecht extracted it from his pom. He refused. They stole the pom and killed him under the guise of an overdose.

Who? How?

"Those questions I can't answer," Trevor admitted to Dorrit, who studied the deputy's report with an unusual silence. "If this was a murder at all."

Dorrit massaged his double chin from behind the desk.

"Therein lies the quandary," the Chief finally said. "We have no direct evidence of foul play. Everything you and Hoshi acquired today points to an arrogant young man who made a fatal mistake. Yet one of his own choosing."

"I know," Trevor conceded. "But that missing pom is a problem."

"You believe Mr. Erdogan's story?"

133

"Inasmuch as he believes it. The kid was wiped out. He said he smokes six digipipes daily to keep a level head. These students ... the entire atmosphere at Maynor School ... they're being pushed to the limit."

"Agree," Hoshi added. She helped Trevor pull together the early evidence into a cohesive presentation. "It was surreal. I'm sure they're hiding something."

Dorrit wagged a demonstrative finger at the Second Deputy.

"Everyone hides things. My wife serves me two small, bland meals each day. She's determined to help me trim the excess in my mid-section. I do not cooperate. Twice a week, I leave home early and take the train to Harmony. I stop into Henwick's and try out a plate of their newest confections."

All member worlds contributed candies, cakes, pies, and chocolates to the famed store outside the Interstellar Congress. Not a kiosk on site – everything was baked inhouse or jumped in by wormhole (an expensive proposition). Trevor took Ana there once a month for a special treat.

"Henwick's is seductive, Chief," Trevor said. "But we're not talking about guilty pleasures. I'm convinced the students in his mentee group know something pertinent."

"Would any have motive to kill Mr. Hann?"

"Motive? Yes. Especially Orval Erdogan. But means? How did they get their hands on Motif with elevated K3? How did they ensure Ulbrecht consumed it? When did they steal his pom? They're smart – probably smarter than the three of us combined – but there's no direct evidence linking them to Ulbrecht's death."

Dorrit nodded full agreement but showed no sign of shutting down the case.

"What is your next step, Trevor?"

"Reinterview the students in his mentee group separately. Talk to his supervisor at Halifax. I want to know more about Ulbrecht's work. This trans-wormhole business concerns me. I thought the IC passed a law decades ago forbidding research into reengaging with the other universes."

Dorrit rocked in his luxuriant chair.

"They passed many reactionary laws after the war, some of which came back to bite them in the proverbial ass. Later Congresses undid most of what that first group bolloxed up. Easy enough to verify."

"I'll run that down," Hoshi said, stifling a yawn.

"Thanks, Hoshi."

Trevor didn't discuss his plans for Raison. He intended to step outside the usual protocols. No need to bring Dorrit into the loop. Likewise for his review of LinkPass histories, not limited to students.

"I'll be straight with you, Chief. This business with the pom leaves me cold. The implications for a program like Orval described is ..."

"Terrifying. I know. But until we have solid evidence the program exists, we don't run this up the chain. If it is on his pom, no one will be able to crack it. Time is with us."

That seemed like a good moment to utter, "Famous last words."

Trevor refrained.

"What about the K3, Chief? When do you expect a response?"

"I submitted the finding to my fellow chiefs, SI, and Central. It's a wakeup call for everyone. I'll know more in the morning, but I expect an emergency session will be called. Have you contacted your man?"

"Tried an hour ago. No luck." Trevor wasn't surprised. His SI friend Oliver often operated undercover in the field. "Deepstream can be tricky, especially for somebody who's ventured off the path, so to speak. I'll try another DS tonight."

Dorrit tapped the chair's arms until he found a rhythm.

Then he yawned.

"In the interest of clear minds and full stomachs, I suggest we call it a day, Deputies. Your first one together has been full, and now you're two hours past shift. Good work. Start again tomorrow."

Pragmatic Trevor cheered those words. Paranoid Trevor wanted to return to his desk and analyze the spools of unexplored data. Did waiting another day make sense when station security might be at risk? Then again, what the hell was he even searching for?

"What do you think?" He asked Hoshi after their dismissal. "Don't hold back."

She stared at the banks of dataflicks in his office.

"I'm glad you showed up when you did, Trev. I wasn't ready to deal with something this big. Thought I was." She chuckled. "If I'd taken that call alone, I wouldn't have entered Ulbrecht's flat. A guy overslept. None of my concern. We would've lost valuable time."

"Lucky us. But you haven't answered the real question. What do you think?"

Her smile vanished.

"To be honest, I don't believe Ulbrecht was murdered. It doesn't seem plausible based on what we know. Maybe something else will change my mind. But at the very least, we know Amity has a major security problem. That's huge."

She wasn't wrong, of course. So what if she couldn't yet see the bigger picture like Trevor did? He wouldn't hold it against her.

"It's important. Yes. We'll see what people at higher pay stamps intend to do about it. So, I'll see you in the morning."

"Yes." Hoshi stammered. "Trev, I ..."

"Talk to me."

"I didn't know if you had plans. You mentioned this morning maybe we could sit down over a drink sometime."

OK, so that was surprisingly fast.

"We will, but not tonight. My plate's full. Among other things, I hope my daughter wakes up soon. I need to ..."

Hoshi waved him off with a grin.

"Of course. What was I thinking? It's been a crazy day. We both need time to decompress. Perhaps when life returns to normal."

Normal. When was that?

Trevor did not allow his paranoia to suggest Hoshi's motives were anything other than pure. If she did have an angle, she wouldn't like his answer. Not in the least.

He ventured home by Swiftrak rather than rifter. Among its many benefits, Amity empowered walkers. He passed many residents in full power-walker posture. Most followed their progress inside hololenses. He encountered no leapers, which was a small relief. No need to stop everything, chase them down, and dish out warnings.

A few residents acknowledged him with a courtesy nod or half-smile, but his uniform and bar appeared to carry no weight. That's how they liked it in Haven, or so Hoshi claimed.

"Live and let live," she said that morning. "That's our charge, Trev. It works."

Until it doesn't.

His gut knotted with the sensation that an unpleasant change was taking place around them. Subtle, quiet, patient.

Pragmatic Trevor warned the alarmist not to get carried away.

He arrived at his brother's flat and sighed. Trevor promised Connor a little heads-up so he could change into ... well, any clothes.

OK. Time for another floor show.

The outer room and kitchenette were empty. A small victory.

"Home, C," he shouted into the bedroom.

"You're late, bruv."

"Busy day. You eaten?"

"Couldn't wait," Connor said, appearing with brush in hand and wearing a maintenance jumpsuit. "Off to my shift in about ten."

Trevor did the math.

"So soon?"

Connor shrugged.

"Those washer fans are calling to me like the sirens of old."

"Hmm. Words I never imagined hearing in the same sentence."

Connor ran the brush through his silver locks.

"Beautiful, ain't it? Poetry." He slapped Trevor on the shoulder. "A gap shift. Seven hours then I'm off for two days. Worse fates."

Trevor held off triggering the kiosk for dinner.

"I was hoping to have a word before you went out again."

"Hey, sure. Why don't we ...?"

Connor cussed under his breath and set down the brush. In one fluid move, he fell upon Trevor, wrapping him in a stern hug.

"Sorry, bruv. I wasn't thinking. Effie told me about Ana's seizure. I'm so sorry."

"Yeah. It's been a tough day."

"I hate it for you, T. I know it's tearing you up inside."

Trevor squirmed out of the hug.

"It's strange. When it happened two or three times a month, it felt routine but killed me to see my little girl like that. Now it's every few months, but the pain's worse."

"I get it. Effie said she thinks each time is the last. Then the next one comes, and she's not sure it will ever end."

"What else did she say?"

"That she was glad you were there." Connor stepped away and grabbed his brush. "I don't want to get your hopes up, bruv, but I have a feeling she's coming around."

"Toward what?"

Connor's comical smile said, "Whatcha think? A reunion. She sees what she's missing."

Oh. That. Trevor sighed and thought of a dinner plan. First, to set the little brother straight.

"C, did you ever meet Reginald Endowi? He's DRC."

"Kidding me? I never drifted with that crowd."

"No, you certainly did not. At any rate, she's been sleeping with him for five, maybe six months."

Connor's cheeks fell.

"The fuck? Effie? I don't buy it."

"It gets worse. She's not going to take me back, C. I have a feeling Reginald will be Ana's stepdad within a couple years."

"No, wait. You two are perfect for each other. Like the universe in balance. And Ana ..."

Trevor refused to ride the wave of Connor's indignance.

"Is *my* daughter and always will be. I love you, Connor, but please don't say anything to Effie. And don't you dare hold it against her. I'm responsible for Ana's condition. Seven years has taken a toll."

"I'm sure it has, but she's juicing some DRC asshole. What are you planning here? You intend to roll over?"

Yes, definitely time to change the subject.

"C, have you ever known me to roll over for anyone?"

"Not once. Not even to Ambassador Pissoff."

Connor knew how to make Trevor smile.

"Pousson," he corrected. "Cost me my job, but I held my ground because I was in the right. I'll do the same where my daughter's concerned, to my last breath. Understand?"

"Sure, bruv. Think so. Hope so."

"Know so, Connor." Little brother meant well but would never understand. "Look, there have been two times in my life when I knew what love truly was. First time, we were standing under that bridge in Redux. UNF on one side, Swarm on the other. Nowhere to run. I thought we were going to die, but the only one I worried about was you. I would've taken a laser bolt for you."

"Shit. Bruv. You don't ..."

"Then I held Ana in my arms for the first time. In that moment, she became my reason to live. She always will be. I will never roll over, C. Not for anyone."

He pushed a finger into Connor's face for final emphasis. Connor nodded approval.

"There you go. That's my big brother. He's still in there."

"Yeah, well. Your big brother is tired and hungry. And I need to talk to you about something before you leave."

Connor retrieved a band for tying up his hair.

"Sure, but be fast about it. I've been tardy one time too many. They're starting to notice in EngSec9."

"I won't hold you up." He decided to hit the high points for a quick shock value. "You can't repeat any of this. Promise?"

"Always, T."

"There was an MOD in Haven last night. Could be murder. Not sure. But we know Motif is entering the station through a gap in Customs or it's being manufactured here. You work in the zone near Halifax and Maynor School. Yes?"

"Ten hells! Yeah. That's the zone."

"I need you to open your eyes and ears."

"For what?"

"Any behavior out of the ordinary. Things you might have overlooked before. It's all fair game. Especially with students. By now, word's spreading. Even the smallest oddity might help."

Connor rebounded from his slack-jawed response to the news and seemed to relish the task.

"So, you want me to gather intel? Be an informant?"

"Judging by your full-throated grin, I think you're up for it.'

"Anything you need, bruv. And no worries: I'll be discreet. Just another drone in a jumpsuit. They'll never notice me."

"Exactly. Stay in the background. *Do not* be proactive."

Connor threw out his arms in a mocking defense.

"Me? I'll be a perfect spy."

"Good. And when you're off tomorrow night, I'd like you to take me to your favorite stomping ground."

"What? *Raison*? I thought you stayed clear of the clubs."

"You know the place inside and out. Yes?"

"All the nooks and crannies."

"Perfect. I'm not going there to have fun, but I need someone who will. Or at least, someone who looks the part."

Connor's eyes ballooned when he saw the big picture.

"I'll be your Second Deputy?"

"You'll be yourself, Connor. That's all I need."

"I'm there, Trev-*or*!"

"Perfect. We'll talk in the morning."

The Stallion brothers used to make a great team when they weren't getting into all manner of trouble. Trevor hoped he wasn't leaning too heavily on nostalgia to unleash their combined forces on the station again.

They weren't kids anymore. This would work. It had to.

He settled down for a quiet dinner. Trevor resisted the temptation to open his wrist plate and pick up work where he left off at HQ. As soon as he started in on all the unfiltered data, he wouldn't let it go. He'd show up at the office without a wink of sleep.

He retreated to bed early, closed his eyes, but couldn't shut off the engine. He turned over often before sitting up in frustration.

"Shit."

There was only one sedative. One way to slow the engine.

Trevor opened his pom and contacted Effie.

The signal dinged six times before she opened the comm.

"Hey, Eff. Sorry. I know it's late. How's she doing?"

"Good, Trev. She woke about an hour ago."

"Can I speak to her?"

Effie looked up and away. Who was with them? Doc Sim? Reginald Endowi? At last, she nodded.

"Ana, it's Papa."

He expanded the holo to see her in wide view. She was still in bed, drinking from a straw. She handed the glass to her mother.

"Hey, Papa."

My angel.

"Evening, sweetheart. Feeling stronger?"

"I am. Mama said you helped me today."

Smile! No tears, asshole.

"I did my best. I'm sorry I had to leave you, sweetheart."

She showed no anger this time.

"It's OK, Papa. I understand now."

Trevor slept well.

19

THE CALL CAME EARLY: Security conference promptly at H8 in Amity Central Administration. "Everyone will be present," Dorrit told him. "Including the President."

That was all the café Trevor needed to power him through his morning routine. President Kieran Haas wouldn't attend unless the stakes extended far beyond elevated K3 in two pads of Motif.

"Got any theories, bruv?"

Bleary-eyed Connor remained in bed, wiping hair from his face. He hit the sack an hour before Trevor received the ding on his wrist plate.

Trevor spit mouthwash into the sink.

"I don't theorize about Presidents. They play by different rules."

Connor squeezed a pillow against his chest.

"You sure rant about them. Especially the last one."

Trevor threw on his jacket and slipped his pom inside.

"She was a criminal, C. Got what she deserved."

"Didn't the inquest clear her name?"

Connor loved to challenge his older brother on the subject of Collectorate Presidents, few of whom Trevor respected. Absolute power transformed people into animals, a topic on which he had no time to debate this morning.

"The Board of Inquiry was stacked with her sycophants. Look, C, I need to leave. How did your shift go? See or hear anything odd?"

Connor talked through an extended yawn.

"Actually, bruv. Yeah."

"Like?"

"Students. Maynor students."

"Go on."

"I was inspecting the ABLs outside the Halifax receiving platform. It was downshift, so there's usually nobody about. Even the drone loaders were quiet. That's when I saw five students. At least, I assume they were. Younger than me."

"They wouldn't be authorized for that location."

Connor moistened his lips.

"Nope."

"Did they see you?"

"Hard to miss the guy in the orange jumpsuit. I don't think they cared. At first, they passed around a digipipe. Conversation got heated. I didn't hear enough to make sense of it, but two went after each other with closed fists."

May be worth a follow-up.

"Would you be able to ID them from glyphs?" Connor gave a thumbs-up. "Good. See you after work. Get some sleep."

Connor hurled a pillow at Trevor.

"Send my best to the President."

Trevor shot back with a sly grin.

"Your name will never come up. Guaranteed."

Connor feigned ignorance, flailing his arms.

"What? The cake accident happened seven years ago. She's forgot about me, bruv."

Trevor wished.

"That woman carries vendettas. Later, C."

Connor lost his residency qualification for Harmony one month after a brief kerfuffle at the Stallion-Labroque wedding reception.

Trevor suspected but never proved Haas – then a Congresswoman – instigated the order as retribution for public embarrassment.

Connor was right, of course. The most powerful woman in the galaxy didn't care squat about anyone with an L3 pay stamp. Trevor presumed her vindictiveness went deeper. She and Grandfather Max butted heads often. Haas fought legislation to help Chancellor refugees establish small colonies on member worlds. Not the only politician with anti-Chancellor bias, but she often wore hers like a badge of honor.

All the more reason Trevor intended to keep his head down.

He met Dorrit at Mogandi Station and was surprised to see Hoshi tag along. Since when did Second Deputies attend a Presidential-level emergency confab?

"It's irregular," the Chief admitted, "but Central requested both investigating officers."

"They couldn't have been happy to see my name attached. I don't have many supporters in Central."

"No, Trev. You do not. As I told Hoshi, say nothing unless called upon."

They entered the train and flashed wrist plates to confirm their destination: Harmony Aleksanyan Station.

"That's the plan, Chief. I've learned my lesson."

Dorrit shot him a skeptical side-eye.

"I dearly hope so."

Trevor watched Hoshi twice check her bar for proper alignment after the train embarked on its short journey.

"Nervous?"

She seemed as antsy as a recruit experiencing Amity for the first time.

"Also excited, Trev. I've never been this high up the chain."

"No worries. Some of these people can be intimidating, but most are interchangeable parts, like us. They do the best they can with what they've got."

"The Chief said something similar. They put their shoes on one foot at a time."

That old saw. Trevor agreed with Dorrit's advice, but the Chief had an ulterior motive: Best no one blame HVSA's lax oversight as a potential culprit. Dorrit wanted a quiet path off Amity.

"When we get there, follow my lead, Hoshi. I know the conference room well. There's protocol to the seating. President Haas on one end, Gov. Murrill on the other. Sec Chiefs and First Deputies on one side; SI and UNF commanders plus Corp Execs on the other. Everyone else gets the kiddie seats against the wall. That'd be you."

The news didn't land. Instead, she asked:

"Gov. Murrill. Don't know anything about him."

Trevor chalked up the question to a brain glitch.

"He keeps a low profile. He's a bureaucrat, more like a glorified city manager, but he's powerful. He signed my transfer order."

She snapped her fingers.

"Oh, yes. Now I remember. Murrill. I haven't paid much attention to Harmony. This is only my third trip there."

"Really? Seat of government. Beautiful gardens. Great restaurants. A history museum. Never thought to visit on a day off?"

Hoshi set her eyes on strangers across the aisle.

"Not especially. Remember what you said yesterday about the seen and unseen? I had time to think about it, Trev. You're right. There's a class system here. I'm more at home with Havenites."

"Nothing wrong with playing tourist. Plus, I did live there for nineteen years. Am I so horrible?"

Her cheeks reddened.

"Not yet."

As the train approached the station, Dorrit made a request.

"Normally, I would take the Swiftrak, but my knee is bothersome today. If you don't mind, I'd prefer we travel by rifter."

Interesting, Trevor thought. He didn't hand it down like an order; he seemed embarrassed. Trevor decided not to pile on.

145

"Perfectly reasonable. It's half a kay. I'll be glad to hold the arms."

"Thank you, Trevor." When the doors opened, Dorrit muttered, "Into the beastly cave we trudge, where monsters breath fire and await our flesh to burn."

Trevor recognized the line from a famous poem. He doubted the Chief meant it for an audience, but the timing surprised him. Or that Dorrit knew poetry.

The docks at Aleksanyan were busier than usual today, with three-fourths of the bays empty. Only one rifter remained among those reserved for security personnel.

"No one's much in the mood for walking today, Chief."

If his words soothed Dorrit's nerves, all the better. In case fingers pointed and accusations arose, Trevor wanted an ally in his new boss. He wouldn't have imagined such a need one day ago.

Trevor dictated the rifter's course and grabbed its steering arms. He navigated among unusually heavy traffic.

"Curious, Chief. I heard you quote Tenochtilan back there. Are you a student of his work?"

Dorrit released a guttural moan.

"Heard that, did you? Dear. I had a passing interest in Tenochtilan when I was fourteen or fifteen. Like so many boys, I found his impression of humanity's darkness a temptation. Then I grew out of it, as most do. And you, Trevor?"

The memories hurt, but the poetry made those years bearable.

"It was complicated. The Chancellory banned his work in our education tiers. They didn't want a lowly Aztecan to undermine Elevation Philosophy. I came to him through the one Solomon friend I made on Earth."

"Ah. Yes. You would have grown up during the Great Transition. Must have been a confusing time."

Trevor heard the term Great Transition used more frequently to explain the twelve-year gap between the fall of the original Collectorate, ruled by his caste, and the rise of an egalitarian People's

146

Collectorate.

"They were instructive years, Chief. I'll leave it at that."

The Amity Central Administration building stood out among its neighbors for its disinterested character. Like the functionaries, bureaucrats, accountants, and solicitors who worked inside, the ACA drew in only those who had no choice. Ten levels of unadorned façade pockmarked by the occasional tiny window hid the nuts and bolts work that kept the three sectors running in orderly fashion.

They took the lift to Level 8: Security and Posture. A cascade barrier greeted them outside Conference Room C. The static field prevented entry until they verified their identity. The wrist plate's LinkPass reader preceded a retinal scan.

Trevor knew the routine. These measures used to strike him as excessive given all the station's safety features. Now, with the undercurrent of change and threat of Black Star infiltration, the paranoia seemed prudent.

Room C, brightly lit beneath radiant ceiling panels, featured a long, clean table with a holoprojector at its center, surrounded by two dozen high-backed leather chairs. Images from Amity's sectors projected along the walls. The "kiddie seats," as Trevor called them, formed two rows at the far end, behind the Governor's chair.

Though Dorrit insisted they arrive early, half the participants beat them. Some took their seats, but most milled about.

"You'll be down there, Hoshi," Trevor pointed. "When you see Haas enter the room, make sure your ass is planted."

"That's the go sign?"

"It means we're at H8. Haas always makes a grand entrance at the last possible second."

"We still have fifteen minutes. Am I allowed to make the rounds and introduce myself?"

He didn't expect a bold play. Dorrit answered for him.

"Absolutely not. We don't use these occasions to network."

Her shoulders sagged.

"Of course, Chief. I never should have ... I'll take my seat."

"Good thinking, Second Deputy."

When Hoshi left earshot, Dorrit leaned over to Trevor.

"She's a fine young woman, but far out of her league."

"With luck, it will be a good learning experience."

Dorrit pointed to the Sec Admin seating, where Episteme Chief Sharif Al-Jani and his First waited patiently. Al-Jani tipped his chin their way. Trevor and Dorrit replied likewise.

"I see we beat Barukh," Dorrit said of his Harmony counterpart, Barukh Tasqur. "Will he think we made it here first at your insistence? To show him up somehow?"

Trevor chuckled at his old boss's reaction.

"Doubtful. Barukh and I worked together for five years. He knows I'm many things, but petty isn't one of them."

"I heard he stood up for you against Ambassador Pousson."

Perception and reality. They never match.

"He didn't support firing me. But he didn't go out of his way to shout down the Ambassador."

Dorrit pointed to their seats beside the Episteme crew.

"This will be awkward for you, Trevor."

"Not so much. We shook hands. He left the door open if conditions changed down the road. Specifically, if I ever agreed to the public apology. Central didn't leave him much choice."

Trevor waved Dorrit ahead.

"If you don't mind, Chief, I need to speak with Director Devonshire about a personal matter."

Dorrit raised a cautious brow.

"You know SI's Forever Queen?"

Trevor stifled a laugh. Lana Devonshire, barely five-foot-six, had run Special Intelligence with an iron fist for more than twenty years. She outlasted many challenges to her post.

"She and I have something in common. We found a job we liked and never left it. I met her through Grandfather."

"Be brief, Trevor."

By all accounts, Devonshire was the most influential woman in the Collectorate who only a few people knew much about. SI operated semi-autonomously, with most of its operations hidden behind veils. Devonshire resisted every attempt by the Interstellar Congress to slash its budget or bring it out into the open.

She sat alone reviewing a tablet when Trevor approached from behind.

"Director, good morning."

She swung about and examined him with a cold demeanor.

"Yes. You are ...?" Recognition brought a twinkle into those aged eyes. "Oh, yes. Trevor Stallion. Of course. How long has it been?"

"Since Grandfather's funeral, I believe. I was hoping I might have a quick word."

"Please." She offered him the next chair. "We'll need to be brief. Admiral Woolsey will want his seat."

Shit.

"The High Admiral's coming?"

"He's in the building."

If Woolsey was attending, then the confab was much bigger than Trevor anticipated.

"I'll be quick. I've been trying to contact an old friend who's an SI field agent. I've been unable to run him down through deepstream. I contacted HQ and they dismissed me out of hand. He's always good at responding to backdoor messages unless he's in deep cover."

Devonshire grunted with a notable disdain.

"You know I can't discuss the whereabouts of our agents."

"I do, but ..."

"What's the name?"

"Oliver Jamison. Last I heard, he was on Earth but ..."

Devonshire was known for her cold, impenetrable exterior, but falling cheeks betrayed her.

"Ah. Jamison. Yes. I seem to recall him mention you some time back. He said you'd make a fine SI agent. He was going to encourage you to apply."

"He did, but I have a young daughter with a medical issue. I wasn't up to the demands of a field agent."

Devonshire touched his hand. He felt the heaviness right away.

"Trevor, we're in the process of notification. I'm sorry. Oliver Jamison died in the line of duty two weeks ago."

A genuine gut punch wouldn't have hurt as much.

"Oliver?"

"One of our best. Remarkable courage. As I recall, he lived here around the time you joined Maxwell."

"Uh ... yes. He, um ... Sorry. His family came to help build out the Episteme infrastructure. He was my best mate."

She gripped his hand tighter.

"I'm not at liberty to discuss the nature of his work, but I will be making a presentation this morning. Put the pieces together. You'll understand what happened."

Devonshire shaded her eyes, a tic signifying the end of their exchange. Trevor meekly thanked her and started around the table to take his place beside Dorrit.

He grabbed an empty chairback for support and gathered his thoughts. *Deep breaths. Calm down.*

Oliver Jamison understood Trevor's paranoid streak better than anyone. He spoke often of the dangers hiding behind the veneer of peace and stability.

"There's going to be another war soon," Oliver told him during that recruiting pitch. "Can't say how it will play out this time, but it's going to be nasty. We won't be ready. SI will be on the front lines. We need men like you, Trev."

So dedicated. If not for Ana, he might have signed up.

Now Oliver's words ripped at his heart. Trevor dreaded what he was about to hear.

20

U NF HIGH ADMIRAL EXETER WOOLSEY entered the room alongside HSA Chief Barukh Tasqur. They shared pleasant words and went to opposite sides of the table. The moment divided Trevor's attention.

He admired few men more than Woolsey, a decorated hero of the Swarm War. Woolsey's medal-laden blue-gray uniform, his elegantly coiffed golden hair, and stern beard delivered a gravitas no one present might match. His history as the first immortal to serve in the UNF and now one of the last elevated his stature.

Trevor had seen the High Admiral from a distance over the years but never had the chance to meet and thank him properly.

However, he couldn't ignore Tasqur, who fell into the seat to Trevor's right and extended a hand. Trevor reciprocated.

"Barukh. Where's your new First?"

The native of Euphrates nodded toward the door.

"Any second now. She was appointed at H22 last night. This meeting is her first assignment with the new bar."

"*Her*? You must've promoted Shireena Balance."

He nodded. "She's put in the work. Of course, Central had to run it past the Ambassador. He demanded right of approval."

Trevor refused to touch that one. He thought Tasqur had more spine. What a disappointment.

"Good for her. She'll make a fine First."

Tasqur acknowledged Dorrit then spoke under his breath.

"I hear you had a hell of a Day One."

"You know me, Barukh. I like to bend gravity."

Trevor detected no hint of the friction or resentment which clogged the office during their farewell. Tasqur was a professional.

So, too, was Shireena Balance, an ex-military on her second rotation. She offered attention to detail and a steady hand. She acknowledged Trevor with a polite smile upon her arrival.

Was it an act for his benefit? Or had they moved on from him so quickly? Fifteen years protecting Harmony, an ugly finish, but no hint of the controversy.

He didn't have time to wallow in pity or paranoia. As predicted, President Kieran Haas arrived seconds before H8. She drifted into the room with the familiar swagger that invited others to clear the way or pay a price. The strawberry blond with coordinating lipstick scanned the participants with a move practiced often on the campaign trail. As Trevor and the others rose to greet her, she signaled for them to refrain.

Haas pulled out her chair and stood in front of it.

"Be seated, everyone. I have fifteen engagements today. This is the only one that intrigues me, for obvious reasons. The findings out of Haven yesterday are troublesome, but Director Devonshire and High Admiral Woolsey are here to provide intelligence they say connects the Haven toxical report to a larger and graver threat.

"One important note." She motioned toward the side where SI and UNF occupied half the seats. "We have excluded the Corp Execs. At Admiral Woolsey's recommendation, we are limiting this classified conference to security personnel. Some may argue we are violating the Amity Charter. They might even have a case. I believe you'll soon understand why the civilian reps should not sit in. Do I hear any enthusiastic objections?"

Trevor heard that question a time or two. It was Haas code for, "Don't you cudfrucking dare!"

No one did.

"Director Devonshire." Haas took her seat. "The room is yours."

The 'Forever Queen' linked her tablet to the projector crystal in the table's center. A four-sided holo arose featuring the logo of Special Intelligence: An eye encircled by forty stars representing the member worlds. It hovered above the grim statistics of the Motif epidemic:

Estimated users: 1.35 billion (3.7 percent of human population)
Verified deaths by overdose: 54,209,166
Estimated indirect deaths through Motif use: 1.1 million
Estimated violent deaths (via Black Star & affiliates): 190,000
Estimated Black Star revenue: 540 billion UCVs
Largest corporate valuation in Collectorate: 710 billion UCVs

"Take a moment," Devonshire said. "Absorb these numbers."

Silence, stares, shaking heads, shaded eyes.

Trevor heard similar statistics from the late Oliver Jamison, who said they weren't being reported widely enough, or the problem's magnitude being given the proper sense of urgency.

But to see them together? His stomach knotted.

"At SI, we obsess over the big picture," Devonshire continued. "Horrific though the death toll may be, those final two numbers terrify us the most. Three years ago, Black Star did not exist. It rose out of a small desert town on Azteca. Within a year, it will become the single richest entity on forty planets. The difference being, Black Star is based on thirty-nine.

"Influence flows out of UCVs, and Black Star has developed a bottomless well of credits to share with any willing partner. Which is precisely their objective, and they're succeeding – both in the public and private arenas. Their tactics are simple: Allies share in the wealth; resisters are summarily executed.

"Until recently, two places in the Collectorate were unspoiled by Black Star. One is Aeterna. The High Admiral's home world remains a powerful shield against the epidemic. Until recently, we believed the same about Amity. Yesterday's report from Haven Sector along with new evidence we uncovered in recent hours tells a different story.

"The precise nature of that narrative — whether Black Star has planted its flag inside this station — remains unclear. But we do know Motif is here, and has been distributed with deadly levels of K3. The High Admiral and I had planned to brief you within the week. We expedited this session after the Haven report came to our attention."

And there it was. The wake-up call. Trevor sensed Dorrit's fear. The "new evidence" almost certainly involved the previous MODs he had covered up. Devonshire turned her eye to Trevor.

"First Deputy Stallion, you are the lead investigator in the case of Ulbrecht Hann?"

Trevor didn't mind being the focus of the audience, especially Gov. Murrill, who approved his transfer to Haven.

"I am, Director. My Second, Hoshi Oda, is also here."

Trevor pointed her out, but Devonshire did not shift focus.

"According to your report, you recognized the signs of an MOD before finding the body. Explain."

Trevor took the room through his analysis of the scene, starting with the blood-soaked impacts on the bedroom walls.

"Deputy, had you previously seen an overdose in person?"

"No. I immersed myself in forensics reports from many worlds."

"At the time, you believed this to be the first MOD on Amity."

"I did, Director."

"Until Chief Dorrit confirmed other reports had been modified."

Trevor never lied to protect anyone above his pay stamp. He did not intend to make an exception.

"Chief Dorrit said it was done to ensure the station's reputation as a Motif-free zone and provide residents a sense of security."

Those were more or less the Chief's words. Perhaps it would score

Dorrit a few brownie points.

"Did Chief Dorrit specify if anyone colluded in this matter?"

Before Trevor answered, Murrill raised an objection.

"Director, is this a presentation or an inquest?"

Trevor heard a long-standing animosity in the governor's tone. Devonshire responded with a simple grin that said he'd never catch up to her.

"I believe an inquest is the last thing Central Administration wants. Chief Dorrit, did you act in conjunction with the other Chiefs and Gov. Murrill in altering the MOD reports?"

Trevor wondered what calculus must've been rushing through Dorrit's mind. Throw his peers into the same wagon and he'd likely save himself, even though the deaths occurred in Haven.

Dorrit cleared his throat and leaned forward.

"We agreed it was in the station's best interest. We determined them to be isolated cases and not a threat."

Of course. Dorrit couldn't have pulled this off himself. But the idea that Barukh Tasqur, who shared Trevor's principles about proper station security, would play along?

You cut me loose!

Murrill rapped the table.

"Enough, Devonshire. These men made a judgment call which I supported. In retrospect, we were wrong. Do you want our heads?"

Trevor noticed the President and High Admiral remained stoic throughout the exchange. Devonshire laid down her tablet.

"I have no power in Amity, nor do I care about your internal affairs – until they affect Collectorate security. The mechanism that delivered two Motif pads with high-dose K3 to an engineering student thrived due to lack of vigilance. As I said, you do not want an inquest. Deputy Stallion, have you reached a conclusion as to how the deceased acquired the Motif?"

"Not yet. We're exploring a number of options, including the possibility that foul play might have been involved."

Apparently, no one outside HVSA knew this angle, judging from the twisted brows and whispers.

"You believe he might have been targeted for murder?"

"We established potential motives." Trevor stopped shy of diving into those, especially the conjecture about Ulbrecht's 'phantom drill.' He had no hard proof the thing actually existed. "Also, I'm not aware of K3 being found at such high levels before, which suggested these pads were manipulated to ensure the victim's death."

Devonshire tapped her tablet, posting a new set of images.

"The information I'm about to disclose is known only to the President and a few members of the security apparatus. Under no circumstance must it leave this room."

She pointed to the holo.

"What you see are five toxicals, all from the past four months and different planets." She expanded the chemical assessment of Motif levels. "Elevated K3, identical to that found inside Ulbrecht Hann. In the other cases, each victim was an influential member of his or her community. They had rebuffed Black Star's efforts to expand its territory. We believe they were assassinated.

"This modified version of Motif will kill almost anyone who ingests it. As that runs counter to Black Star's bottom line, we believe they have manufactured a small subset of pads to use as weapons. We have found evidence suggesting the other deaths were staged to resemble MODs."

Trevor thought now was a good time to speak without being called upon. He raised his hand.

"The LinkPass data from Ulbrecht's flat shows no one entered his home to pull off such a feat."

"Understood, Deputy. Black Star's agents are clever. They may have found a way around Amity's unique tracking system."

That's what worried him.

"So, you're saying they've infiltrated Amity?"

The question had to be front and center to everyone's thoughts.

"Almost certainly." Devonshire didn't miss a beat. Whispers intensified. "What we don't know is the shape of it. The common rabble they employ – the front-line dealers, the termination squads, the smugglers – would never slip the net. They wouldn't try. But Black Star's reach is staggering. Many of their allies come from a specialized class. People with no criminal record. No suspicion to their name. But their accounts are lined with Black Star UCVs."

Murrill interjected.

"No one enters this station without thorough vetting."

Devonshire seemed amused. She and the President shared a glance that set Trevor ill at ease.

"Governor, have you tightened those background checks in the past three years?"

Hell, no.

Murrill shifted in his chair.

"We work with many planetary partners and SI. Our process has always worked, even if it is not entirely consistent."

Haas replied. "Director, I feel certain the Governor will institute any changes you propose."

"Thank you, Madam President. We'll send recommendations in the coming days. Now, I illustrate the case of young Mr. Hann to indicate the immediate threat to Amity. However, you did have four other MODs that did not involve elevated K3. On the surface, they were standard overdoses. What I'm about to tell you illustrates a larger issue we may not be able to contain much longer."

She changed the projection to a representation of the human genome. The double helix twisted in vibrant color, with a tiny section cut out and highlighted.

"The fatality rate among Motif users has remained constant at four percent, regardless of age, gender, ethnicity, social class, or home world. For every hundred thousand users on Catalan, about four thousand die. For every hundred users on a small world like Inuit Kingdom, four die. More than a year ago, SI began compiling toxicals to search for the common thread.

"Three months ago, we found the solution." She expanded the genetic slice, which included a variety of statistical data. "Ninety-nine percent of MODs occur in people possessing this aberrant genetic marker. Everyone born with this marker has a high risk of structural defects in the circulatory system. Exposure to Motif is an effective death sentence. And yes, our expanded studies prove: This marker resides in roughly four percent of all humans."

Out of the stunned silence, Barukh Tasqur said:

"The implications are incredible. If this data went public, it would be ..."

"A disaster," President Haas cut him short.

"How so, Madame President? Fifty-four million have died. It's a simple matter for anyone to have a gene scan searching for the marker. Everyone in that category would stay clear of Motif."

"And what of those who don't possess the marker, Chief?"

Trevor understood the moral dilemma. On the face of it, users should be allowed to know the risk factor. Devonshire countered the argument.

"If the thirty-five billion who have not tried it believe they can use Motif without fear of death, what happens next? How many billions will clamor for it? Black Star's operations will expand faster than we have any hope of slowing. Their financial and emotional hold over the human race will become absolute."

"What are you saying?" Murrill asked.

"It's a simple matter of causality. The obsession for this drug will lead to a fundamental breakdown of the interstellar economy. Regional and federal governments will bow to pressure from Black Star and its affiliates. Wars between forces loyal to the narco-states will fight a diminished opposition. The UNF, which has been hamstrung by the Constitution and a weak-kneed Congress, will not have sufficient tools to restore order. In a few years, the Collectorate will cease to exist. Anything after that will make our worst fears about the Swarm invasion seem minor."

"Alarmist," Murrill said. "You produce a study that will save lives, but you claim it will bring doom upon us all. You people in SI live in a constant state of fear and cynicism. You have no faith in the better nature of the human race."

Devonshire nodded. "We're paid to be frightened and cynical. You can pretend humanity has reached its zenith. We know better."

Other voices entered the fray, sending the room into a temporary verbal skirmish. Dorrit's considerable cheeks turned white. Hoshi locked eyes on Trevor. He felt her disbelief.

Had they fallen so far that preserving a four percent death rate was acceptable policy?

Haas banged the table until the room fell silent.

"The decision has been made," she said. "The Director informed me days ago. I allowed her to pass along the information to this station's chief security officers in order for you to understand the depth of our problem." She saved her sharpest glare for Murrill. "Governor, if you're unable to run Central Administration under these conditions, I'll be happy to accept your unconditional resignation."

Trevor had seen men of stature cower – and he usually took pleasure in the moment – but he felt for Murrill. The Governor sought to preserve Amity's reputation but had been kept out of the intelligence loop.

"I swore my life to upholding the Amity Charter," Murrill said. "I have no interest in resigning."

"Excellent. As you were saying, Director?"

Devonshire scoffed at Murrill and continued.

"Black Star has known about the genetic marker for at least two years. Their leadership hid the data. That seems counterintuitive to good business. Not to Black Star. Profits only fuel a piece of their agenda. The rest is bent toward chaos and a slow collapse of civilization itself. They are nihilists. They seek to end the rule of law, to see us turn against each other, until we are so weakened that no force can stand against them. Their leader seeks to create a new empire built on the blood and ash of billions."

OK, that's dramatic.

Trevor raised his hand.

"Director, I believe we've all heard horrific stories about Black Star, but what you're predicting is an apocalypse. If I may, how would SI know this information unless ..."

Devonshire smiled, as if anticipating the question.

"We have agents on the inside."

"Yes. But they'd have to be embedded close to leadership."

"And no one has gotten close, or so the public believes."

Devonshire laid a hand on Admiral Woolsey's shoulder. They shared a nod. Woolsey sighed.

"Sixteen standard days ago," Woolsey said, "we captured the man who invented Motif. Number Three in Black Star leadership. What he revealed changed our outlook on this fight. Unless we take quick and decisive action, all we fought for in defeating the Swarm may be lost."

21

THE HOLO SHIFTED TO THE FACE of a man in his early thirties. He stared at the vid with a wild-eyed expression of joy though his right eye was battered and shut. His bleached hair was frazzled, and the scraggly black goatee did not hide a bloodied lip.

"This man was born Marcus Gallego," Woolsey said. "He's an Aztecan who adopted the pseudonym Elian. Part biotech genius, part psychopath. Several months ago, one of SI's field agents began tracking his movements. Like others in the Black Star leadership, Elian was well practiced in the art of living in the shadows.

"Fortunately, he was not so expert as to elude the field agent. He sent word of Elian's location, but the agent and his partner needed backup to secure the target. We sent in our best interdiction unit. Elian was captured after a firefight in which we lost several good soldiers. The team took him to what they believed to be a secure facility for interrogation.

"It was not. Ten hours later, Black Star jumped in a cruiser and overwhelmed the facility. They slaughtered the agent and our team."

Now it made sense.

Trevor set his eyes upon Devonshire, who nodded.

Oliver! I'm sorry, my friend.

161

"So," said Murrill, "Elian is free again?"

"No. The enemy forces had two objectives. One, to take out our people. Two, to execute Elian. They succeeded on both counts."

"Why would they kill a man so important to Black Star?"

Woolsey's eyes lingered on Murrill, as if he should've known the answer. Trevor did. He assumed the other security officers reached the same conclusion.

"He was not important anymore, Governor. Though Black Star would not exist without him, Elian served his purpose. He became a security risk if captured. We held him for ten hours. And in fact, he did talk. Not to the extent we hoped, but Black Star assumed he was a traitor. We have secure cam footage.

"They shot Elian repeatedly then decapitated him. They left with his head, like a prize. Needless to say, they were acting on orders from the top."

"Their leader?" Al-Jani asked. "The one called Raul."

Woolsey nodded with resignation.

"We believe that's also a pseudonym, but yes."

"Did the interrogation give us any hope of finding the man?"

Devonshire shook her head.

"Elian praised Raul endlessly, as we've seen before among these Black Star fanatics. He said, 'Raul's a god. You'll never be able to stop him.'" Devonshire chuckled. "As you see, their devotion is absolute. Black Star is as much a cult of personality as a delivery system for death and chaos."

Al-Jani voiced the rumor that Trevor and others heard.

"Is it true he might be one of your kind, Admiral? An immortal."

Woolsey had to know the topic would rear its head. Wild speculation surrounded Black Star's leader. There were no images or vids; only human imagination run amok.

"Possible, Chief, but unlikely. It's been thirty-five years since my people settled on Aeterna. Of the hundreds then unaccounted for, all but a dozen have come forward. The others are presumed dead or simply unaware of what they are. All our combined efforts have generated little more than wild tales about Raul. Our best witnesses were the survivors from the Orpheus terrorism incident three years ago on Azteca. They made claims about Raul that stretch credibility. Frankly, we're not sure he exists at all."

Devonshire added, "He's such an elusive figure, we suspect he's a myth created by Black Star leadership to perpetuate their agenda."

Al-Jani rubbed his hands together, apparently as dissatisfied with that response as everyone else.

"It sounds to me like the four of us who covered up the MODs are not the only ones who have been negligent."

Devonshire and Woolsey shared a glance, as if waiting to see who wanted to take that accusation. Woolsey stepped up.

"Chief, I respect the difficulty of your job." He scanned the entire opposite side of the table. "Everyone here has to make hard choices. But our interdiction teams and SI's field agents – as much as they're allowed to fight with one hand tied – are sacrificing their lives to make headway against the enemy." He shifted his focus to Haas. "We lack the personnel, warships, materiel, and the will of Congress to fight a proper war. This is not news." Back again to Al-Jani, he added, "Yes, we came to the battle late. But respectfully, *negligent* is the wrong word."

Haas jumped in.

"I've made my position clear to the High Admiral and the Director. More funding and less handcuffing will come ... in time. The process is complicated."

Really? Trevor didn't understand how but held his tongue. Shooting down the President's claim would not endear him or protect his job.

Woolsey also did not take the bait.

"Elian only talked to his interrogator when asked about Motif specifically. He happily explained the techniques he used to create it. He confirmed the four percent fatality rate. He admitted the drug

163

could be easily manipulated into a weapon. He was proud of his work. He talked of his place in history and how his name would be remembered for centuries."

Devonshire added, "In his final report before the attack, my agent said Elian no longer cared if he died. All the man wanted was fame, no matter how he came about it. He succeeded.

"We're fighting a cancer for which there is no cure and which intends to ravage the whole of civilization. Earlier, Governor, you called me an alarmist. Right now, my people and Admiral Woolsey's forces are holding the gates. The enemy hordes are growing faster than we can withstand. In time, we won't be able to keep them at bay."

Woolsey said, "We recommend Amity tighten security protocols. Freeze Customs activity until everyone in the spaceports can be investigated and cleared for further duty. Expedite the inquiry into Ulbrecht Hann's death. Determine how he acquired Motif and track it back to its origin."

"I can provide a field agent to assist," Devonshire said. "The Admiral can send in a small, inconspicuous interdiction team. Of course, these measures will require your authorization, Governor."

Murrill reared his back up, but a quick visual exchange with the President softened his features.

"You'll have it today."

"Perfect," Haas said. "I trust our sector Chiefs and their Firsts now understand the urgency. Each Chief will meet with your team today and tighten protocols. At the Director's suggestion, I will sign a classified Presidential Order authorizing station security to access all LinkPass history under the umbrella of probable cause.

"This will provide wide latitude, but it is a temporary measure. Do not abuse it. Understood? Now, if there's nothing else, I have another engagement in ten minutes. I'd prefer to miss it, but my absence at public events tends to draw unwanted scrutiny."

Trevor reckoned if the President had a gavel, she would have used

164

it. Instead, she rose from her chair; all others followed suit and held their position until she departed.

"Right," Tasqur said to break the silent aftermath. "I propose the Chiefs spend a few minutes with Gov. Murrill then assemble with our sector teams. Anyone opposed?"

Murrill waited a beat before agreeing. He turned to Devonshire and Woolsey.

"How long do you intend to remain on station?"

"I'm consulting within my attaches," Woolsey said. "I'll return to Central Command in six hours."

Devonshire sighed. "Like the President, my day is full. I'll be jumping straightaway. You know where to find me."

In other words, one hundred sixty light-years to another empty star system. Like Amity, Central Command's permanent home showed no favor to any member world.

Dorrit huddled with Trevor and Hoshi.

"We won't be long. You heard the Admiral. Ramp up your work on the Hann case. We need results. Explore LinkPass histories. Whatever tools you need."

If Dorrit was relieved at not being hung out to dry for his MOD decisions, he didn't show it.

"Right away, Chief," Trevor said.

"You can count on us," Hoshi nodded.

Outside the room, she leaned into Trevor and mumbled as if she didn't want the other departing deputies to hear.

"Are you as stunned?"

"Not especially. When you know things are bad, you can be sure the truth is worse. I doubt they told us everything."

"I can't believe they're allowing us to violate the Charter. It's one thing to investigate when there's a crime; now all we need is to claim probable cause? Someone can look at me funny, and I decide that's enough reason."

Trevor scoffed. This wasn't the time for moralizing.

165

"It's not martial law, Hoshi, and we won't endanger anyone who's clean. Better yet, the LinkPass will help us rule out suspects. Sooner we nail this down, sooner we zero in on Black Star's infiltrators. There has to be a connection."

She grabbed his arm.

"You think we're looking at an assassination, like the others she mentioned?"

"It's too early to go there, Hoshi. Everything about Ulbrecht says he had a brilliant future, but he wasn't influential that I can see. Did anyone else know about his so-called phantom drill? Did the damn thing do what Orval Erdogan claimed? Who would benefit by killing him? Was he somehow connected to Black Star?"

They exited the security perimeter and drifted into Central's primary atrium.

"I don't know, Trev. From all we've learned, he doesn't seem like the type."

He was disappointed in his Second.

"You heard Devonshire. They're recruiting people with clean histories. No criminal record. Upstanding citizens. And if Orval was telling the truth, Ulbrecht knew how to cheat the system. Wouldn't that make him a perfect candidate?"

"Maybe. What's the plan?"

Trevor stared past his partner to a tempting scene across the atrium, where Devonshire and Woolsey chatted. His opportunity might never come again.

I have to do it now.

"Go on ahead, Hoshi. I need to stop in and check on my daughter. I won't be fifteen minutes behind. You can get things rolling. Open LinkPass histories for everyone in Ulbrecht's mentee group. Same for Orval."

She couldn't feign her disappointment. Her frown screamed.

"Oh. OK. After that, I guess I'll wait for you, Trev."

Like with yesterday's awkward invite for after-hours drinks, Trevor thought she was trying too hard.

"Grab some kiosk snacks. We'll be putting in long hours."

Did he really think the first woman in his life not named Effie had developed a fast crush?

You're imagining things. Let it go, Trevor.

He purged his mind of those petty concerns and set a course for the two most powerful people in the Collectorate not named Kieran Haas. He had rehearsed the words for years, gradually assuming the opportunity might never arise.

As he approached Woolsey and Devonshire, the tiny woman bid farewell to the Admiral. She turned into Trevor's path and stared up at the First Deputy, who bested her by eighteen inches.

To his surprise, she reached for his hand.

"Deputy. I'm so sorry you had to learn about Agent Jamison that way. He was a good man. One of our best. I intend to add you to the notifications list. You'll be welcomed to attend his memorial at Central Command when we set a date."

A place he always wanted to visit.

"Thank you, Director. Ollie was a good mate and a true hero. I'll be honored to attend."

Soon as he said the words, Trevor realized he had committed to leaving Amity Station for the first time in nineteen years.

Devonshire wished him all the best with the investigation and rushed away. The true object of Trevor's attention had begun walking in a different direction and with some urgency.

Come on, Trevor. You can do this.

He caught up.

"Admiral Woolsey, may I have a moment?"

The face of the UNF was much younger in closeup. The beard did not hide Woolsey's eternal youth.

"Of course." The Admiral extended his hand. Trevor responded with a firm, military grip, as he rehearsed. "What can I do for you, Deputy Stallion?"

"Well, to be honest, sir, I'm a bit out of sorts at the moment. You might know my history. My grandfather was Maximillian Vanover."

Trevor berated himself for name-dropping straightaway.

"Of course. I respected his commitment to Amity. Very interesting man. Very *confident* man. Yes?"

They shared a chuckle.

"An understatement, Admiral. Sir, I've seen you on station from time to time, but I never felt right approaching you."

"Why?" Woolsey laughed. "I generally try to be approachable."

"Maybe it's the uniform. I don't ... oh, I'm screwing the pooch on this one. Admiral, I wanted to thank you personally. Both for me and my brother, Connor. Sir, you saved our lives twenty-three years ago."

Trevor saw the gears churning as Woolsey reflected.

"You're from Earth?"

"Yes, sir. Philadelphia Redux. We were there when the Swarm invaded."

"Ah. That. A difficult day, in many ways."

"Yes, sir. I didn't know it at the time, but your wormhole maneuver as Captain of the Lightfoot saved us and likely everyone in Redux. Your forces landed just in time. My brother and I were trapped underneath a bridge while the battle raged. We lost our mother that day, and our father died in combat. I ..."

Woolsey settled a hand on Trevor's shoulder.

"I'm terribly sorry."

"Lucky for us, we had Grandfather Max. After the war, I learned about the Woolsey Maneuver, and I've followed your career ever since. I'll admit I'm something of an overzealous admirer. I just wanted to shake the hand of a genuine hero."

The gushing felt over the top but also long overdue.

Woolsey took it with the steady lip and humble smile of a man who heard these stories often.

"I appreciate the kind words, Deputy Stallion. Trevor. We were lucky that day. Also unlucky. Twelve hundred and nineteen. That's the number of Redux civilians who were killed because the plan wasn't good enough. You see, I don't forget who died on my watch."

Woolsey tapped his chest.

"These bars have taught me many things. One of which: There's never a clean victory. I take solace in what we accomplished, and I love that fate somehow brought us together in this moment. But I don't consider myself a hero. I fought for a cause bigger than me, and I survived when so many did not."

Trevor felt the conversation reach a tipping point. He had so much more to say, but was it appropriate? Had the Admiral tired of talking about the old days?

"I understand what you mean, Admiral. I do this job because it's my way of contributing to everything Amity stands for. I also do it for my daughter. I want her to be proud of me."

Woolsey shrugged. "What else is there?"

"There shouldn't be, except ..." His voice almost cracked. "When you sat across from me, I couldn't help but think, 'I'm on the same team with a living legend.' More or less. I mean, sir, you've fought in three universes. The life you've led is ... well, it's mind-boggling."

Woolsey nodded. "On that point, we agree. I sometimes have a hard time believing it myself. One battle after the next. But I'm a soldier. All I know is the fight ahead. And frankly, I think another war is inevitable. I'm glad to know we're on the same team, Trevor."

That sounded like 'thank you, but I have to work to do.' Trevor knew he'd overstayed the moment. They shook again, yet right when Woolsey pivoted to leave ...

"I ... I don't want to keep you, sir. Just two things."

"Sure."

"You really think it will come to war?"

"In a few years."

"Even if you're able to expand the fleet and truly go after these bastards?"

The Admiral sighed, but it didn't sound like impatience.

"We knew who the Swarm were. We built a remarkable navy to meet them. There won't be front lines with Black Star. They'll be unpredictable and cold blooded. Worse than the Swarm."

"I see. And what about the rumors of their leader? I saw how you reacted when Chief Al-Jani brought it up. I get the sense you think he might actually be an immortal."

Woolsey tossed him a dubious glare, as if Trevor overstepped.

"I can't discuss the particulars. I hope you understand."

"Absolutely. You're a light-year above my pay stamp. I'm just happy you gave me a moment to embarrass myself. I also hope you'll be leading the UNF for a long time. We need you, Admiral Woolsey."

"Thank you, Trevor. I don't hear that kind of support as often as I'd wish. All the best."

Trevor saw genuine pain in the Admiral's eyes as he walked away. The burden must have been unrelenting.

He thought of Ana, whose young lifetime of pain tore at his heart every day, and magnified the weight tenfold. What must it have been like to oversee the protection of forty worlds and watch the enemy take root everywhere?

If he can manage, what have I got to complain about?

Trevor set his mind to making a difference in the only way he knew how: Solving Ulbrecht Hann's murder.

"Time to finish this."

22

MAXIMILLIAN VANOVER PREACHED interstellar unity after the Swarm War. Yet the public face did not match the one Trevor and Connor saw in private. Every night they remained under his care, Maximillian told them great tales of Chancellor history.

"Legacy, my boys, is defined by how we use these memories to take control of our future."

Connor's attention waned, his mind searching for something new and shiny. Trevor, on the other hand, processed every message, but not out of blind faith. He sorted the ideas into mental boxes.

Accept. Reject. Reconsider.

"Gramp," Trevor said, "what you're telling us is nothing new. If we don't learn from history, we'll repeat the mistakes. According to you, the Chancellors did everything right for three thousand years. You talk of nothing else. Yet the empire collapsed overnight. That can't happen unless our caste made huge mistakes. They didn't learn."

Trevor, then eighteen and tired of dwelling on the past, watched with increasing impatience as Max opened a data spool containing testimonials about the fall of the Collectorate in 5357-58.

"We were set upon by a tiny group of malcontents who made weapons like no one had seen. Singularity bombs. They mastered mobile wormholes, a technology we knew nothing of. They hit the Carriers without warning. The slaughter was unprecedented and unforeseeable."

Trevor stood his ground.

"I read about Salvation. The hybrids and the bioengineered immortals were children. Our caste fell to a thousand kids in a fleet of seven ships. Gramp, an empire doesn't allow that to happen if it's paying attention. The Chancellory lost its way. It stopped doing 'all the right things' long before then."

"You were not there, boy."

Max's tone showed no regret or shame, either of which Trevor thought appropriate. He despised his caste's ancient legacy of oppression and opportunism. They enriched themselves at the expense of ninety percent of the human race.

"Gramp, you're saying we were wronged without doing wrong ourselves. We share none of the blame. Is that your position?"

"Trevor, my boy, I'd hate to think you've grown into a self-loathing Chancellor."

"I won't allow the past to define me. The Chancellors' time ended. Connor and I were born too late. We have to be defined by something other than our caste, or we'll be miserable."

Max crossed his legs and stared quizzically at his oldest grandson. He massaged his beard.

"You're wrong, my boy. The caste itself may no longer guarantee the life of your dreams, but your genetic profile does."

Trevor side-eyed Connor. The ten-year-old played with a tablet.

"How, Gramp? Our genes are so flawed, we take VT 460."

"Those genes contain the intellectual traits that elevated our caste above the human race."

The old man popped up from his comfy chair. He snapped his fingers at Connor and told the boy to put down his tablet. Connor rolled his eyes but complied.

"You have the innate ability to reassemble the intricate details of the present to extrapolate a future you intend to create. It's more than merely thinking ten steps ahead of a competitor. It is a level of perspicacity that's rare to anyone not born of Chancellor blood."

Connor scrunched his lips together.

"Perspi-what?"

"Insight, my boy. Perceptiveness. For example, I display a hundred dataflicks in front of you. Each one contains a random piece of news from somewhere in the Collectorate."

Connor wasn't a big fan of reading, but his eyes locked in. He must have thought Gramp was introducing a game.

The boy loved his games.

"All the planets or just a few?"

"All forty. Now, a quick read might suggest few similarities. But what if *you* saw them all as connected? What if *you* could reassemble them to forecast the future?"

Trevor heard this nugget before, so he gladly let Connor take it.

"That would be wild, Gramp," little brother said. "But why would I want to?"

"Simple, my boy. To leverage the future. It's one thing to dream of what you want to do when you're old enough. It's another to actively build your plan from its foundation. For instance, look around! This station emerged from our Civil War. I anticipated the decline of our caste and the inevitable reshuffling of life on the colonies."

Trevor sighed. The speech would go on a bit, a testimonial to Max's greatness. How he knew Earth would reorganize into an egalitarian society, how it would need strong trade with its former colonies, how a new interstellar alliance would rise and require a centralized government. How Ark Carriers could be refashioned to house the government in a neutral system. Presto! Legacy!

Connor tuned in, perhaps more attentive than the previous times he only appeared to show interest in Gramp's tales of glory.

"You saying Chancellors can see the future?" He asked.

"No. We're not mystics or conjurers, but we are gifted with the

173

ability to see patterns and understand their relevance. We use that ability to nurture our own ambitions, as Chancellors have since the first of us, Johannes Ericsson."

Trevor took a turn rolling his eyes.

Ugh. The Ericsson myth. Again.

"He was imbued with a divine intelligence that allowed him to map out three thousand years of human endeavor. He saw every strategy necessary to conquer and subjugate all ethnics not of his kind. That intelligence was not only passed down through his line, but engineered into the countless family branches. Just because the Chancellory no longer rules humanity does not mean you lack the tools to gain similar leverage over the future."

Trevor had read it all, from the propaganda to documented history. Yes, his ancestors were visionary; they learned how to crush every opponent and lord over them for centuries. They seemed to have special insight into the weaknesses of anyone not born to the caste. The wealth, the military might, the technology – it was all theirs. They controlled the stars unchallenged.

Yet they fell from power in a blink.

Trevor heard quite enough.

"Connor, what Gramp is saying: Pay attention to everything going on around you. Read and study. Learn from history. It will help you understand how to manage your own life."

Connor tucked his tongue inside his cheek.

"Oh. I get it now. But that sounds like a lot of work, Trev-*or*."

Max glared at Trevor as if he were a third leg. Perhaps Max knew the oldest was a lost cause but remained hopeful Connor might fall for his indoctrination.

"I'm disappointed, Trevor. You often display the best traits of a quality Chancellor. Your obsession with detail. Your ability to solve the most complex problems in your Tier III studies. Your paranoia. The way you analyze everyone who comes into your orbit."

"What does that even mean, Gramp?"

"You hear life's underlying melody. You are constantly trying to make sense of a puzzle ordinary humans don't know exists. You are the most voracious reader I've ever encountered, Trevor. You are searching for ways to rearrange the pieces."

Trevor would've laughed, but he didn't want to piss off Gramp. Instead, he settled for the lazy reply.

"And why am I doing that, Gramp?"

"Because it was engineered into your genes. Move past this self-loathing Chancellor phase. You'll see what I mean."

"OK. Will I experience a sudden revelation?"

Max sneered at his grandson's snark.

"Mock me. It will make no difference. But a day will come when you are staring at all the tiny swaths of fabric meant to form a tapestry. You will see how to stitch them together. That moment will change your life, perhaps even history itself."

Then the old man roundly sighed.

"Unless, of course, you continue with this cynical deconstruction of your ancestors. Such a shame if you fell short of your potential."

"Yeah, Trevor." Connor stuck out his tongue. "A real shame."

Trevor didn't talk back. Instead, he realized just how much Connor would have to be untaught.

Which is precisely what he tried to do while Connor remained under Max's influence. After they moved into their own flat together, the brothers stopped talking about the past. Trevor realized Connor didn't especially care one way or the other. The past felt as irrelevant to him as the future. The wild child was always happy but aimless.

Just once did Max sit down with Trevor and voice concern about Connor's future. Five months later, his heart stopped while he slept.

At the service, Trevor listened to the eulogies and admitted the one thing he never told Gramp:

"You were right."

Trevor never pinpointed when the trait first took shape, but it guided every important decision. It drew him to Effie and told him to give his whole heart to Ana Marie.

No detail bypassed him. Subtle body language, inartful tics, perceived slights, secondhand rumors, circumstantial evidence. He recognized Amity's class divide, the hubris of the ruling elite, and their pursuit of personal agendas over the greater welfare. He felt a slow, inexorable shift from the station's original, noble mission.

Life's underlying melody.

"You were right."

The variant swaths of fabric tightened into a more definable tapestry when Black Star entered the picture. All news about the emerging threat drew him deeper into research. His dreams spoke of a new darkness sweeping between the star systems. The transition away from enlightenment and hope gathered steam.

Pieces realigned. A picture formed.

If any leverage was to be had, as Max always insisted, the time for it was slipping away.

Trevor dismissed his nightmares as paranoia run amok. He carried them alone. Why frighten Effie? Why bore or confuse Connor? They needed a clear-headed husband, father, brother.

Now Ulbrecht Hann was dead. Black Star encroached on this great sanctuary, but it had yet to win.

Solving this murder was vital. Proving the link to Black Star and uncovering its agents on the inside even more critical.

Dozens of dataflicks and the AI-generated trend waves from LinkPass histories hovered around Trevor in his Sec Admin office.

"You were right, Gramp."

Trevor let go of his last inhibition and saw the tapestry emerge.

Six hours after the security conference at Central, the case came together. When it was solved, they'd call him a hero. His good name would be restored.

But Amity Station's reputation would be destroyed.

23

TREVOR FOUND THE SOLUTION when he realized his biggest mistake. It was a foolish oversight, made clear after he had time alone to deep-dive into the evidence without distraction. He had sent Hoshi and two other Second Deputies to Maynor School to interview more students about Ulbrecht, whose death went public overnight.

"If you receive pushback from Thet or the mentors, tell them to complain to Central. We won't tolerate interference."

Hoshi played along like a pro, but Trevor sensed reluctance.

"Should we reinterview his mentee group? They've had a day to sit on this. They might be more forthcoming."

Trevor considered what the LinkPass history had already revealed and wagged a finger.

"No. Not yet. I need to connect a few dots first."

Trevor burrowed into the data. Instinct screamed: The answers are here! Two hours later, feeling on the cusp of seeing the full tapestry, Trevor slammed a fist on his desk.

"I had it backwards," he muttered. "Why didn't I see it sooner?"

"See what?"

Shit. Back already? You should've been gone another hour.

Hoshi stood in the open door with her colleagues.

"Sorry, Trev. Only caught that last bit. Have you figured it out?"

"Could be. Learn anything at Maynor?"

"Well, we confirmed that the place is every bit as surreal as it seemed yesterday. The students are strange, Trev."

He needed to pursue the evidence. Enough with the diversions.

"How so?"

"They're carrying too big a weight."

"Exhaustion? Stress? Or good old fashioned secrets?"

"We can't put a finger on it. They didn't have much to say about Ulbrecht. Most knew of him by reputation but no more. And the ones who did, offered nothing of value. The news hit hard."

"Good. File your reports and uplink them to the case spool."

Hoshi sent her colleagues away to do just that then took a seat beside Trevor. If she had just given him another ten minutes ...

"OK, Trev. They're gone. What didn't you see sooner?"

You got nowhere to send her. Out with it, jackass!

"I know how the killer did it," he said.

Hoshi gasped. "Someone forced him to take Motif?"

"That we won't know until we catch the suspect. Here's the issue: We trusted the LinkPass history to tell us who entered Ulbrecht's flat and when. Since no one entered with or after Ulbrecht, we assumed he already possessed the Motif when he returned from Raison Club."

She nodded. "Naturally."

"I should know better than to trust a foolproof system."

"What do you mean?"

"When Ulbrecht came home, the suspect was waiting for him inside the flat."

Hoshi's double-take fit the moment.

"Whoa. Wait, Trev. You're saying someone accessed his flat while he was out. How? LinkPass shows no one except Ulbrecht."

"Correct. That's what it shows. It's wrong."

"How?"

"Hoshi, we have close to a million access points on Amity." He held up his right thumb. "No entry without a verified gene stamp. It's the law. There's never been one verifiable error in the reporting matrix."

"Because it's foolproof."

Trevor snapped his fingers.

"Unless you happen to be equipped with a program that skirts around even a perfect system."

Clarity slapped Hoshi upside the head, but she didn't show it with the wide-eyed fascination Trevor expected.

"You can't be serious, Trev. Ulbrecht's secret program?"

"Yes. His phantom drill. I believe Ulbrecht sold it a while ago. Either the buyer or an associate used the phantom drill to enter Flat 529, overriding the required gene stamp. It wouldn't have been detected by the LinkPass reporting system. The suspect waited for Ulbrecht then either convinced or forced him to ingest the Motif."

Hoshi buried her face in her hands and took a deep breath.

"That's an incredible stretch. Can you prove it?"

"I will. Hoshi, do you remember how immaculate his flat was when we entered? Other than the bedroom, it was spotless."

"Sure, but what that does prove?"

"When I went back there yesterday to look for his pom, I checked everywhere, even inside his kiosk. I thought maybe if he wanted to hide it from a thief ..."

Grandfather Max would've been proud of his attention to detail.

"I know, I know. Long odds. But I reviewed the kiosk production log. I was curious when he last used it."

"And?"

"The night before he died, roughly the same timeframe, he made a cup of Flojot."

Hoshi grimaced. "Never heard of it."

"It's a restorative health drink, popular on Yaniff. Supposed to guarantee better sleep. Here's the thing, Hoshi: He made Flojot for sixty nights in a row after returning home. Ulbrecht was a creature of habit. The night he died, no Flojot. Why? I don't believe he had the

179

chance. Someone was waiting for him."

Trevor thought he'd pulled off a feat of superb detective work. Hoshi couldn't restrain her giddiness.

"That one, I give you, Trev. Very impressive. But it's just an aberration in a man's routine. You need proof."

"I have it."

He flipped a wrist toward the dataflicks like a conjurer in the midst of a magic trick.

"The patterns are here, Hoshi. They line up. I'd say their plan was brilliant. They were patient, careful, and deliberate, but there was an oversight. That's all you need. An entire empire fell due to one oversight."

"I'm confused, Trev. Who and what are you talking about?"

Fair enough. If Hoshi was to see the tapestry as he did, Trevor would have to start from the beginning. It would be a good test run. A verbal explanation would confirm the strengths and gaps in his theory.

"Follow along. If I go too fast or ramble off the path, stop me and ask questions. Ready?"

"Can't wait."

He pulled forward the bundled interview logs from the students in Ulbrecht's mentee group.

"These students are smart, exhausted, but also bad liars."

"Is that why you told us not to reinterview them?"

"Yep. Here we are: Eliza Hutton, Sil Mariputti, Jor Kerrindos, Freddie Lighthorne, and Ashraf Diep." Their facial glyphs and official biographies accompanied the text of their interviews, recorded by Trevor's wrist plate. "They agreed Ulbrecht was brilliant and spent his nights at Raison, and none of these people had the wherewithal to match his lifestyle. Sound right to you?"

"Yes."

"Let's start with Jor. His first reaction was to call Ulbrecht an idiot. He volunteered that they were incompatible lab partners but otherwise didn't know him. Later, he said Ulbrecht had the energy for three people. He called it 'some kind of magic.'

"Next, there's Sil. He claimed to have shared a few drinks with Ulbrecht at Raison, but Sil never stayed long.

"Then there's Freddie. Said they were 'fair friends.' He called Ulbrecht *intense* and said he spent one night at Raison with the guy, and that was enough. Following?"

"I am. I assume you're going somewhere with this."

"Oh, yes. Next is Ashraf. He said they had little in common but he admired the man.

"Finally, Eliza. She had an immediate emotional reaction. Based on what she told us later, Eliza was shocked but not surprised by Ulbrecht's death. She told us not to trust the others in the group – they were jealous of Ulbrecht. When we discussed Raison, she said he invited her many times, but she couldn't manage that lifestyle."

Hoshi nodded. "I remember. She all but confessed to being in love with him."

"It went further. But let's start with Raison." Trevor pushed away the bundled biographies and reached for trend waves he created from LinkPass histories. "That club is the key. I filtered histories to focus on every time any of these five entered Raison. Watch carefully. I'm going to set Ulbrecht's club entries beside theirs."

A series of horizontal bars illuminated the date and timestamps of Ulbrecht's club appearances.

"They were right about him," Hoshi said in an astonished tone. "How many times is that?"

"He visited on a hundred fifty-five standard days. Including same-day returns, a total of two hundred thirty entries. The man was a regular. But his fellow mentees were no slouches."

Trevor moved their bar charts into place, each with a different color scheme. Though none had as many bars, almost every visit corresponded with Ulbrecht.

"Ninety-eight visits between the five. Sil and Freddie eighteen each. Jor twenty-one. Ashraf seventeen. Eliza? Twenty-nine! They arrived within ten minutes of Ulbrecht almost every time. Sil, Ashraf, and Eliza came as a threesome sixteen times. Jor and Freddie as a pair, but ten times. These people loved the club and Ulbrecht's company."

Trevor gave her a moment to reach the inevitable conclusion.

"They all lied," she said, sounding naïve enough to be shocked.

"Which begs the obvious question: Why?"

"I assume you have an answer, Trev."

"Getting there. First, I want to back up. There's a problem with Eliza. She claimed to have Bucher's Syndrome. Yes?"

"Sure. Eliza said it acted up when she was emotional."

"I fell for it. She mimicked the symptoms perfectly."

He yanked her dataflick from the bundle, flipped it around, and displayed a window topped by EXIGENT MEDICAL SUMMARY. Hoshi reacted as if a monster leaped out of the holo.

"Trevor. What in ten hells are you doing? These are her medical records. We had authorization to open LinkPass history, not this. You could be fired if they ..."

Oh, enough with the hysterics. Please.

"Have a seat. This is Eliza's IMER. OK? Intersystem Medical Emergency Referral. It's primary data if she needed emergency treatment on any member world."

Hoshi groaned. "I know what an IMER is, Trev. But only authorized doctors or phasic techs can open it without approval."

"By the letter of the law, you're right. But she had a medical emergency yesterday. As authorized officers of the court on site, we provided assistance. Synchwater. That's our story."

He tried to lighten the tone with a mischievous lilt, but she wasn't buying.

"You better hope no one finds out about this."

"Doubt it, unless you intend to screw me over."

"Trev, I ..."

"You wouldn't be the first. Hoshi, listen. Bucher's Syndrome is serious. Everyone is tested for it, especially from high-risk worlds. But it's not listed on Eliza's IMER."

"What?"

"Not everyone from a high-gravity planet suffers from it. Nor does Eliza." He scrolled down the page to a different diagnosis. "She's pregnant."

Hoshi grabbed the flick and expanded the text, her jaw agape.

"Fifty-one standard days! Why did she claim it was Bucher's?"

"Best guess? She'd compromise her status at Maynor. Abortions aren't permitted on Amity, so she'd have to return home. I checked the student calendar. They have a short quarter break coming up. I ran down the manifests for outbound liners on those days. Guess who is booked for a quick jump to Hansen's Landing?"

Hoshi backed down and told Trevor to give her a moment.

"Feeling all right?" He asked.

"I'm fine. So, she's pregnant. We assume Ulbrecht is the father."

"Oh, yeah. She never confirmed they slept together, but her LinkPass shows seven visits to his flat, the last one eight days ago, but the second was fifty-one days ago."

"Seems obvious enough, Trev. I understand why she lied to us about it. She's trying to protect her place at Maynor. That's all."

Dare he berate his Second for an obvious bias?

"Doesn't change a simple truth: She's a liar. She visited Raison more than anyone outside of Ulbrecht. She's a problem, Hoshi. A big one. That group is working together. They're connected to Ulbrecht's murder if not directly involved."

"What? How?"

Time for the tricky bits. Was she open-minded enough?

"Remember this morning when Devonshire was asked whether Black Star had infiltrated Amity? She said, 'Almost certainly.'"

He pointed to the five biographies, to which Hoshi responded with a dumbfounded stare. Somewhere deep down, Trevor assumed, she stifled laughter.

"You cannot be serious. The students? Working for Black Star?"

"Devonshire said they recruited people with no criminal record. Beyond reproach. She said we'd find the evidence in their accounts. A massive influx of UCVs."

"Trev, these students are in their early twenties. They have brilliant futures. Why would they take creds from Black Star?"

It was a fair, predictable question.

"They wouldn't. But what if it was their only ticket into Maynor? A third party promises to guarantee selection and then support the student and his family. Simply repay the kindness with certain favors. An allegiance. If you don't hold up your end, deal's off. Everything goes away."

Hoshi wasn't buying. She shook her head with vigorous disdain then smirked.

"I just found a hole in your theory. Headmaster Thet picks the applicants. He said millions apply each year. What was the ratio for Yaniff? Three out of ...?"

"Seventy-four thousand. Very exclusive. A man with that sort of power has remarkable leverage, don't you think?"

Trevor allowed her to mull the implication. She came to it slowly, with a growing awareness in flustered cheeks.

"Thet? He's taking bribes?"

"Him or administrators close to him. A selection committee chooses the finalists. The application process is publicly listed on their stream, but the criteria for selecting winners is not."

Hoshi waved off the idea.

"I can't believe he'd do it. Why risk his stature?"

"Hoshi, I spent nineteen years in Harmony. Corruption comes naturally to people who live on the mountaintop. Back home on Hokkaido, your people still revere President Aleksanyan. Yes?"

"Of course."

"And why not? She was a war hero, a founding member of

184

Congress, her husband was High Admiral for years. She'd probably still be President if she wasn't assassinated. Admirable, honorable, above reproach. Yes?"

Taking Hoshi down this road was distasteful, but Trevor decided it had to be done.

"Where are you going with this, Trev?"

"I happen to believe she was the most corrupt President we've ever had. The inquest about her financial endeavors aside, I heard valid rumors from a close friend in SI that Aleksanyan kept a small unit of assassins on a secret payroll. They quietly eliminated problems for her. I'm not saying it's true, Hoshi, but that friend died two weeks ago after he captured the man who invented Motif. He knew the Collectorate like few people."

Trevor tried to be supportive, laying a hand on her arm.

"The people we most admire aren't always bad. Some come as advertised, but others lose their way. There are things about Thet that worry me."

Hoshi sat up straight.

"Like what?"

"Indonesia Prime. His home world is base for Black Star's largest operations. The five planets within the Perseus Cluster have seen the most violence related to Motif. Sil Mariputti is also from Indy Prime. Ashraf Diep is from New Bangkok, which is inside the Cluster."

"A coincidence. Thirty-eight planets are represented at Maynor. There's no evidence of corruption, Trev."

"Not yet. I submitted a criminal probable cause order to the Interstellar Banking Exchange for an ROA on Thet, everyone in the mentee group – including Ulbrecht – and Orval Erdogan."

"ROA?"

"Review of Assets. I asked for the past three years. It's a small wealth estimate based on UCVs lodged in protected depositories. It won't say where any of the credits came from, and it will take several days to push through the system. But here's the thing: None of those students were born to wealthy families. Not even close. In fact, they'd be the perfect marks."

She studied him as if he was a stranger. Of course, they'd only known each other for two days, so it made sense.

"I'm trying to believe in you, Trev. I really am."

"Fair enough. Then what d'ya say I push on through the rest, and then you can tell me I've lost my faculties."

Hoshi rubbed the back of her neck.

"I'll try. But I'm going to warn you now: If you present this to Dorrit, he'll laugh you out of his office."

"We'll see."

Trevor gathered Orval Erdogan's profile. The young Turk's glyph beamed with an energy not present in the guy Trevor interviewed.

"Orval said he hadn't visited Raison in months. The LinkPass history confirms his story, so it's doubtful he had relations with Ulbrecht's mentee group. But he did have a relationship with Ulbrecht, and that's where he lied."

"What kind of relationship?"

"They were business partners."

Her double-take returned on cue.

"Wait. Your notes said he claimed Ulbrecht was a fraud. Ulbrecht threatened his life."

"Oh, sure. Ulbrecht *was* a fraud. No doubt. He cheated his way onto Amity. But he also skirted the Housing Authority to make sure his and Orval's flats were nearby. Why? To keep his enemy close?" Trevor chuckled. "Not likely. Nor would he have told Orval about the phantom drill unless he trusted the man. They went into business together and started hunting for buyers. Think someone in Episteme with a deep account might see its value?"

"Like who?"

This was the part where uncertainty entered the fray. Too many potential options for Trevor's taste, but he remained satisfied with his theory's internal logic.

"Difficult to say. But we know of six people who were obligated to pay back the kindness of a benefactor. Yes? And one of them slept with Ulbrecht."

"Whoa. *Eliza Hutton?* You think she ..."

"Acted as a conduit. Aside from Orval, she's the one person Ulbrecht would trust. He introduced her to the program, and she knew the right people to contact. Hoshi, I believe Ulbrecht sold the program weeks ago, but he betrayed his business partner. Orval realized he'd been cut out – that's why they argued. When we spoke to Eliza, she played it down. Said it wasn't important.

"She had too much to lose if the truth were known. As for Orval, that guy was a mess when I spoke to him. Now I know why: With Ulbrecht dead, he lost his chance at seeing any UCVs from the sale."

Trevor gave her a moment to digest the latest twist.

"If you're right, then Orval wasn't the killer."

"Nope."

"Who then?"

Trevor relished the question, even though the answer eluded him.

24

TREVOR SURVEYED THE DOZENS of dataflicks. Unmasking everything but the killer's identity by the second day wasn't bad at all. He felt buoyant. Trevor knew how to resolve the mystery, and where to find the answer. That last bit he kept under wraps for now.

"A ghost," he told Hoshi. "A ghost killed Ulbrecht Hann."
She didn't laugh. Perhaps it was his somber tone.
"Does the ghost have a name?"
"From birth, I'd assume."
"Are you playing with my mind, Trev?"
"Not at all. One part is simple: Ulbrecht's killer owns the phantom drill. This person was the buyer or the buyer's agent. He or she entered Flat 529 without detection, introduced him to a deadly pad of Motif, and left as quietly. The bigger question is: Who would be so audacious? That's trickier.

"By law, there are no secure cams inside residential properties. Only two verified residential crimes have taken place in the past ten years. They were quickly solved because of LinkPass. It's brilliant security – unless someone can move about with impunity."
Hoshi shaded her eyes at the implication.
"That's frightening if true. Amity has always prided itself on being

the safest place in the Collectorate."

"For the most part, it still is. Hoshi, I don't believe the killer is in these dataflicks."

"OK. Explain."

Time to go down the conspiracy well.

"Black Star has too much at stake. They expect a return on their investment. They need a way to monitor the students. To direct them. Make sure no one goes rogue. The students have a minder."

She paused to mull the idea.

"Like an official contact or a watcher?"

"Yes. It would also be someone of high repute. Slipped into the station without fanfare through the normal application process. That's likely what happened with their agent in Customs."

Hoshi clapped her hands together in a moment of clarity.

"The mentor! Mustafa Chait. He's with them more than probably anyone. He could use their time together to receive updates or make new demands. It would be a perfect cover."

Under normal circumstances, Trevor would have congratulated her. OK, so it wasn't the biggest leap. At least she was thinking along the proper lines.

"He was my top suspect, until I saw this."

Trevor pulled up the man's LinkPass history, academic schedule, and transport manifests from the Episteme Spaceport.

"Chait teaches four classes and meets with his mentee group three times a week. Then, with regular precision, he takes a liner to Euphrates and stays for two days. He's been doing this for more than a year. His biography lists a huge family. He spends a fortune jumping back and forth to be with them.

"Here's a vid of Chait disembarking the Dallaquin three hours before we discovered Ulbrecht's body. He took a rifter directly to school. An hour later, his mentees reported in – except for Ulbrecht. That's when Chait called in his absence. Chait lives on campus, along with some other faculty. He hasn't traveled to Haven or Harmony in months. He's not our guy."

Her shoulders sagged with the same frustration Trevor felt when he first ruled out Chait.

"Perhaps you're wrong, Trev. Perhaps there isn't a minder."

"Oh, there is. It would be someone who feels free to travel between the sectors, meet with the students during off-hours, and have no fear of being outed. And now, with the phantom drill, feeling more confident than ever."

"But why kill Ulbrecht? He sold the program. He did his part."

"Ulbrecht learned the truth about his group's benefactors. Eliza said he was afraid. I think she encouraged him to keep quiet. But the minder — or perhaps someone above this person — ordered his death. Black Star uses modified K3 as a weapon, so they smuggled it onboard through their Customs agent. The minder received it and finished the job. Might have worked, too, but they weren't counting on me to show up at his door."

Trevor didn't mind if that came across like braggadocio. Those other Haven deputies wouldn't have dared to escalate the situation and enter the flat. Hoshi's reticence proved as much.

"You see, K3 is interesting. It decays slowly. Within a standard day, its blood concentration is barely noticeable. If he hadn't been found in the morning, the levels would have been so low, we would have written it off as a standard MOD. That, I believe, was the plan all along. His killer stole the pom. By now, it's likely off station or incinerated. And that is where we stand. Thoughts?"

Hoshi hopped up and paced the tiny office, hands to her hips. She scanned the breadth of the evidence and shook her head.

"How did you manage all this so quickly, Trev? I'd have spent days staring at these flicks, and ... I don't know. I'm honestly overwhelmed."

"And impressed, I hope."

She scoffed at his snark.

"Who wouldn't be? Didn't you tell me your wife said you ought to be an SI agent? She's right."

Trevor thought of Oliver; he couldn't shake the sorrow.

"Maybe when all this is over, I'll take a look at a career change. In the meantime, Hoshi, do you see cracks in my narrative?"

Her blank expression betrayed nothing, like a doctor unsure of her diagnosis.

"I think it could work. The only weak link is this so-called minder. He's the only one not on the board. The way you described him – there could be thousands of suspects."

Fair point, to which Trevor rebutted:

"We'll narrow the search. The minder would have arrived within the past thirteen or fourteen months. He'd need time to blend in. Based on the timeline for the other MODs, we can assume the Customs agent arrived shortly thereafter. Then the students followed seven to eight months ago. Black Star is playing a long game, putting their pieces in place carefully."

She nodded. "Good, but that's still a lot of suspects."

"To meet all my criteria? Not so many. I have ideas where to start, but the key is the credit trail. The ROA requests will establish a firm timeline for all the players."

"But you said they'll take days."

He chuckled. "If we're lucky. They might be more useful for a prosecutor. I hope to nab the minder before then."

"When do you intend to bring this before the Chief?"

"The morning, I'd think. I need to conduct some solo interviews at Halifax. Something tells me the trans-wormhole business ties into the case. After that, I'll go to Dorrit."

Hoshi crossed her arms in understandable frustration. Trevor knew she hated being left behind again.

"If you won't let me tag along to Halifax, can I help some other way? You've been doing all the heavy lifting."

"Sure. Run a search on potential suspects. All who arrived after SD 140 last year. Eliminate administrators and corp execs. Only roles that involve regular contact with the public. Highlight anyone with a modest background who came from the Perseus Cluster. That should narrow it to a few hundred."

"And then?"

"The difficult bit. Find connections with Ulbrecht and the mentees. Remember, LinkPass is your friend."

Trevor smushed his holos into a giant bundle and gathered them against his chest. Hoshi opened her wrist plate to elevate the case spool, into which Trevor dumped his work.

"For quick reference," he said. "I'm going to head over to Halifax. If you hit the motherlode, call me at once."

"Will do, Trev."

He didn't expect her to find a solid link anytime soon. Resolution required a different approach.

"You're a good partner, Hoshi."

She stared at the accumulated evidence and no doubt thought of the grind which lay ahead.

"You can count on me."

He winked on the way out. Anything to make Hoshi feel valued. She was an earnest deputy but also green. Trevor doubted she could navigate the course he intended. Better she sit it out.

En route to the Crossway, Trevor opened his pom and tapped the InComm. Connor, who did not respond for a full minute, was bare-chested.

"Sorry, bruv. I was deep in Loutah."

No commentary. No snark. Play it straight, jackass.

"Apologies for ruining your session, C."

"Not to worry. I'm a man at peace."

"OK then. One question: Are you too much at peace for a wild night out at Raison?"

Connor's big, beautiful smile – the one that usually heralded trouble since age three – emerged through a forest of teeth.

"That's an offer I'd never turn down, bruv. When?"

"I want to be there by H10. Show me around."

"It don't get hopping until around H11. You solid with that?"

"Perfect. Only thing is, my wardrobe's not club appropriate. Would you ...?"

Connor's eyes twinkled.

"You have to ask? Trust me, bruv. You will be the talk of Haven."

"I'd rather it not come to that, but thanks, C."

Trevor didn't dwell on what type of ensemble Connor might lay out for him. He trusted his brother to show at least a little decorum. He wanted to blend in at Raison, not make a name for himself. Trevor thought of the LinkPass trend waves he didn't show to Hoshi, the ones he hoped would prove beneficial tonight.

Timing was essential.

He hopped aboard a train bound for Episteme Kallcunik Station, last on the line. The nearest points of interest: Episteme Spaceport and Halifax Research & Development.

Entering Halifax would be simple, but getting them to come clean about an apprentice and his work might require more a bullish approach than he used at Maynor School.

Trevor opened his wrist plate and searched the Episteme Sec Admin directory. He choked down his pride and contacted the last person he ever expected to call an ally.

25

SECOND DEPUTY THOMAS QUINLAN, Trevor's childhood bully, greeted him inside the Halifax lobby. Hands tucked behind his back and legs spread, Thomas exuded the same arrogance that intimidated the Stallion brothers long ago. Yet as a man of forty with gently receding hairline, he lacked the same aura of danger.

"Thank you for this," Trevor said reluctantly as he extended a hand. "I won't forget the assist."

"I would hope not."

Despite having five inches on his old nemesis, Trevor couldn't shake how Thomas managed to meet him square in the eye.

Thomas continued.

"I appreciate you thinking of me before Chief Al-Jani."

"Not a tough choice. I respect Al-Jani, but he's too close to the corp execs. And frankly, you owed me a debt I never called in."

When Thomas chuckled, one corner of his lips folded down as if struck by a palsy. Something to do with an injury he sustained after a bar fight years ago. Trevor forgot the details.

"I always assumed you'd attach strings, Trevor. I'm surprised you waited three years."

"Honestly, I forgot about you, Thomas. Life was always better when we steered clear of each other."

Thomas showed zero hint of offense.

"No argument. But look at us! Twice in two days."

He led Trevor inside the Halifax lobby.

"Al-Jani briefed us. You caused quite the stir."

"I was in the wrong place at the right time. If there's a stir, Black Star is behind it."

Thomas nodded toward reception and led them to the lifts.

"Regardless, the spotlight shines upon you, old friend. We've been told to assist the investigation however necessary."

"Perfect. Do they know to expect us?"

"I spoke to a mate who promised to alert the department chief."

They entered the lift, where Thomas requested Level 4. Trevor did not feign surprise.

"You have a mate in Interstellar Cartography?"

Thomas straightened his jacket with a flourish.

"I'm a much more gregarious man these days. Episteme brings out my better side."

"Ah. So the old fixture — four-word sentences and the underlying tone of impatience — long gone?"

"Indeed," he said as the lift opened. "The man of mystery routine did me no favors." He stopped in the threshold. "A confession. I almost left the station after one week on the job. I found out what it means to be the most limited man in Episteme. Even among Sec Admin, I'm an intellectual dwarf. My own mistake for never giving two shits about my education."

Trevor wondered if that was why Thomas applied for promotions early on. Was he looking for a way out of Episteme?

"Appears you've compensated, Thomas."

"More like, I learned the secret to existing among these people. A smile, a certain swagger, followed by well-timed worship of their considerable talent, tends to set them at ease."

"Ah. Sucking up."

"At every opportunity."

For the first time Trevor could recall, they laughed together ... and it wasn't staged for the other's benefit. Perhaps they experienced a sudden thaw in their relationship – or maybe Thomas had merely demonstrated the technique that allowed him to flourish on Episteme.

"Pleased to see it's working out. For the record, I always found this sector imposing." The door opened, and he motioned for Thomas to lead the way into a maze of labs. "I don't understand much of what they do here. They can be a strange lot."

They walked abreast along a wide avenue lightly populated with scientists in lab coats and full-body tunics, all bearing the Halifax logo featuring a red bird of prey and a spiral galaxy.

"Strange in what sense, old friend?"

"Maynor, for a start. Interact with the students much?"

"Only when they test boundaries."

He thought of Connor's report about a group out of place on Halifax's loading dock.

"Often?"

"They can be a wild bunch. When called on their violations, downright obnoxious. They've even tried to bully me on occasion."

"Huh. Now there's some irony."

Thomas had no witty retort. Perhaps he didn't want to touch that part of their shared history. Instead, he led Trevor through a door simply labeled *IC*.

A small, bespectacled man with a shiny dome greeted them in an anteroom with one chair, a kiosk, and a pair of sconces.

"My mate," Thomas said. "Ivan Detzler."

Ivan removed the smile meant for Thomas and studied Trevor with clear suspicion. He couldn't have cleared five feet by an inch.

"You need to know," Ivan told Thomas, "she's not happy about this. Not in the least. You she trusts. But this one?"

"Now, now, Ivan. First Deputy Stallion is a veteran of great repute. I'd hate to think he'd be subjected to anti-Chancellor bias. Such an esteemed woman must avoid outdated attitudes."

In another context, Trevor would've verbalized his amusement at the irony which thickened into hypocrisy.

The man almost sounds reformed. Nope. All part of the act.

Ivan's cheeks turned cherry red.

"OK. Yes. She has a problem with his ... with the Deputy's kind. And with good reason. But that's not her issue. She's grappling with the loss of her best apprentice. She's having a difficult day."

He delivered the explanation without once eyeing Trevor, who might as well have vanished.

"Show me inside," Trevor said. "I'll be gentle. I only have a few questions, Mr. Detzler. Promise."

"I vouch for him completely," Thomas added. "In fact, if there's even the slightest conflict, I'll be waiting here."

Trevor felt a wave of relief. He did not want to conduct this interview while his old nemesis observed.

Ivan shuttered and waved Trevor onward.

"Eh. Let's get it over with."

Trevor saluted Thomas, who settled into the lonely chair.

The IC lab caught him off-guard. It was far from anything like he'd expect of a facility for mapmakers. At its core, three narrow bases at least ten meters long supported dark, translucent cylinders, the ends of which mounted into titanium frames. A series of phasic plates lined the bases, with low-back swiveled chairs completing the workstations.

Ivan led him between two such cylinders toward the lab's rear, where a blond woman in her forties ate a sandwich. Between bites, she stared at her visitor unblinking.

The little man made a mess of introductions.

"Madam Cass, this is Deputy ... what's your name, again?"

Trevor ignored him, stepping forward with hand extended.

"First Deputy Trevor Stallion, Haven Sec Admin. I apologize for barging in at a difficult time, but I have pressing questions."

The woman, whose blue eyes reminded Trevor of an Earth sky he hadn't seen in two decades, set down her sandwich and wiped her hands with a napkin. She sighed at the trouble of standing before conceding to the shake.

"Cassandra Latin, Chief Cartographer. My staff have taken to calling me Madam Cass. From you, I'll accept Chief Latin."

Huh. She's not condescending at all.

He felt these vibes on rare occasions. Anyone with a lingering sentiment against Chancellors got their jollies by playing linguistic power games. Latin's impressive stature, facial bone structure, and piercing eyes provided the clue to her animosity.

"Of course, Chief. If I'm not mistaken, you're Aeternan."

"I don't see how that's germane, but yes."

Perfect. One of only ten immortals based on the station, less than a fifth of its peak years ago.

"I only bring it up because I rarely have the pleasure. I sat in on a meeting this morning with High Admiral Woolsey."

Latin offered no reaction.

"Ivan, activate SIM2. Let's rerun yesterday's algorithmics."

"Certainly, Madam. If you need anything, I'm close." He flicked a side-eye at Trevor. "Also, Deputy Quinlan is waiting outside."

She thanked her diminutive assistant and carefully wrapped the second half of her sandwich inside a fresh napkin.

"You're here to ask about Ulbrecht. You want to know about his work for IC and whether I thought he was a drug addict."

Wasting no time. Good!

"I'm sure your answer to the second part is no because he wasn't. Ulbrecht led an interesting life, but what happened to him was a one-time affair. Chief, we believe Ulbrecht was murdered."

He let the revelation lay heavy between them. Latin shaded her eyes for a few seconds. Trevor looked for any tic, no matter how small, but this woman gave away nothing.

"Someone killed him? Why?"

"I thought we might explore that subject, Chief. I need to know

198

what sort of work Trevor did for you. Mr. Detzler said Ulbrecht was your best apprentice."

She motioned for Trevor to take a seat.

"Apprentice?" Latin tapped her desk. "That title belittles him."

"How so?"

"From the moment he entered my lab, I knew Ulbrecht was a generational talent. Within the first hour, he called into question the very algorithmics that form the basis of our research. Within a month, we made more progress than the previous two years."

OK, so he might have cheated his way onto Amity, but he wasn't necessarily a fraud.

"Ulbrecht's public biography states he was studying trans-wormhole shielding tech. I've heard different perspectives on its validity. Perhaps you can shed some light."

"Oh, me. That Ulbrecht. Wrote it on his public bio, did he?"

"His headmaster said it was intended as a joke."

She scoffed, her first visible show of emotion.

"Bien Thet is a moron who disguises himself as a guru. The cleaning staff know more about what we do than Thet. Take his word at your peril, Deputy Stallion."

Brutal honesty or great dramatics, Trevor wasn't sure. But he got her riled, which meant she'd lead him down the necessary path.

"I understand from other sources that your department is attempting to map black matter substrata, where wormholes are formed. Was that where Ulbrecht influenced your algorithmics?"

"Deputy, we're not *attempting* to map anything. In fact, we're achieving it. We long ago shifted our focus from the visible universe to the dark regions underneath. Most human space travel is spent inside regions we've only begun to understand.

"More than four thousand wormholes are generated each standard day. We can cross the farthest length between member worlds in three hours. It's the single greatest achievement in human history. Now, I dare you to ask a thousand captains what they know about black substrata. If you're fortunate, five will offer a cogent answer. As long as their worm drive catalyzers plot the course and open the aperture, they don't care."

A speech already. Impressive.

Trevor pressed his luck.

"You think they should."

"What kind of a lunatic pilots a ship wearing blinders?"

"Probably the kind who has a valuable cargo onboard, and profit waits on the other side of a quick jump."

Latin relaxed until hinting at a smile.

"They would be the ones. We believe this is reckless. Humans have pressed forward anyway. We map the substrata to better understand its environmental stability and precisely why it allows us to open wormholes inside it. Ulbrecht's work was invaluable. His mind interpreted algorithmics like poetry."

Trevor stopped her.

"Back up, please. You said, 'it allows us.' *It?*"

She draped a hand over her mouth, perhaps realizing she said too much. When it fell away, Latin sighed.

"At this point, pretenders like Bien Thet claim we're a fringe science. You might too after hearing my answer."

"Chief Latin, the only people I don't buy are the ones who won't give me a straight answer."

Her smile suggested she believed Trevor.

"Deputy, are you open-minded?"

"I try to think so."

He wasn't prepared for what came next.

26

L ATIN GAZED AT TREVOR, as if inspecting him to ensure he had the proper intellect to understand her answer.

"I'm sure you realize," she began, "that the universe has to be far more than an infinite collection of molecules, some of which miraculously evolved into complex life. Yes?"

"We know there are nine universes, and they once connected to each other through fissures. I'm open to all sorts of possibilities."

Latin shifted her gaze and shouted.

"Ivan, adjust SIM2 to the base matrix. I'll be there in a moment."

"Yes, Madam!"

She recalibrated.

"Deputy, the need to understand black substrata is critical for one simple reason: It's alive, and it's sentient."

Not the first time he'd come across the farfetched idea, but never heard it from anyone of Latin's credentials.

"You said it *allows us* to travel through. Is it a lifeform? A species? For the lack of a better word: God?"

"Deputy, the universe is too carefully designed to have been brought about by random acts of molecular generation and decay. The tissue that binds existence but remains hidden to the naked eye contains a sentience we may never fully understand. What we know: Worm drive algorithmics are a language that speaks to and receives confirmation from the substrata.

"There is no other viable explanation. We cannot open tunnels beneath the visible universe on demand. Predictable and reliable? No. Our technology works because an intelligence beyond our limited comprehension cooperates. To what end? We'll never know. Please, Deputy. Follow me."

Already, the interview had taken him to places far afield of his purpose, and he still hadn't asked the two most critical questions. Trevor played along and followed her to the middle cylinder, the inside of which now glowed with smoke in varied colors.

"Deputy, have you ever seen a full simulation of a wormhole inside and out?"

"Not outside. I wasn't aware anyone's ever witnessed it."

Ivan stifled a laugh; his boss seemed bemused.

"Nor will we. Ivan, launch the base matrix. What you'll see is a product of more than a decade of data-gathering from hundreds of unmanned probes. Some recorded the wave energy of the inner walls while others created disturbances to corrupt those walls."

"Huh. You mean crashing out of the wormhole?"

"Correct."

"Like the Lightfoot incident during the war. Woolsey's ship."

The clouds took form, generating a rapidly spinning gray mass.

"After a fashion," she confirmed. "Capt. Woolsey's ship took an indirect hit from an enemy missile which followed them through the aperture. Not a model we dare replicate. Look here."

Latin pointed out the wormhole's hyperfast rotation. Data from the phasic plate projected numbers that made Trevor's brain spin faster. A physicist, he was not.

"What you see, Deputy, is a staggering release of energy to provide stability until the ship has safely passed through the exit aperture. It does this by holding back the turbulence inside black matter. The science is likely beyond you, but think of it this way: Have you ever cut a pie slice, and the filling was so fluid that it instantly flooded the gap?" She did not wait for an answer. "There are no gaps in substrata. It's the glue, the cartilage if you will, that holds the universe together. And yet, it will spin up all that energy to allow humans to travel the stars like genuine gods."

Trevor reckoned if he thought about it long enough, the implications might hurt his brain. The people in this little lab didn't get much notice, but their research went to the ultimate of cutting edges. He didn't come for a lesson on wormhole mechanics, yet he couldn't let this go without asking:

"Are you saying a lifeform beyond comprehension is generating that energy four thousand times a standard day across nine hundred light-years? We don't know it's motivation. Only that it apparently wants to help."

She crossed her arms and huffed.

"You oversimplified the relationship. My counter is speculative. However, I stand on solid footing. We did not create wormhole drives on their own. That we know for a fact."

She caught Trevor by surprise.

"We do? How?"

"I assume you were born around the fall of the first Collectorate."

"5358."

"A turning point in history. I was eleven. My people – not one of them yet in their twenties – aligned with a small group of hybrids to form Salvation. You might have heard of it?"

Shit. Of course. She must have been one of them.

"We never would've succeeded without mobile worm drives. Our leader at the time – a man whose name my people are forbidden from uttering – devised the technology. He was among a small group who were engineered from infancy with an artificial intelligence."

Trevor remembered reading the reports of that era. Horrifying.

"Yes. The hybrids called themselves the Jewels."

He knew the infamous names of their leaders but decided not to embarrass Latin by mentioning the head lunatic.

"They did," she said, "but the AI inside them were the true Jewels of Eternity. The genuine masterminds. A million years old, traveled the galaxy, crossed fissures between universes, terraformed many of our worlds before humans knew how to stand on two feet. The hybrids were killed – fortunately for everyone – but the Jewels of Eternity live deep inside Aeterna. We haven't heard from them in more than twenty years. Might be preferable if we never do.

"My point, Deputy: The Jewels knew many secrets about the universe, including the mechanics of wormholes. They provided the monster who led Salvation with the algorithmics. Without the drive, we wouldn't have killed millions with singularity bombs or claimed Aeterna for ourselves. The Collectorate wouldn't have fallen, and we wouldn't have been able to defend our home when your ancestors came after us in 5358. I was there, a blast rifle in hand, fighting off the Unification Guard. Soldiers bigger than you."

There it was: The smoldering resentment toward Chancellors. He read the stories about the Chancellory's disastrous assault on Aeterna; ten thousand soldiers killed in an hour trying to take down a single enclave of immortals. The Last Day's War, they called it.

"Those were difficult times, Chief Latin. I'm glad you survived. The People's Collectorate owes a debt to Aeterna." He pointed to the cylinder. "Your simulation is impressive. Your theories even more so. Now, let's go back to why I'm here. What is trans-wormhole shielding tech?"

She answered with a raised finger.

"Ivan, insert the cross current." As her assistant navigated the phasic panel, Latin said, "Deputy, we have a theory: Black substrata binds not just this universe but all. While the physical fissures have been closed, we hold that the black matter allows for cross currents which flow between universes. Here."

Vortices opened along the simulation and intersected new tunnels flowing perpendicular to the original wormhole. Those tunnels demonstrated the same hyperfast rotation.

"Crossroads with off ramps," Trevor mumbled.

"Very good, Deputy. The Lightfoot incident opened the door to this possibility."

"You plan to design worm drives capable of doing this?"

Latin shook her head.

"Engaging with other universes would violate Collectorate law."

Trevor's paranoia took charge.

"Science always finds a way around the law. But this would be insanity. The Swarm almost destroyed us. You wouldn't actually try to open new doors?"

"Of course not."

He didn't like her tone. Hesitant, uncertain.

"What's the shielding tech?"

"A theoretical design we would use on our probes to test the larger proposition."

"Right. The one you'll definitely not do."

"As I said, Deputy ..."

She went on at length about the ethics of their work, defending the need for science to push new boundaries while balancing the needs of the many. Trevor ignored the details as he made the connection between Ulbrecht, this lab, and why he was killed.

"Chief Latin, what would happen if your research fell into the wrong hands?"

She and Ivan laughed.

"Nothing, of course. Thieves wouldn't know what to do with it."

"You sure there's no one out there with your expertise on the subject? No one at all?"

Her smile vanished.

"Your point, Deputy?"

"You said Ulbrecht advanced your work by two years in a month. Now, what if a group bent on destroying civilization could make this work? What sort of chaos might they cause?"

Latin ordered Ivan to shut down the simulation.

"I do not care for your implication."

"Neither do I, but I can't ignore it. Did Ulbrecht often discuss the practical application of your work?"

Latin shaded her eyes, while Ivan reasserted the same level of suspicion with which he greeted Trevor.

"Madam Cass has given enough of her time. And been generous about it. You should leave, Deputy."

She silenced her diminutive assistant.

"I can speak for myself, Ivan. But yes, Deputy, he's right. Any discussions of that nature are proprietary and will not help your investigation. I have a sandwich to finish and a long day ahead. Please. Ivan will show you out."

OK, so that's where they zip shut. Interesting.

"No worries, Ivan. I can handle the complicated journey."

The little man sneered at Trevor's dose of snark.

"You heard her. Go."

"I never overstay a welcome."

Not usually, at any rate.

Trevor thanked her on the way out. Latin called after him.

"Will there be a service for Ulbrecht?"

"Don't know, Chief. You might want to contact Maynor, see if they're planning anything. Thank you again. Sorry for your loss."

Truth was, anything else Latin revealed would've made little difference. She offered enough detail for Trevor to fill in a gap.

Ulbrecht was out of control. That's why they killed him.

Trevor locked the final pieces into place as Thomas greeted him in the anteroom.

"Productive?"

"Oh. Yes. Very."

He said little to Thomas on the way out of Halifax, but his old adversary did not hold back after they entered the lift.

"It's nasty business, old friend. I trust you'll put it to bed soon."

"What? Oh. Yeah. That's the plan."

"I'd like to think my helping you sidestep the Halifax barriers will not go unnoticed."

Lovely. Now he comes clean.

"I'm grateful, Thomas. You saved me valuable time."

"Good. I know we have a dense history, but I'll soon be applying for a position in Harmony. I hoped you might put in a good word with Central. They've been cold to my previous applications."

Can't imagine why.

"I'll certainly include you in my case notes. Of course, I haven't been in favor with Central lately."

Thomas grinned as the door at Level 1 slipped open.

"Soon to change, I'm sure."

He extended a hand, which Trevor accepted.

"We'll see."

"Also, Trevor, I've been contemplating our shared journey. We're due for a fresh start. We might have been friends if I hadn't bolloxed it up. I thought perhaps dinner ... my treat ... when you're free."

If Trevor suspected the man was sincere, he would've agreed on the spot. Yet the temperature seemed to fall a couple of degrees in Thomas's vicinity. Better to leave things alone.

"You know, Thomas, when I turned fourteen, I had you by a good three inches. I could've beaten you to the edge of your life."

Thomas smirked. "You might have tried, but I was quite handy, especially with my right hook."

"I didn't care. I wanted to hurt you every time you walked into the room. I held back because it would've broken your parents' hearts, and I loved them for giving us a home. Plus, I had to set a standard for Connor."

"Hmm. Still want to hurt me?"

"No. But friendship? Not happening."

Thomas nodded with faux resignation.

"Too bad. I thought maybe ..."

"Tell me something, Thomas. How are your parents doing?"

"They're ... uh ... getting on with life in reasonable health."

Trevor saw the truth in his blank features.

"When was the last time you deepstreamed them?"

"Very expensive to DS."

"Huh. Yeah. When did you last visit Earth?"

"Even pricier. They're fine, Trevor. Just fine."

What was left to say? Trevor hadn't spoken to them in years. Perhaps he'd DS the Quinlans after this crisis ended.

"Spend a few credits, Thomas. Don't take them for granted."

He didn't wait for the man's response. Didn't care.

Trevor made a beeline for the public docks. As he put distance between himself and Halifax, the last nagging bits of the puzzle slid together. One question remained: Who waited for Ulbrecht in Flat 529?

That answer, he concluded, would greet him in the place Ulbrecht used to treat like a second home.

Raison Club.

Here we go, Connor. I hope I know what I'm doing.

27

TREVOR'S HEART TOOK A DIP when he saw the ensemble Connor laid out for him. The blood-red jacket cast a waxy sheen that reflected light. Its black buttons glowed at a touch. Connor insisted the matching elastic pants and form-fitting collarless black shirt were perfect for the dance floor.

"You can check the jacket if it's too hot, bruv."

Not much chance of that. Trevor needed the internal pockets for his pom and pistol.

The decorative glasses were the coup de grace. Thick, jagged frames surrounded lenses shaded in between the jacket and shirt. Flippers, Connor called them. They hid the bearer's eyes without dimming the natural light.

Trevor slicked back his gelled hair in a single wave. Connor, also grooming in front of the water room mirror, didn't care for the look and swiped his brother's comb.

"Hold still," he said, parting Trevor's hair down the middle.

"I look ridiculous, C. Like a child."

"It's the rage on Catalan."

"We're not on Catalan."

Connor shrugged as he applied rouge to his own cheeks.

"I thought Amity was every planet, bruv."

So went the mantra, to which Trevor dared not argue. Connor painted beneath his eyes, added sparkles along his jaw line, and tied up his hair. The effect seemed to work with the shimmering one-piece tunic that accentuated his considerable muscles.

"You always go to this much trouble for the clubs?"

"I'm following the plan, bruv. You said we had to look like two guys out for a good time. Draw no attention."

"Oh, and these getups won't turn eyes?"

"We'll blend in." Connor set down his makeup brush. "Damn. How long since you last had a night out on the station?"

A fair question, although Trevor didn't care for the tone.

"Dinner with the wife and little girl tend to be subdued."

"Prison much?"

Trevor sighed. His brother never cared for the domestic life.

"I hope you experience the joy one day, C. It can be like magic. Sometimes."

Until it all goes wrong.

"I hear you, bruv. I do. But kids? Not my style. That's why I love little Ana. I can play Uncle C for an hour and go home. No. When I find a husband worthy of me, we're gonna celebrate each other without the extra luggage. No offense."

"None taken."

Trevor shifted uneasily in the heavy jacket while Connor finished his touchup. Connor grinned at his brother's discomfort.

"It's sitting a little loose on your shoulders. Sorry about that, Trev-*or*. You're not so buff anymore."

"Eh. Only have but so many hours to spend in the fit room."

"Now you're making excuses. Every married man on my crew is just like you. Anal to the core, bruv."

Trevor stepped out into the bedroom.

"*Practical.* That's the word you're looking for."

Connor came at him with the makeup brush.

"I choose my words with loving care. *Anal.*"

What was the point of arguing?

"Connor, I'm the same man I've always been."

"You said it, bruv. Anal for as long as I can remember. Guess I loved and respected you so much, I reckoned you'd grow out of it by now. But they say folks don't ever really change."

Nope. No argument. Just brothers. Trevor's tension subsided.

"That *is* what they say."

Connor slapped Trevor on the shoulder.

"Whoever in ten hells *they* are. Am I right? But anytime you want me to teach you the Loutah ... it might help. Metamorphosis. Cocoon to butterfly. Anytime."

"I love you, C, but I doubt I'll ever be a man at peace. It's not in my fiber."

"Bullshit. We all got the right stuff. Just have to dig, bruv. Who knows? Maybe that's what you need to win Effie back."

Trevor drew the line at marriage advice.

"My burden, Connor. You tend to yours. Fair?"

OK, settle down, jackass. He didn't deserve that. He's doing you a hell of a favor.

Connor retreated to the water room.

"I hear you, Trev. I overstepped."

Trevor paced while Connor attended to the last details. It was half past H9, giving him enough time to explain the night's strategy and hit Raison by the top of the hour. If their patterns held true, Ulbrecht's fellow mentees would arrive soon after. Surely, they'd link up with their minder at some point in the evening.

You people have a lot to talk about. Don't you?

"Time to let it rip," Connor soon announced. "Have some drinks, hit the dance floor, solve a murder. What a night. Ready?"

Trevor surveyed his always-astounding brother.

"Your pom?"

Connor winked and tucked at his left side, where Trevor saw a slight bump camouflaged against the tunic.

211

"Matching pack. Designed it myself. You like?"

"Clever. You'll need it." Trevor opened a thumb-sized case to reveal two translucent ear beads. "Very sensitive to paired voices. Great at filtering out distractions. I hear Raison is loud."

Connor took a bead and smiled.

"On a bad night. The rest of the time? Nobody talks on the prime floor. No point. You just let go and dance."

"We'll hear each other with these. Word of warning: If I'm in your ear while you're in conversation with someone else, play it cool. I've seen newbs struggle with these at first."

Connor pushed the bead into his ear.

"Bruv. Please. I'm all over it. You may not know this about me, but I'm a brilliant actor. I could star in popvids."

He sounded sincere, to which Trevor shook his head and pointed to the door.

"You do know popvids are outlawed on seven planets?"

"Yeah, but that leaves a big market. I have every attribute the producers want."

Trevor stopped in the open doorway.

"This nudity phase of yours ... you didn't get it from the Loutah. Did you?"

Connor's cheeks likely reddened beneath that makeup.

"I compiled a healthy library, bruv. Share a watch sometime. The Inuits? They're the best."

"OK. That's more than I needed to know. We're going to walk to Raison. Put the popvids out of your mind and pay attention, C. I need this plan to work."

Connor saluted.

"I'm your Second. Nothing comes before the plan."

Technically, Connor became a de facto employee of Haven Sec Admin. Trevor executed a little-known and never used clause inside the Amity Charter to deputize his brother. He doubted Central would buy Trevor's action as properly pursuant to the Emergency

Declaration exemption, but he'd deal with their ruling on another day. If this plan went awry, they'd fire Trevor for using a civilian in a law enforcement capacity. Clause 26-G gave him cover.

Heading down the lift, Connor said:

"I feel incomplete without a pistol and a bar, bruv."

"Sorry. I'd have to justify the acquisition to Dorrit. Be happy with the field appointment. If the pieces fall into place, my pistol will be enough. We don't want laser bolts set loose inside a nightclub."

"No argument on that score, but I'm a good shot. I went through all the training. Remember?"

And walked away from a steady career.

"Ten years ago, C. That's a lot of rust."

To which Connor snorted.

"Bruv, they're aim and press. Anyone can learn in ten seconds."

"Which is why they're restricted to security personnel."

"I hear most planets have open carry laws. Not just for pistols. Blast rifles, too."

The lift mercifully opened.

"Thank you, C. I'll be sure to bring that before Central at our next roundtable discussion of how we *increase* the crime rate on Amity."

He suspected Connor used the banter to mask anxiety about tonight. Even before Trevor explained his theory about Ulbrecht's death and the connection to Black Star, Connor had to know he wouldn't have been deputized unless the stakes were high.

Trevor considered teaming with Hoshi for about ten seconds, but the Second Deputy played too close to the regs for this operation. He needed a fearless partner who'd approach any stranger and play a role. Moreover, if matters went sideways, Hoshi's record would remain clean. Before he checked out for the day, Trevor briefed Hoshi on his interview at Halifax.

"It's not conclusive, but I think we're on the right track," he said, glancing at her search results of newer Amity residents.

His narrow parameters for unmasking the minder produced three hundred names. Hoshi had yet to find connections to Ulbrecht.

"Finish this for homework, and we'll sit down with it tomorrow morning. After that, I'll lay out the case to Dorrit."

She couldn't mask her disappointment.

"This might take hours, Trev. I was hoping maybe we could work on it over a light dinner."

Subtlety was not her thing, apparently. Trevor allowed for the occasional white lie, even to colleagues.

"I arranged a call with my little girl in about an hour. I haven't had quality time with her since she returned home. So sorry."

"No worries. Family comes first. My brothers DS'd me a few days ago, and we went on for hours. They pooled their creds to afford the call. But we had the best time."

"How many?"

Her disappointment morphed into a wistful buoyance.

"Six. All younger. They surprised me. And the things they talk about ... you have to know my brothers."

"I'm sure they're proud of their big sister. You miss home?"

"I feel like I never left. If it happened in Puratoon in the past year, my brothers passed it on."

That seemed like a fine note to leave things. He didn't want to hear insider reports from a backwater on Hokkaido. Trevor promised the Chief a full presentation by H2. Yes, he added, we'll have enough to update Central.

If this gambit failed ...

The Stallion brothers earned many bemused stares on their way out. Actually, the glimmering man to Trevor's right drew most of the attention. Even at his most outrageous, Connor cut an astonishing figure. His broad shoulders and rock hard pectorals combined with a swagger that told onlookers who possessed the superior genes. Connor acknowledged everyone with a wink.

"You can't get enough of it, C."

"People appreciate beauty and art, bruv."

"Yes. And as long as they're looking at you, they don't give ten hells about me. I'll take it."

When they stepped onto the Swiftrak, Trevor told Connor to ignore public adulation and focus on the mission. Walking at a steady but unhurried pace, he rehashed the plan's details. Connor never broke stride.

"We'll need the breaks to slide our way, Trev. Gotta have proof to score a win."

Therein laid the crux of the problem.

"There's an easy way and a hard way to do this. Easy: We unmask the minder tonight. We bring them all in. At least one will confess. Those five students are on edge. If the minder killed Ulbrecht ..."

Connor got the picture but also raised his voice.

"The others will have to wonder if they're next."

"Bring it down a decibel, C. We're in public."

"Sorry."

"At first, I thought they lied about not partying with Ulbrecht. No. They came because the minder demanded it. If they show, it's because they weren't given a choice."

Connor nodded.

"It's not a bad arrangement, actually. Raison lets people lose themselves. They use the Recon tubes for disguises. On the prime floor, it's all about the music and the dance. Bodies smashing into each other, and you don't care who. People disappear into the Spin Rooms. Every kind of fun you can think of. Had my share of sweet adventure. Yeah, bruv. Meeting there makes sense."

The frequency of previous mentee visits predicted at least three of the five students would be there tonight. They always arrived fifteen to thirty minutes after H11.

"I've only been in Raison one time," Trevor said. "A year before I met Effie. You invited me. Remember?"

Connor frowned. "Really?"

"Yep. Although I more or less dragged you out a few hours later.

You weren't cogent."

"Shit. Must have hung one on."

"More like three, four, or ten. At any rate, you know the place as well as anyone. Don't lose yourself in there. Or me. Got it?"

"I'm your man. Um, you mentioned before about an easy way and a hard way to do this. What's the hard way?"

Before Trevor laid out his backup plan, a human flew above him, legs flailing. He screamed for those ahead to clear a path.

The teenager landed with a thud, rolled over twice, and continued running. He ignored the curses from those close by.

"Leaper," Connor said. "Good thing you're not in uniform. You'd have to chase the little asshole."

Instinct told him to chase anyway. Common sense won out.

"I thought this only happened during off-shift hours. That's what my Second told me yesterday."

"They don't care. I hate Natives. Entitled little monsters."

"Huh. And you were any better at their age?"

Connor conceded the point through a pregnant pause.

"So, about the hard way?"

"Yeah. It starts with me being wrong tonight. I regroup tomorrow, present my theory, hope Dorrit buys it and allows me to bring in the students for questioning. That won't be easy. Maynor will fight it. We'll have to do an end-run on the Charter. And frankly, it might put these students in real danger if their benefactors think they'll break. Otherwise, we'll have to follow the UCVs. There are no guarantees it will prove anything."

Connor wrapped an arm around his brother.

"Remember how you laid into me when I decided not to join Sec Admin?"

"Yep. Wasn't my finest hour."

"Truth is, I wanted to say yes, but I wasn't cut out for it. You knew it, too; just weren't willing to admit it. You're good at this job, bruv. The best. I wish we'd been able to work together. So happy you're trusting me tonight. Don't worry. We'll find this bastard and solve your case. The Stallion brothers will do it the easy way."

As with many of Connor's declarations, that sounded like a candidate for famous last words. It did not lessen Trevor's unease.

Trevor opened his pom to search files transferred from his wrist plate, which remained hidden beneath his jacket. The plate would give him away. He expanded a small holo with the mentees' glyphs.

"Have you committed them to memory?"

"You only gave me an hour heads-up." Connor laughed. "Of course, T. If I spot one, you'll know in a flash."

To Trevor's disappointment, none of the five matched the students Connor had seen fighting on the Halifax loading dock. That lead had always been a longshot, but Trevor needed some luck, and soon. After all, no one counted on him to solve the case – just Chief Dorrit, Central Administration, SI, and President Haas.

No one at all.

"They're on your pom," he told Connor. "If there's any doubt, check the glyphs first. Understood?"

"No worries, Trev-or. I might be a rookie, but I'm no moron."

That proposition was about to be tested.

They arrived at Raison five minutes later.

28

T HE CLUB INTRODUCED ITSELF with a genteel aura. The Paradise Lounge cast dim blue lighting from translucent ceiling panels. Several dozen tables and booths, each lit by a spectral glow lamp, slowly revolved around the bar, where crowds ordered their beverages from kiosks. Drones with delicate mechanical tentacles poured and mixed drinks faster than human bartenders.

"Slow for now," Connor said, pointing out the half-empty tables. "Give it an hour, bruv. They'll line up three deep for drinks."

Trevor studied the layout. He wanted the best vantage for watching the entrance, but the revolving floor created a strategic problem. He pointed out an empty booth on the periphery.

"We'll start there."

Connor shrugged.

"You're the boss. What's your flavor?"

"Not here to drink. Have to keep a clear head."

"Everybody drinks in Raison. You'll look like an ass. Plus, there's a forty-cred top charge."

Shit. He could think of a hundred better ways to spend forty credits, but he already lost the money when he tapped the entry's LinkPass sensor. Yet Connor hit the mark on a different count: No drink in hand meant he'd stand out.

"Yeah. Sure. Order me a white wine."

Connor glared at Trevor as if he'd been scandalized.

"Bruv, you're a Chancellor. You can do better. They got drinks from all forty planets."

He might have visited Raison only once before, but Trevor knew their game: Sauce up the patrons before sending them onto the dance halls, the drifting opera, and the Spin Rooms, where they'd spend hundreds more credits. Though the lounge was subdued – soft instrumentals blended with the crowd's banter and clinking glasses – the faint rumble from the primary dance floor's industrial music was unmistakable. Connor pressed him again to order a stronger drink.

"No surprises, C. Got it?"

He fully expected to be surprised.

"Damn, Trev. You used to be a creature of the night."

"Then I grew up. I'll be waiting in that booth."

Trevor settled in and watched Connor activate his social butterfly drive. Rather than ordering drinks, he accosted familiar faces at the bar. They exchanged pleasantries which Trevor endured through the ear bead.

For a moment, he took his eyes off the shimmering Stallion at the bar to study other patrons. Most belonged to the younger set, and their costumes were louder than Trevor's, lessening his discomfort. He saw a few couples with romantic notions, but most were clearly friends or colleagues unleashing the pent-up tension after a workday in Amity. A few wore flippers to hide their eyes, and a couple had already dipped into the Recon tubes, judging from their animal skins and face paint. The dress trend for most: Short, low-cut, loose-fitting – perfect for the physical requirements of drifting opera.

Opposite to the double-wide entrance, six labeled doorways with LinkPass sensors led into serpentine corridors connecting Paradise Lounge to Raison's most popular attractions. There were too many doors for Trevor's comfort. If the mentees and their minder met

219

further inside the club, would he lose track?

Trevor made sure he drew no one's attention before dipping his left arm beneath the table. He pulled back his jacket sleeve and tapped the wrist plate without being conspicuous. He activated a live status update on the mentees' LinkPass profiles. The tiny holo was a viable tracking mechanism, but also a blatant violation of the Charter, which allowed its use only to pursue a criminal or aid someone suffering a health emergency.

It also screamed, "Sec Admin on the case!" to any who saw the plate in action. Blown cover would not be helpful.

None had arrived at the club early, but three students were on the move. Two checked out rifters, while another exited the train at Mogandi Station. The others? They could've been walking. Hard to say. There were no access points along the Swiftraks.

"Assuming all five received the same orders," he muttered.

"What's that, bruv?"

Trevor forgot about the ear bead. He pulled down his sleeve.

"Nothing, C. How are those drinks coming?"

"On their way."

Along with company, as it turned out.

Connor was shocked to discover his coworker Jeon at the club. As those two bantered by the bar, Trevor made a connection: This man taught Connor the Loutah.

Ridiculous timing, but it didn't stop Connor from inviting Jeon to the Stallions' booth. Trevor cursed then added:

"No, C. Make an excuse. Send him on his way."

Connor did not reply.

"Sure he won't mind?" Jeon was heard to say. "I am not one to intrude on family time."

Connor scoffed. "My big bruv loves to make friends. He has a wife and kid. Doesn't get out much."

Connor's facial sparkles glistened in the passing glow of spectral lamps en route to the booth. He carried a tall drink in each hand. His

EngSec9 coworker followed.

Trevor sighed. *I made a terrible mistake.*

As they approached, Trevor slid to the corner of the booth, giving him the best perspective on the entrance. He hoped Connor would have the foresight to slide in from the opposite side.

No such luck.

Connor handed Trevor a tall, thin glass with a dark liquor. Was it purple? What was the brown foam on top? *Cudfrucker!*

"Slide in, bruv. Got a friend I want you to meet. Best man I know not named Stallion."

Trevor forced a muted grin and complied.

"This is Jeon Phee. He's my mate from work. I wouldn't be at peace if he didn't show me the path."

Trevor nodded but did not extend his hand.

"Ah. Yes. Connor mentioned you. The Loutah, right? You're from the Shailin tribe on Indonesia Prime?"

Jeon, about Connor's age, dipped his chin in confirmation. He bore a semblance to Headmaster Bien Thet and student Ashraf Diep, both of whom hailed from the same world.

"Your brother spoke of me? How good of you to remember."

"Connor seems to think the Loutah has changed his life." Before Jeon replied, Trevor held up the purple liquor. "C, I recall asking for white wine. What is this?"

"A real drink, T." He nudged Jeon. "Tell him."

Jeon shook his head, as if to say Connor had been naughty.

"Trevor, it's a drink from my world. In our ancient tongue, it's called *M'juhti.* Today, most people know it as horse nip."

This mission got better by the moment.

"Should I even ask?"

"Yeah, you better," Connor said, chuckling.

"Not to worry," Jeon said. "It's a refreshing beverage, fermented from wild henberries. It's believed the berries drive horses mad with extreme sexual appetite. Or so the legend goes."

"You'll love it," Connor added. "Aftertaste lingers, but it'll make you feel ten years younger."

"Great. Horse nip. Debited to *your* account. Yes?"

"My treat, bruv."

Connor raised his glass, as did Jeon. Trevor hated being boxed into a corner, so he played along.

"Full hearts," Connor said.

Glasses clanked and Trevor sipped.

He wiped foam from his lips and stifled a laugh. *Fermented henberries, my ass.* It tasted like forty proof grape juice.

"Whatcha think, T? Great, huh?"

"Good thing I'm not a horse. It will do." Shifting eyes between the entrance and the guest, Trevor added: "Popular in your tribe?"

Jeon reared back.

"No, not at all. Most Shailin reject fermented beverages."

"You're different?"

"I have learned to adapt since I came to Amity. There are only two other Shailin on the station, and they live in Harmony. I never see them."

Connor leaned into Trevor like he was about to deliver a secret.

"You two have something in common. This is also Jeon's second visit to Raison. Ask him why."

Trevor overheard earlier. Jeon answered without prompting.

"I recently made the acquaintance of a lovely woman from New Bangkok. We are exploring the future. I hope, that is. She is outgoing. Loves to dance. She should be here very soon."

"Ah. A date. Well, good luck to you, Jeon."

He thought Connor might get the message and create an excuse to send Jeon on his way. Instead, the opposite occurred.

"Jeon has an amazing life story, bruv. It's remarkable he's even alive today to meet a nice girl. Ask him about it."

Jeon grabbed at Connor.

"No, no. We are all here to enjoy ourselves. Your brother does not wish to listen to my sad tales."

That's the cudfrucking truth.

Connor didn't give up.

"No, really. Jeon, you should tell him. Or I will, if that suits."

Jeon shaded his eyes in obvious embarrassment before nodding.

"Trevor, has your brother always been this way? Putting others in awkward positions?"

"Since he learned to talk."

Connor beamed with satisfaction.

"It's my special gift. So, Jeon's family used to live in the Ularu Province on Indy Prime. Three years ago, Black Star came in there and effectively took over."

The mention of Black Star piqued Trevor's interest.

"They sent extermination squads around to kill anybody who refused to work for them. They burned Jeon's village. His family escaped with the clothes on their backs. Jeon's father encouraged him to seek a better life off world. Long story short, he entered the Amity lottery. He didn't make the cut. Guess what happened?"

"No idea," Trevor said.

"Two months later, the shuttle carrying the winners crashed on its way to the spaceport. Jeon got the call."

Of all the luck.

"That *is* amazing, Jeon. Is your family well?"

"Spoke with Father last week. Life is hard in Elaxis, but the city has many jobs not in service of Black Star."

Connor picked up from there.

"Jeon had to be trained from scratch on the air recycling system but now he's our team leader. He's come a long way in eleven months. Agree, bruv?"

The twinkle in Connor's eyes opened Trevor's. Connor told the man's story to make a point.

"Jeon, do you plan to reapply when your rotation is up?"

"I may, Trevor. No one in my family has ever made this many

UCVs. Half of it goes back home to support the others."

Trevor had taken his eyes off the entrance. Did the first mentees slip past him?

"I've heard a great deal about what Black Star has done to your people. I'm so sorry, Jeon."

"Thank you, Trevor. I ..."

A somber tone turned buoyant when Jeon spotted someone and waved across the lounge.

"My young lady has arrived. If you will excuse me. Trevor, so wonderful to meet you. Control this brother of yours!"

"I'll do my best, Jeon."

Trevor followed the man until he kissed a woman in her early twenties. She dressed like a business professional.

"Come clean, Connor. What just happened?"

Connor threw back his drink, a muted yellow liquor that vaguely resembled a healthy urine sample.

"I remembered what you told me about the minder's profile."

"Oh?"

"Someone with no criminal history, family not affluent, arrived here in the past thirteen or fourteen months, free to move around and worried about being recognized. It was a hell of a coincidence running into Jeon. Here. Tonight. He never mentioned a girlfriend before. You get me?"

"Huh. You made the leap to ... Connor, do you seriously suspect *he* is the minder? And she's his cover?"

"No, but he could be. That's my point, bruv. The minder is an enemy agent hiding in plain sight. Nobody suspects him. That means he'd have to be a great actor. Somebody people trust."

Connor posited nothing Trevor hadn't already considered, but he applauded his brother's instinct. And the remarkable reversal of fortune that brought Jeon here struck a wrong chord.

"Do you want me to check his LinkPass history? If he's been here more than twice, then we've caught him in a lie."

Connor stared at his empty glass. Did Trevor sense apprehension?

"I'd know if he was playing me for a fool. Believe it or not, T, I learned a few things from you about studying people. But, uh, if tonight's mission doesn't work out, maybe you run his history."

Trevor committed to doing so even if they found the actual agent. Jeon's story was problematic. He watched the man buy his girlfriend a drink and take her to a small table across the lounge.

"Strong instinct, C. I should've known you wouldn't compromise the mission without a good damn reason."

"Compromise? That's what you think I did, bruv?"

"You improvised not five minutes after we arrived. What was I supposed to think?"

"Dunno. Maybe give your brother a little more credit?"

He made a good point; Trevor did not argue.

"I'm sorry." Trevor reached for his glass of surprisingly decent horse nip. "Is there anything they serve you haven't tried?"

Connor crossed his arms and mulled the question.

"Hmm. I used to keep track. There's probably four or five planets I haven't hit yet. Mostly variations on whiskey. I'm not much for whiskey. Too bitter."

Trevor sipped the horse nip and tried to think of a witty response. He never had the chance.

Connor slipped out of the booth.

"Looks like it's game on, bruv."

"What are you ...?"

Connor nodded toward the entrance. There they were.

Sil Mariputti, Ashraf Diep, and Eliza Hutton. He hadn't seen her on the LinkPass profile. The others took rifters; she must have walked. But their grouping followed a pattern. His research showed them arrive as a threesome on sixteen previous occasions.

"Where are you going, Connor?"

He smiled. "To say hello."

29

"N O WORRIES," CONNOR SAID. "I won't compromise the mission. They have no idea who I am."

"Fine, C, but don't push them. If you come across heavy-handed, they'll know something's off."

"Gotcha, bruv."

He straddled up to the bar, ordering from the kiosk nearest to the mentees. Connor didn't hesitant to engage.

"Before you put in that order, I'll say two words: Horse nip."

Sil, Ashraf, and Eliza glared up at Connor. From his angle, Trevor couldn't see the looks on their faces, but he thought abject horror might be expected.

"You drink that sludge?" Ashraf scoffed.

"Every chance I get, friend. Tonight, they're having a special. Order it with extra foam." Connor threw an air-kiss. "The best."

Ashraf turned his back and huddled with the others. Their voices were too low for Connor's ear bead to consume.

"You three look like newbs," he added, opening a kiosk order. "Special treat. Three horse nips on me. What d'ya say?"

Trevor felt a knot in his chest.

"You're laying it on too thick, C. Back away before you scare them out of the club."

"We're not newbs," Sil said loud enough for the bead to hear. "And you look ridiculous. Go away."

"Listen to him, C."

Connor finished his order, grabbed his drink, and complied. Yet he didn't leave their company without a passing remark.

"When someone offers to buy you a drink, smile and be grateful. Generosity does not have to come with a price stamp."

Trevor saw Ashraf mutter a reply but outside the bead's range. Connor rejoined his brother with a tall horse nip plus extra foam.

"That could've gone better," Trevor said, to which Connor laughed.

"Whatcha talking about, bruv? That was perfect."

"How so?"

Their eyes followed the threesome to another booth.

"I got a closeup. Those three are wound so tight, their assholes are sewed shut. That woman ... Eliza ... she looks pale. Either that, or she's wearing the worst makeup in human history. Take a look at how they're dressed. Hardly made an effort. They're not planning to dance. They plan to meet their contact here or in a Spin Room."

Connor's theory made sense. The students wore casual tunics more suited to lounging at home. Moreover, they sipped their drinks without appearing to talk to each other.

They're waiting. Where are the other two?

"I've heard about the Spin Rooms but never seen one. They use sims to replicate other environments. Yes?"

"Those are the most popular. You can go damn near anywhere in the Collectorate. A tropical beach on Earth or a jungle on Indy Prime. Mostly for the same purpose: Hang out and fuck."

"When did they become sex parlors?"

Connor let slip a wicked smile.

"Hard to say, Trev-*or*. They're whatever you make them. But once you register and pay up, what happens inside is nobody's business."

"That seems like a shocking violation of the Charter. I assume criminal behavior is not exempted."

"I wouldn't know, but I get your point. If we lose them inside a

Spin Room, we can't prove anything."

"Not necessarily. I have an ace up my sleeve. It's not strictly ethical, but ..."

Connor sipped his drink.

"No need to explain, T. You're hunting for a killer. Can't let a little thing like ethics stand in the way."

He refused to feel guilty.

"I guarantee Black Star has no ethical quandaries."

"Yeah. Well. I'll say this much. I'm not a detective, and I don't have your knack for sizing up folks. But those three over there? Not killers."

Trevor held up his glass, which was almost empty.

"You just got through telling me what great actors these agents must be. Who's to say one of them ..."

"Liars maybe, bruv. Frauds. Spies. Whatever. But right now, those three are scared."

"Let's stay put, C. We don't move until they do."

"Gotcha."

The lounge grew more crowded over the next fifteen minutes, but Trevor zoned out the distractions. The other mentees not only were no-shows, but their LinkPass profiles displayed no movement since entering their respective flats earlier in the evening. They weren't coming. Not invited? Refused to accept the invitation?

Trevor wondered whether he misread the group dynamic.

He checked in on Orval Erdogan and found a similar result. Ulbrecht's likely-jilted business partner had not left his flat since returning home from school.

"Take a look at that," Connor said, snapping Trevor out of his LinkPass surveillance. He nodded toward one of the six doorways leading deeper into Raison.

A guest passing into Paradise Lounge imitated a birdman. Black feathers dominated the waist, scaled the arms, and cushioned the neck. The guest wore black flippers and a white headdress.

A few heads turned, but such a sight wasn't out of bounds for Raison. Connor puzzled on it, though.

"Looks like a woman, bruv. She came down from the prime dance floor, but she ain't dressed for it. Too hot in there for extra frills."

Trevor would have let Connor's analysis and his attention wander – until she slowed at the mentees' booth. They moved over as she slipped in, leaving a large enough gap for two others.

"This could be our target," he mumbled, hoping his luck had taken a sudden bounce. "What kind of guest dresses like that?"

"Might be drifting opera but depends on the theme. She looks more like a character you'd bring to a Spin Room. People like to role play as animals. Probably found the costume in a Recon tube."

"Or maybe she doesn't want to be recognized."

Trevor stumbled on an idea he never considered. What if the mentees did not know the minder's identity?

"Maybe, T, but those three are buttoned up. They haven't opened their mouths since she arrived. Look at them."

They listened to the birdwoman without moving a muscle.

"Connor, are there any entrances besides the lounge?"

"Staff, as far as I know. Not patrons."

"So, either she works here or she arrived before us. Let's take the second option for now. What does that tell you?"

"She set up a Spin Room."

"But that door ..."

"Yeah. She took the indirect route. Maybe that's part of the game she's playing. Dunno, Trevor. I'm making this shit up as I go."

"Me, too. Perhaps if ..."

Movement. Finally.

The mentees slid out from the booth and walked past birdwoman in silent order: Eliza, Sil, Ashraf. They said nothing to each other as they quietly passed through the entry to the Spin Rooms.

"They're in no mood for dancing," Connor mused. "Follow?"

"You go. Quick. Don't draw suspicion. Keep a safe distance. I want to see what the minder does."

Connor swiftly but discreetly complied. His parting words before leaving the lounge:

"Don't wait too long, bruv. She might just be a messenger."

Trevor worried the same. He left the booth and wandered casually between tables toward the bar, his eye drifting toward the feathered woman. Was she waiting for someone else? Following another's orders? Or was this how every encounter with the mentees transpired?

Birdwoman left two minutes after the students. Trevor avoided eye contact as she started toward the interior doors, yet the side profile made him question Connor's conclusion. Was this actually a woman? The suit hid any distinctive gender curves.

He or she passed through the first entry en route to the prime dance floor. Why a different route? Was Connor right? Was this merely a messenger now going about other business?

"Headed a different way," Trevor said, just loud enough for the bead to hear. "Prime floor."

"Hard to keep track of anyone in there, bruv. Let me know if you lose her."

"Never mind me. Keep on those three."

"Gotcha."

The corridor greeted Trevor with a sea of black, but his worries of losing the minder dissipated quickly. A sharp left turn brought him to an escalator. A psychedelic wave of color embedded in the walls accompanied a warm mist. His target ascended, now halfway toward the dance floor. Vibrations turned to merciless pounding.

The minder stepped off the escalator. Beyond, whirling spotlights and an army of drums awaited. As he reached the top, Trevor wondered if he had miscalculated the ear beads' ability to filter out background noise in favor of his voice.

A violent cacophony poured down from the catwalk above the prime floor. Dozens of bald men in red tunics pounded on Damascene bowel drums, each two meters deep and equipped with speakers to intensity the effect. Patrons danced in hysterics on the main floor and on two catwalks parallel to the drummers. The spotlights cast red beams from the rafters.

Connor was right: These people appeared insane, arms flailing, crashing into each other without care. Some tripped, fell, and quickly recouped. Others took incidental blows but never responded with violence. They lost themselves in the moment, a total break from the rigid life outside Raison.

Trevor felt the rush, understood why they'd surrender to it. There was something primitive here. Savage. Perfect.

Shit.

He lost track of his target. He only looked away for a second.

Trevor tested his ear bead, unafraid to shout – as if any of these people would notice.

"Connor, can you hear me?"

"Gotcha, bruv. Are those drums?"

His brother's clear voice brought a flicker of relief.

"Listen, C. I lost the target."

"It's OK. She's not dressed for prime. All the other dancers, they're wearing skin-tights. Am I right?"

Of course. The minder will stand out.

If he pushed through the lunatics without getting knocked around, he'd spot her. For certain, no one else here wore feathers.

"I'm going in, C. Have you reached the Spin Rooms?"

"Just now. It's a maze back here. I'll let you know what's up when they choose a room. Be careful."

A sudden special effect heightened Trevor's anxiety.

"What in ten hells?"

"Talk to me, bruv. What's happening?"

A flock of tall, rail-thin and entirely pink birds dive-bombed from the rafters, aiming for the dancers below. A storm of fire chased the birds, exhaled from a serpentine dragon.

231

The aerial combatants screeched and roared, passing through dancers along the catwalks, flying in loops around the drummers, and descending to the prime floor.

When Trevor described the precision holograms, Connor cursed.

"You have to be joking! The Pink Flamingoes are back. How didn't I know they were on tonight?"

"Never heard of them."

"They're the best. They play the station every few months. You're a lucky man. Is it a beautiful sight?"

Trevor shuddered as several flamingoes attacked him.

They weren't real. Yet ...

Their squawks rang in his ears, and his stomach knotted.

"I'm too old for this shit, Connor."

"No, you're not. You're just married with a kid, is all. Hold it together, bruv. First time is always a bit off."

"I made a huge mistake. If I don't find the minder soon, I'm out of here. What about the students?"

Connor didn't reply straightaway. When he did, his voice lowered, barely a whisper against this madness.

"They're heading into a room now."

"Did anyone greet them?"

"Dunno. I'm not close enough."

"Fine. Do what you can. I'll search for the minder."

What have I gotten myself into?

Those words remained front and center as he navigated through the sea of dancers, many of whom were much older than he expected. Perhaps Connor was right; he'd shed all sense of adventure. Ten years ago, wouldn't he have embraced a scene like this? Or had he ever been capable of releasing his inhibitions?

Grandfather Max would've had none of it. A silly indulgence, a pointless and fleeting escape. The business of life and legacy required a precise pursuit of tangible objectives. The attainment of glory was every serious Chancellor's endgame.

No. Trevor was nothing like Max, but he also couldn't imagine life as Connor did: A series of random journeys to test the inner soul.

"You're the middle man," Effie once told Trevor, back when her love and fealty were firm. "The one we can always count on."

At the time, it seemed like a compliment, a fair reading of his disposition. Now, it grated under his skin.

In this moment, he couldn't count on anything. His instinct had betrayed him. He walked the breadth of the prime floor. How in ten hells had he lost the target? Why even follow? The students were key. As long as he had them cornered and asked the right questions, they'd lead him to the minder.

Or was it all a game of misdirection? Was it possible the minder knew someone might follow? Was he being led away from the students for a reason?

What if, what if, what if ...

Then, as he prepared to give up, Trevor glanced toward the rafters. His eye caught the nearest catwalk parallel to the drummers.

A feathered human danced among scantily dressed patrons.

How did?

Of course. He was an idiot. A pressure lift scaled the far wall at each end of the prime floor. They had to go up and down somehow!

The simplest logic having eluded him, and the feathered dancer content above him, Trevor reached the only logical conclusion.

"It's not the minder," he told Connor. "It was a messenger."

"That's gotta mean your real target is inside the Spin Room."

"I'm going back down, C. Guide me to your location."

"On it, bruv."

He tried to shed the embarrassment of being deceived, but it was his own damn fault. So certain he was. Surely, his instinct couldn't betray him, not this close to a resolution.

After he descended the escalator and returned to Paradise Lounge, his body vibrated. The squawk of birds and the maniacal pounding of drums haunted him. How did normal humans survive such things and go to work in the morning?

Yes, he *was* too old for this shit.

It's not a total loss, Trevor coached himself en route to the Spin Rooms. The minder and her agents couldn't stay inside that room forever. Once they appeared, he'd have a lock on the killer's identity. Unless, of course, this person intended to play yet another sleight of hand.

The Spin Rooms were shielded from the earthquakes of the prime floor and the drifting opera gallery. Additionally, each room featured soundproof walls to protect the privacy of those engaging in a wild variety of fantasies. As such, this sector of Raison was as quiet as a hotel after midnight. Trevor walked narrow corridors past rooms with alphanumeric designations, all of which were arranged on a bizarre, four-diamond grid pattern.

Connor whispered instructions. Trevor made a wrong turn and had to reset his path. Ten minutes after he left the madness of prime – though his ears still rang – Trevor rounded a sharp corner and ran into his brother.

"You made it," Connor said. "I was worried about you, bruv."

"Where are they?"

Connor nodded up the corridor.

"Far end."

"That's got to be ten or twelve rooms down."

"Fifteen. I've been pacing. Can't just stand idle out here. People stare at you like you're trouble. Didn't want anyone reporting me to house security."

"Good thinking, C. Any traffic in or out?"

"Nothing. Tried putting an ear to the door once. Lot of good that would've done. What's the plan, bruv? We wait them out?"

Trevor didn't hesitate. He had one shot at this.

"We go in."

"What? How?"

Trevor pulled back his jacket sleeve to reveal the wrist plate.

"Same way I entered Ulbrecht Hann's flat."

"Override LinkPass? Trevor, these doors only accept gene stamps from invited participants. Wouldn't you be breaking the law?"

He used a clause within the Charter to gain access to Ulbrecht's residence. He did not have evidence of a health emergency this time.

"Risk-reward, Connor. The risk is acceptable. Worst case: We walk in, surprise them, claim we were invited. The students won't question it at first because they'll assume our gene stamps were accepted."

Trevor started walking toward the target room, Connor abreast.

"Then what, T?"

"The rest depends on whether the minder is with them. If he is, we go all in. I'll show my bar."

"And me?"

Good point. Connor's size was intimidating, but his sparkly complexion and shimmering one-piece undercut his gravitas.

"You'll stand inside the door. Block their exit."

"If the minder's there, are we sure he's unarmed?"

"No. We're not. I've got an idea."

They stopped outside room AL-43. Trevor grabbed his pistol.

"Remember your training?"

Connor reached for the weapon with a simple nod.

"Good. You don't have a pocket, so hold it behind your back until we know the situation."

So much for the regs. So much for the law.

"If this goes bad, Trevor, you'll ruin your career. Maybe there's another way."

No, not this time.

Trevor began the entry override.

He never imagined what lay on the other side of that door.

30

A SIMULATED PORCH overlooked a lake. Emerald green water sparkled in sunlight, and spindly young trees swayed in a light breeze. String music filled the room. Mandolins, perhaps? Incense burned, the smoke rising in tiny whiffs from a low, bamboo table in the center. Trevor understood the gravity of the moment when no one reacted to his surprise entrance.

Sil Mariputti and Ashraf Diep laid close to the table as if having been tipped over. Trevor spotted Eliza Hutton on the far side, face down in a contorted mess.

"Cudfrucker!"

Trevor raced to the students but didn't need to guess. Sil and Ashraf stared into the infinite. He checked their pulses anyway.

"Dead?" Connor asked.

Two tea cups laid at their feet along with a tiny puddle of spilled brown liquid.

A survivor moaned.

"Eliza?"

Trevor rushed to the pregnant student.

"Help ... please ..."

He rolled Eliza over. Her eyes bled.

"It hurts. Please ..."

Trevor glanced up at Connor, who said:

"We need to call the front. Raison has a house doc."

He was right, but Trevor decided it wouldn't matter. Her tea cup lay shattered at the table's base.

"Eliza, what happened here? Who did this?"

Her head spun, her eyes wandered. She was close now.

"My baby. I wanted my baby."

"Listen to me, Eliza. Who is responsible? Who is your minder?"

Eliza shook her head, but Trevor sensed she was far away. Were his questions even getting through?

"We were going to have a family. He loved me. I ..."

She fell limp in Trevor's arms.

He laid her down with care and backed away.

Connor squatted.

"Bruv, what in ten hells have we walked into?"

Trevor's heart raced as he tried to reset for a new strategy. He looked past the carnage and assessed the room. The bamboo table, surrounded by thin mats, featured a formal tea service with two small trays of cookies. Dark wood panels lined the interior walls, which were decorated with calligraphy, paintings of birds soaring above ocean waves, plus tropical settings dominated by beaches, palms, and seashells. Those items remained static, but the holographic paintings at the entrance morphed between cityscapes.

He began to make sense of it.

"They're cleaning up loose ends."

"Who?"

"Ulbrecht's death didn't go down the way they hoped. We weren't supposed to find the elevated K3. It drew too much attention. Now they're afraid the students will crack. They'd sooner kill their own agents than risk exposure."

"Black Star?"

He nodded. "Or whoever's running their operation here."

"Something about this feels off. We saw that birdwoman ..."

"Or man ..."

"Whichever. We saw that person talk to the students. They came straight here. Had to be under orders. Right?"

"Not a doubt."

"I followed them. OK? I don't think they said a word to each other the entire way. No one entered the room afterward, no one left. That means the poison tea was sitting here waiting for them."

Trevor understood Connor's point, even if his brother had yet to unravel the entire picture.

"It's not an effective way to murder three people, is it? If even one decided not to drink, and nobody was holding a pistol against his head ..."

Connor's eyes ballooned.

"Suicide! They knew it was poison."

Damn it. She was pregnant. Why, Eliza? What would be so horrible you'd see no other way?

Then the truth stitched together. The wild stories about Black Star, the intel he heard in the security conference.

"Connor, the man who invented Motif – number three in Black Star leadership – was recently captured. His own people executed him rather than save him because they thought he might have talked to SI. If they'd take out someone that far up the chain ..."

"That's ruthless shit, bruv. But this weren't an execution, so to speak. If you're right, they drank the tea willingly. Why not just run? Get protection from Sec Admin?"

He asked the right questions, to which Trevor knew the answer.

"Family. That's why. These agents weren't the only ones to benefit. Black Star is helping their families, too. When the ROAs come back in a few days, we'll see the proof. If I were to bet, I'd say the minder gave them no option. Drink the tea, and we don't kill your family." He stared at the bodies of those young, promising fools. "I saw how they walked out of the lounge. They showed no emotion.

They'd given up."

"So, that feathered cunt who killed them – it wasn't a messenger."

Why hadn't Trevor stayed true to his instinct? It wouldn't have saved these students, but the minder never would have left his sight. Why did the bastard choose the prime dance floor? Passing time? Letting off steam while the students said their goodbyes?

Wait a minute ...

"He'll be back," Trevor whispered.

"What's that, bruv?"

"The minder. He sent them here to kill themselves, but he'll need to make sure of it and remove evidence." Trevor reached for his pistol. "We're going to surprise him. What do you think, C?"

Connor scratched his head.

"Two against one? Sure. I can buy that. But I don't understand how he planned to get away with it. Raison will know who reserved the room."

"I'd lay odds it will be listed under one of these three." He reconsidered. "Or Ulbrecht. He was a regular."

"Can you find out, T? Do your magic and break into their system?"

"Not that simple. I can check LinkPass histories, not internal records of private business. I guarantee LinkPass will only show their three gene stamps. The minder got in here the same way he entered Ulbrecht's flat. Like a ghost."

"That phantom drill program you talked about?"

Trevor studied the room again and developed a plan.

"Connor, as I understand it, Spin Rooms can be fully customized by whoever reserves it. Yes?"

"Anyone on the invite list can alter it with permissions."

"So why this design? The wall art, the bamboo table and tea service ... it's something you might find on one of the planets in the Perseus Cluster. But I can't nail down the precise style."

"Why does it matter?"

Trevor focused on the door's morphing cityscapes.

"Here's how we're going to do this, C. I need you back in the corridor. Pace about like you did before. Play it cool. Anyone passes by, smile and keep walking. When the minder returns, say, 'What a night!' Got it?"

"And then?"

"Wait until he enters before you follow. I'll do the rest."

Connor started for the door.

"Sure about this, bruv? We got three dead students, and we're laying in wait instead of reporting what happened here? Trev, I have a bad feeling this is gonna blow back on you."

"It's my choice, Connor. I need to finish this. Are you onboard?"

Mr. Sparkly Face gave Trevor a hug.

"The Stallion brothers ride together."

"Always, C. Now get the hell out. I've got work to do and probably not much time."

Connor winked.

"I'm on the case."

Trevor assumed the minder crafted this environment to provide the students a peaceful sendoff. A touch of mercy, perhaps. He might also have given them a time frame in which to say their goodbyes. Did they send delayed messages to their families through their poms? No way he could check; the devices were protected by gene stamp.

He flipped open his own pom and scrolled the holographic menu until he found the People's Collectorate Central Archives. He raised the pom's Optic Translator program and linked to the device's vidcam. Trevor spoke to the pom's AI.

"Search all public data spools to match the imagery in this room." When the AI confirmed the request, Trevor flipped the flashing red holo around to face the door. He held it there until four cityscapes recorded. "Proceed with a full-room scan."

Like the snapdrone that analyzed Ulbrecht's flat yesterday, the pom-powered holo began careful work, projecting a red field as it moved methodically about. While it scanned, Trevor studied the tragedy at his feet and recalled yesterday's brief interviews at Maynor. At the time, he thought the pressure of a brutal curriculum was pushing these students to their limits. How naïve.

Schoolwork must have felt like a breeze. Black Star had you inside a vice with no way out. Follow orders or we'll kill your families.

What was the endgame had they survived their rotation?

That answer eluded him.

For now.

The minder might provide insight, although he was likely much more committed to Black Star's cause. No point raising hope.

Trevor removed the lid from the teapot and took a strong whiff of the contents. Bitter and acrid.

The poison wasn't even disguised.

A voice – no, a recent memory – grabbed Trevor's attention.

"The leaf is less mature and a touch bitter at first taste. But the finale enriches mind and body."

Trevor fumbled and almost dropped the pot. He replaced the lid and set it on the table.

Bien Thet. Yesterday.

They entered the headmaster's office. Thet had a tall ceramic pot on his desk. He offered them a cup of ...

Pearl tea.

Hoshi waited for Trevor's permission before accepting a cup. Then she ... what was it? Yes, he recalled her reply.

She grew up on pearl tea but added, "You'll be hard-pressed to match the quality. We're known for our blend in New Seoul."

Thet said they approached the blend differently in his region on Indonesia Prime. "The leaf is less mature and a touch bitter at first taste. But the finale enriches mind and body."

Hoshi took a cup; Trevor refused. "Not much of a tea drinker."

She said the tea "was lovely. I can't help but miss the sweetness."

Thet is the minder?

It should've been a mic-drop moment, the final piece of the

puzzle. Thet sat in the perfect position to oversee the students. They could talk business during private consults. Bien Thet was the perfect conduit for Black Star to infiltrate the station.

Moreover, this Spin Room could have been inspired by the same man whose office consisted of hanging plants, panoramic nature views from across the Collectorate, and antiques.

And Thet's reaction to news of Ulbrecht's death? Muted. Surprised but not shocked. Instantly assumed it was drugs.

He already knew. It's him. Has to be.

So, why didn't the answer feel right? What was missing?

Trust your instincts, jackass. Come on now. You're overthinking it. Thet is logical. Impeccable reputation. Can move freely about ...

No. There's the problem. He was too recognizable for all these meetings at Raison. Even if he entered the Recon tubes and disguised himself, why would he take the chance of being seen in this sector so often?

Trevor thought back to the feathered creature dancing on a catwalk. A bit too spry for a sixty-year-old academic.

What am I missing?

The AI made an announcement.

"Optical Translations complete."

Trevor regrouped and spread the results into an orderly grid, like so many dataflicks. He started with the cities. Then the artwork. Then the lake that dominated the view. Finally, the maps.

A hard chill ran through his blood.

He didn't want to believe it.

Cities: *Inchon Redux. New Seoul. Puratoon. Gwang-si.*

Artists: *Cho Ji-Lin. Yanna Syung. Luna Baek.*

Lake: *Sonang, thirty kilometers from Puratoon.*

Maps: *Gangwou Province. Puratoon Metro Zone.*

He read them a second time, hoping for a different result. But Trevor wasn't insane, and these names had one common thread.

Hokkaido.

Second largest planet of the Perseus Cluster. Home of President Aleksanyan before she was assassinated.

Everything in this room was Hokki design. Likely the teapot, too.

Of all the possibilities, this one never occurred to him. Yet the answer screamed in his face from the moment he entered Ulbrecht Hann's building.

Reply after nervous reply, tic after nervous tic, every panicked, suspicious, or knee-jerk reaction. Resistance disguised as assistance.

Connor said it best:

What in ten hells have we walked into?

Trevor closed the hologrid and stowed his pom.

OK. Get it together. What now?

The implications would extend far beyond Sec Admin and Maynor. He needed time to sort out the next steps. He needed ...

"What a night!" Connor said with gusto.

So much for planning.

He grabbed his pistol, took a position behind Eliza's corpse, and held the weapon at his side.

What would he say first? Where would the questions begin?

The answers terrified Trevor.

After the door slipped open, the birdwoman stopped in the threshold and jerked back half a step. She froze for a few awkward seconds. Trevor wondered whether she was armed. Though his eyes were hidden behind the flippers, might she have recognized him?

"Who are you?" A guttural male voice shouted. "What have you done to them?"

Trevor raised his pistol and aimed between her eyes.

"You can drop the voice modulator. It might have fooled *them*, but not me. Step into the room, Hoshi."

31

HE GAVE HIS SECOND DEPUTY few options, but Trevor did not expect her to choose the most foolish. Rule number one for criminals on a space station: Don't run. There's no escape. Unless, of course, you fancy an airlock.

Hoshi sprinted as far as the mountainous younger Stallion brother allowed – about a meter. Connor grabbed her with both arms and shoved her back into the doorway. To Hoshi's credit, she employed the defensive techniques learned in UNF basic training.

She broke free of Connor's right arm, reached inside her outfit, and retrieved her pistol. A green bolt exploded from the plasma chamber and smashed into the center of Lake Sonang.

Connor chopped down on her free arm. Hoshi grunted and dropped the weapon. Connor yanked both arms around her back and pushed her forward.

"This little coit's got an edge, bruv. Jabbed me in the jewels."

"You did great, C. Hold her tight."

Trevor stowed his weapon and patted her down. He found her pom and removed the voice modulator from beneath the feathered collar. He didn't want to see her face; Trevor wasn't sure he'd be able to control his actions.

Like he had a choice.

244

He removed the neck feathers, the wig, and the flippers. Her disguise gone, only Hoshi Oda remained. And yet, it wasn't her.

Sweat poured down her face. Her eyes belonged to a different animal from the one who wore the bar. Was it fear? Rage? Insanity? Simple bewilderment?

Trevor thought she aged twenty years from the woman he'd known for all of two days. He grabbed her by the chin and squeezed.

"You called me 'sir' the first time we met. Then said, 'Ready when you are.'" She didn't reply, not a single hint of pain even as he tightened his grip. "You made a fool of me. All of us. I sat in my office today and described the killer's profile. I told you what parameters to search for."

Trevor's chest hurt, or maybe it was just his pride.

He laughed in her face before he turned away.

"I was describing *you*! And the shame of it is, I never suspected you for a nanosecond. I saw the entire picture, but I was too fucking arrogant to think someone wearing the bar was behind it all."

As Trevor tried to regain self-control, soft string music filled the silence. Under any other circumstance, it might have soothed his battered ego and lessened his roiling fury.

Trevor grabbed Hoshi's weapon, which lay near the door.

"Throw her down, C. Don't be gentle."

"With pleasure, bruv."

She hit the floor on her side and came up holding her right wrist. Trevor handed the extra pistol to his brother.

"I can't play this by the regs," he whispered to Connor. "There's never been a situation like it before."

"Uh, you want to tell me who she is?"

Trevor realized his oversight.

"My Second Deputy, Hoshi Oda."

Connor's double-take was a fitting capper to the night.

"Whoa. Wait. This is your partner? T, I don't know what ..."

"Don't bother. I'm at a loss myself. Look, earlier you mentioned there's a staff entrance to Raison. Right?"

"I think it's Level 2, directly under the Spin Rooms."

"Thanks, C. For now, why don't you guard the door? I doubt she has an accomplice, but let's play it safe."

Connor laid a hand on his shoulder, the supportive kind one gives in lieu of saying, "Sorry for your loss. Here if you need me." Did Connor ask the logical question: "How could you not know?"

Trevor refused to fall back on the easiest excuse: "She was my partner for two days."

Two days, two hours. It shouldn't have mattered. The clues were there at every stage. He refused to accept them.

Trevor grabbed a mat beside Ashraf's body and dropped it a few feet in front of Hoshi. He took a seat and crossed his legs.

His venom subsided.

"You were good," he told Hoshi. "Almost pulled it off. Anything you'd like to say before we begin?"

She scrunched her face as if trying to hold back tears. Her teeth chattered.

"Why did it have to be you?" She said, spitting her words. "I'm dead because of you. They'll kill me, Trev. I'm dead."

Rage and fear. A usable combination.

He pointed to the corpses.

"No, Hoshi. They're dead. Ulbrecht's dead. But you? I'll damn well make sure you live."

"You can't stop them, Trev."

"I disagree. Unlike the Motif mastermind, your people don't know what's happened here. We can play it differently. Yes?"

As he said the words, a horrible realization took over.

Shit. She was at the security conference. She knows everything. How much did she report? Shit.

Just another problem to face, but not the immediate one.

Trevor flipped open his pom.

"I recall you said yesterday that Chief Dorrit isn't fond of wrist

246

plates and impersonal forms of communication. He likes to be on site and take charge of the scene. You said that, yes?" She eyed him with understandable suspicion but did not reply. "Before I left the office today, he and I reached an understanding, given the urgency."

Trevor tapped his comm link and scrolled. He glared at Hoshi while waiting for an answer to his call. A blubbering voice responded.

"What? *Trevor?* What time is it?"

"Sorry to bother you at home, Chief. This is your personal pom?"

"Yes. I was asleep for ten minutes. This had best be important."

"Today, I made you a promise. Now I'm keeping it. Chief, I'm with Ulbrecht's killer. There have been complications. Three more bodies."

Dorrit's shock echoed far beyond the pom.

"Three? What in ten hells!"

"Listen to me, Chief. We can't do this on an official line. You need to come alone."

"I don't understand. What are you ...?"

"We're in a Spin Room at Raison. There's a staff entrance on Level 2. You need to enter through an override protocol. Ignore the regs and do not wear your uniform." Trevor glanced over his shoulder. "My brother will be waiting. He'll escort you up."

Connor nodded, but Dorrit sounded flustered.

"Your brother? Trevor, you are not making sense."

"Fine, Chief. Here's our killer."

Trevor activated the pom's cam and flipped the device around. Hoshi looked away, as if that might do any good.

After a predictable pause, Dorrit's tone softened.

"No. Not her. You must be ..."

"She's a Black Star agent. She killed three students, also working for Black Star. You understand our problem?"

Trevor took the only practical course. If word got out that Sec Admin had been compromised ...

"I'll be there in ten," Dorrit said, ending the call.

Trevor stowed his pom.

"You know how to get there?" He asked Connor.

"No worries, T. But what if she's working with someone?"

"I'll be fine. Stow the pistol in your side pouch."

"On it, bruv. Good luck with this coit."

Trevor glared at what his partner had been reduced to.

"Luck," he said for Hoshi's benefit, "won't play a role."

Alone now, Trevor gave the Hokki woman a moment to come to her senses. Might she think logically about her predicament?

"It's only going to get worse, Hoshi. You'll be handed over to SI. They'll bury you in a prison moon so deep, Black Star won't waste their resources hunting you down."

He saw her gears churn. Perhaps she was searching for an escape mechanism.

"I know my rights as a citizen of the Collectorate. You have to arrest me and charge me before a public panel."

"If I were playing this game by the regs? Sure. Then you'd likely join these three fools in the abyss. Hoshi, you have one chance at ever seeing the light of day. Right here, right now. Everything. Names, locations, dates."

He expected her features to soften with even the distant hope of freedom. Instead, Hoshi burrowed her eyes into tiny daggers.

"Never. If I crack, they'll go after my family. They'll wipe out my entire neighborhood."

She seemed convinced, but Trevor wasn't persuaded.

"Oh, I'm sure the good guys will get to them first. Then again, maybe it doesn't matter. Maybe they're like you ... committed to the cause. Or whatever the fuck it is Black Star stands for."

Hoshi spit, but her pitiful effort fell short. The saliva formed a little puddle at his feet.

"You don't know, Trevor. People like you don't know."

"Really? Tell me. We've got some time."

The same innocent smile she greeted him with yesterday now felt like the byproduct of a deranged mind.

"My family were farmers for generations. My parents lost their land because it was poisoned by the seamasters. No one helped. We moved to the city and scraped by. We had nothing, but the seamasters and the elite classes, they rode high. They ignored us.

"Until Black Star came. Now my brothers have jobs. My parents have dignity. We owed them, so I gladly took this assignment."

Gratitude. That's her motivation? Great.

"Your benefactors are ruthless killers, anarchists, and psychopaths. It's dignified to work for that lot?"

She sat up straight. Her crooked smile revealed the human beneath the human. That's when Trevor understood: *She's been conditioned. How else could she have hid this rage for so long?*

"Dignity is having solid ground beneath your feet, Trevor. Dignity is knowing people give a damn what happens to you. Remember what you said yesterday about the seen and unseen on this station? When you said that, I almost thought you'd be an ally."

"Or at the very least, someone you could con. Yes?"

She licked her lips. Did her eyes shift toward the bodies?

"Ah," he said. "Thirsty, I'd wager. The dance must have taken it out of you. Sorry I can't help. Bad tea."

"Hah. Hah. People like you are so smug. You should hear yourself. Every time you announced a new theory about who did what to whom, you strutted around like the smartest man on the station. I wanted to laugh and throw it back in your face."

The notion was humbling. Trevor remembered Effie's ironic words before he took the Haven job: "Build trust equity." His wife meant well. Yet like every diplomat, she was far too self-assured.

Trevor wasn't certain how he'd learn to trust anyone again.

"I imagine you had a private chuckle, Hoshi. For all the worlds, you tried to slow me down at every turn." He softened his tone, delivering a feminine touch. "Oh, no, Trev. Don't go in Ulbrecht's flat. You're violating his rights. Oh, no, Trev. Don't report an MOD. Oh, no, Trev. You can't access private medical records. Oh, no, Trev. You can't research their financial assets."

He sighed. "That's when it fell apart. Right? You saw me getting close, but when I requested the ROAs, it was game over. You knew what the money would show. You also knew your name would turn up on the search I ordered. You probably scrubbed it, but it was too late. The person you report to agreed. He ordered you to take out these three before we brought them in. Yes?"

Her chin raised in open defiance.

"You have everything figured out, Trev. You know nothing."

"This is your chance to enlightenment me."

"Fuck. You."

"So, that's it then? Nothing more to confess?"

She crossed her arms and pursed her lips. Trevor might have thought her stance amusing were it not for the three bodies lying close by.

"Fine, Hoshi. Then let's do it this way. I'll confess *for you* now that I've slipped the last pieces into place. When I'm done, tell me where I went wrong. OK?"

The string music filled a long gap, after which Trevor decided he needed to work off the nervous energy. He hopped up and stretched his legs.

"You didn't kill Ulbrecht because he learned about Black Star's role in buying his phantom drill. That story Eliza gave us? Utter bullshit. Ulbrecht was a genius but also ambitious. He didn't care who paid him. See, this guy was shooting for the big time. The biggest of all. He intended to steal Halifax's research on trans-wormhole drives and partner with like-minded geniuses who dreamed of opening new fissures to the other universes.

"That possibility works against Black Star's goals. It wants control of *this* universe. It wants to destroy the Collectorate and run a savage new regime. So, when word of Ulbrecht's plan got out, your supervisor ordered you to kill him. Right so far?"

She was a totem, unbending and silent.

"I'll take that as a yes," he continued. "Ulbrecht would not have accepted Motif voluntarily, and threats of killing his family wouldn't have worked because he only has a mother, and they haven't spoken since he arrived on Amity. She verified as much when she received the death notice. So, you had to try a novel approach. You entered with his phantom drill, hid in his bedroom, and attacked him. He wasn't a big man. You have UNF training. While he was subdued, you planted the pad on his tongue. Nature took its course.

"You closed the bedroom door and waited outside. Afterward, you planted the other pad in the end table and stole his pom. If his mentor hadn't reported Ulbrecht late to class, or if I wasn't your partner, he wouldn't have been found until the K3 level had dropped. Whatcha think? Perfect score so far?"

Yeah, she wasn't going to be any help.

"Excellent. On we go then. At first, I assumed Bien Thet was the minder. Then I saw you at work in the prime dance hall."

Her cheeks fell. *Ah, she's paying attention.* Hoshi must have wondered how he snagged her.

"But now I realize Thet isn't excused. On the contrary, he's your contact. He gave the order. You see, I've been thinking about yesterday when we arrived at Maynor. The greeter tried to put us off. Something about Thet being much too busy. She didn't count on me making myself at home in his office. Nor did you, Hoshi.

"We went after lunch. Ample time for you to warn him. That little exchange about the pearl tea? You two were talking in code. You said, 'We're renowned for our blend in New Seoul.' Funny that. You grew up in Puratoon. That's fifteen hundred kilometers from New Seoul. I didn't understand how you'd mix up that city with the place you claimed to love. Until it made sense: It was coded language. Kind of like my brother out in the hall when he told you, 'What a night.'"

Trevor tapped his ear bead twice, no doubt answering her last, lingering question about the trap but also reminding him that Connor heard the entire soliloquy. As if on cue, and no doubt proud of himself, Connor replied in his ear:

"Damn, we're the best, bruv."

"We are, C. Now, Hoshi, we come to this mess. When Thet ordered you to kill these three, you had serious reservations. You thought the timing would draw too many eyes to Maynor. I'm sure Thet agreed, but I doubt he had much choice. He has a master, too, and I'm sure they had a plan to weather the storm.

"You knew the Motif strategy wouldn't work, and a part of you related to Sil, Ashraf, and Eliza. They also came from humble backgrounds. You didn't want them to die violently, so you came up with this plan." He looked around the room at its many Hokki trappings. "You ordered a simulation with all the best features from home. A beautiful view, sweet music, and a chance for them to die with ... what did you call it? Dignity?"

He walked over to Eliza.

"I remember how shocked you were when I proved she was pregnant. It must've torn you up inside to know you'd have to kill a pregnant woman. Or maybe not. I don't think it matters. What I do believe is you couldn't stick around to see them drink. Not after Ulbrecht. You'll kill, but only if you don't have to watch.

"You went to the prime hall because you didn't want to think about it. That's what people do in there. Lose themselves. When time was up, you returned. You had to make sure. Just like with Ulbrecht. We'll have to touch base with the others in Ulbrecht's mentee group – Freddie Lighthorne and Jor Kerrindos – but I'm sure they're innocent. Otherwise, I'd be staring at five bodies.

"Which brings me to Orval Erdogan. He wasn't obligated to Black Star, either, but he was in deep. Ulbrecht cut him out of their partnership when he sold the phantom drill. I believe you helped negotiate the sale. You or someone up the chain decided Orval would be a liability as a partner. He didn't fit Black Star's profile. If he wasn't cut out, he'd be killed. Yep. Except for a few other minor details, I believe that's a perfect score. Thoughts?"

OK, so maybe he *was* strutting. Unseemly given the context, but Trevor didn't care. Given the past several days, ever since an arrogant ambassador tried to ruin his career and good name, Trevor needed to bag a victory, no matter how small.

"Doesn't matter what I think," she said at long last. "My life's over. My family will be dead in a few days. But if you really need to know, Trevor? Fine. You don't have a perfect score. You made a mistake."

"Hmm. Just one?"

"Yes."

"Which is?"

Something new washed over Hoshi's features. Trevor recognized it, but not in a way that excited him.

Pride.

She beamed with pride.

"You're wrong about me. I'm a soldier. I *can* watch." Then, after a pregnant pause for obvious dramatic effect: "I have watched."

He felt an awkward chill.

"Who else? The other four MODs? Were you the one who ...?"

Hoshi laughed. "He's long gone from Amity."

"Then who?"

"You'll know when you find him. The rest is for you to figure out. You're never wrong, Trevor, so I'm sure you'll solve the case."

He wanted to believe it was a bluff. Wishful thinking.

"I'll hand it to you, Hoshi. You had everybody in this station fooled. Your act was so well crafted. Saluting Dorrit, making him feel like a big man. Throwing me just enough complimentary bones to feed my ego. And then those strange attempts at roping me into dinner and ... well, who knows what? Was there an endgame with me, too? Was I going to turn up dead in the near future?"

Her eyes deadened into the place where bluffers do not go.

"Don't assume you won't."

Trevor found one consolation that others in Sec Admin might not: He didn't know her long enough to care about her.

Now, he wanted to beat her senseless.

Instead, he walked away and waited for Dorrit.

A moment later, Connor provided the heads-up.

"On our way in."

He gave Dorrit a moment to absorb the breathtaking scene. The big man grabbed at his considerable chest. For a second, Trevor thought he was having a heart attack, but Dorrit waved him off.

"I ... I don't know what to say. Hoshi? How could you ...?"

"Chief, no."

Trevor pulled Dorrit away. Much of his color had vanished. Teeing off on Hoshi wouldn't do him any favors.

"Stand guard, C. She might make a run for the tea."

Connor found the line funny.

"She ain't getting off that easy on my watch."

Trevor escorted Dorrit to the far end of the room.

"Listen, I'll explain everything. But right now, we need to act fast. She and Bien Thet are in this together."

"Headmaster Thet? I can't believe he'd ..."

"Thet doesn't know what's happened here. We have to keep it that way. We need to sneak both of them off the station as soon as possible. If we ..."

Dorrit's eyes ballooned to an apoplectic state.

"Are you insane? We have three dead students. You want their killer gone?"

"Sneak them onto a warship outside. Ship them to SI. Admiral Woolsey and Director Devonshire can make it happen. Chief, we don't know how many agents Black Star has on Amity, or how connected they are. I guarantee they'll be activated when word gets out. You heard what happened to the Motif inventor. If Black Star comes for these two, we'll have a bloodbath on this station."

Trevor saw terror in the man so close to his gentle retirement.

"Chief, you told me yesterday that sometimes we have to fight a quiet war. Now I understand. Those three students killed themselves.

It was a ritual suicide. We can explain it that way. Yes, the school will take a hit. So will Amity. But we'll move forward. We'll have a chance to hunt down their agents. Amity Station will still be safe."

Dorrit balanced one arm on Trevor.

"I ... dear ... I don't know. I should speak with the other chiefs. What about the President? If she learns what we did ..."

"She won't say a cudfrucking word. She needs Amity cleaned. We have to act now."

He nodded in reluctant agreement.

"What about the bodies? If we bring in a team of lifetechs, it will cause a stir. People will ask questions."

"I know. You won't like my solution, but I think it's our best bet."

Dorrit's color drained when he heard the plan. Trevor didn't blame him. All remaining regs had effectively been abandoned.

"Tell me, Trevor, how could I have been so deceived for a year?"

They glared at Hoshi, who bore no resemblance to the woman Dorrit thought he knew.

"We all have blinders, Chief. I know that's little comfort. They played us, and now we're facing a hell of a fight."

After several dicey hours working with Dorrit to pull off a sleight of hand, the exhausted brothers sat down at home and reflected. Connor poured them both a drink.

"It was the right move, T."

"Depends upon who screams first and loudest."

They clanked glasses.

"You're the smartest guy I know. Where would this station be without you?"

"I love you, too, Connor."

It *was* a good plan. It covered the bases and bought them time. And it almost worked.

32

OVER THE NEXT EIGHT DAYS, filled with perilous maneuvers, contentious security meetings, and a few moments of earned peace with Ana in his arms, Trevor couldn't shake what he witnessed in Spin Room AL-43.

They were so young, walking a path toward certain prosperity. And yet, their commitment to savages who would destroy that future felt inviolate. They'd give their lives for the cause. Kill for it. And along the way, hide their true face in pursuit of ... *what?*

Madness? Chaos? Anarchy?

Hoshi said nothing else before she was sedated and boxed as cargo. Didn't have to. Her eyes, dark and lost, spoke a language he'd never comprehend. *Radicalized*, SI Director Devonshire called her. A growing phenomenon among Black Star converts.

"How do we fight it?" He asked her.

"We can't. Not yet."

"Why?"

"We don't have the resources. Until we take out the leadership, this disease will spread."

The interim solution – a painful necessity – plugged the leaks. Station personnel underwent a security reevaluation, not one vestige of their lives left uncovered. The Maynor student body came next.

The general population would soon follow. President Haas quietly suspended the Amity Charter's personal privacy clauses. She hoped their efforts would not run afoul of Constitutional diehards among the Interstellar Congress.

They might not have resorted to such extreme measures were it not for Orval Erdogan.

Fourteen hours after Hoshi Oda and Bien Thet quietly vanished from the station, someone reported Orval missing. Trevor took lead on the search. He knew what they'd find inside the man's flat.

"I *can* watch," Hoshi told him. "I *have* watched."

This time, it wasn't Motif with elevated K3. Trevor found Orval shot through the head. He lay sprawled against cabinetry beneath the kiosk, his brains splattered behind him.

He might not have belonged to Black Star, but he knew too much about Ulbrecht's business. Poor kid was doomed the moment his ex-business partner died.

The radiant charge inside his wound matched the energy signature of the pistol Hoshi carried into the Spin Room. It wasn't Sec Admin-issued; just another piece of contraband passed through Customs.

That particular leak was closed within a day. The agent wasn't a Black Star loyalist, just an asshole who received a huge payoff and never asked questions.

It did not, however, erase the furor sparked by Orval's death. A critical truth could not be whitewashed: A resident of Amity had been killed in his own home, and Sec Admin had no suspects. A murderer walked among them. Did Orval know his killer? Was it connected to the triple suicide at Raison?

The debate lingered on how to solve the case. Reveal the killer's true identity? If so, a false story awaited approval: Hoshi and Orval had a personal relationship. She killed him in a crime of passion.

Trevor agreed it might work, but how to explain her absence? Was she distraught afterward? Space herself through an airlock?

No. Her body would have been detected by station sensors or

warship surveillance drones.

Eight days gone, and still the loose threads dangled. Two parts of Trevor's strategy did hold up, however.

His financial requests showed huge influxes of UCVs far beyond salary into accounts belonging to the students, Hoshi, and their families. The largest, steadiest income went to Bien Thet, whose coffers swelled fifty percent in the past standard year. Linking the credits directly to Black Star would take months if not years, but that task belonged to people far above Trevor's pay stamp.

In the short term, his plan to deal with the triple suicide held up against scrutiny.

That night, Dorrit called in a veteran lifetech he trusted. The man arrived in nightclub attire, as requested, along with a pair of snapdrones. He used the devices to selectively sterilize the Spin Room, leaving only the students' fingerprints and genetic residue.

Trevor and Connor restored Hoshi's full birdwoman attire and carried her out the front door, pretending she was drunk. Staff did not bat an eye.

Trevor never lied to more people about more things than he did those following days. When he visited his little girl, Effie asked leading questions; she knew something was afoot when he replied with non-answers or simply, "It's a need-to-know basis."

Not the most endearing quality if he ever contemplated winning her back into his arms.

Dorrit buckled under the pressure. Twice, he called in sick. Fatigue, he claimed. Trevor thought it was the fat man's heart. He advised checking in with a doc. Dorrit refused; quiet time with his wife would do the trick, he insisted.

"He might retire early," Trevor told his brother. "Or Central will force him out. They're looking for a scapegoat."

"You don't think ..." Connor didn't finish the sentence, but Trevor knew where he was headed.

"No, C. They won't come after me. I saved their asses. Plus, I've got Devonshire and Woolsey on my side."

"Maybe, bruv, but they're not the President."

"She won't move against them. Right now, Haas needs the UNF and SI firmly in her corner."

Connor's instincts weren't wrong. The political game trumped every other machination. Trevor uncovered the most serious threat to station security since Amity opened for business; yet only eight people knew. There'd be no special commendations or a public ceremony honoring his feat.

If Grandfather Max were alive, he'd have insisted on public redemption filled with pomp and circumstance.

Just as well, Trevor thought. He wanted his good name restored, but not in a way that might make him a target.

"Was there an endgame with me, too?" He asked Hoshi that night. "Was I going to turn up dead in the near future?"

"Don't assume you won't," she replied.

Hoshi never spoke to him again.

Soon after their conversation about scapegoats, the brothers sat down for dinner, during which Connor – unusually quiet – broached a subject Trevor did not see coming.

"Remember how I told you I was close to making a big decision about my life?"

"Sure. You said the Loutah was helping you work it out, but you were scared."

Connor set his dinner plate aside.

"I've made a decision, and I'm not scared anymore. I know what I've got to do with my life."

"Oh?"

"I need your help, but I don't think you're going to be keen on it."

"Hey, you were there for me, C. Anything I can do, just ask."

Connor called it: Trevor wasn't keen.

He also refused to stand in his little brother's way.

The next day, Trevor spoke with Admiral Woolsey at a security conference, bypassing military bureaucracy for a quick resolution.

Five days later, the Stallion brothers celebrated their last hours together in the company of their only family. Connor showed up at the Stallion-Labroque flat with hair cropped above his ears for the first time in twenty years. He carried one small satchel – all the possessions he'd need for his next destination.

They celebrated with Ana's favorite cake, Effie's preferred wine, and Catalan-style lamb balls that Connor loved when he was a kid. Trevor tried to bear up with a smile and a hearty laugh, mostly for Ana, who didn't seem to understand at first what was happening.

"You're going away, Uncle C?" She said, a tear on her cheek. "You can't leave."

Connor sat her on his knee.

"I'm going on a long trip, Annie-M. Just like your Mama sometimes. I'll be back."

"When?"

"Might be a while, but I promise to deepstream when I can. What do you think about that?"

She wiped away the tears.

"Mama brings me gifts when she visits the planets. You promise to do the same?"

"I'm all over it, kiddo. What do you prefer? Candy? Furry things? Jewelry?"

Ana looked to her parents as if asking permission.

"Painted rocks."

Connor scrunched his eyes in momentary confusion before reality hit.

"Oh, so that's what your collection's about."

"Mama brought me nine so far."

Effie intervened, speaking to her daughter.

"Connor won't have control over what planets he visits. So, if he sends you one, it might be from a place where I've already been. That's OK, Ana. Right?"

The girl beamed.

"Oh, sure. As long as it's from you, Uncle C, I'll treasure it."

Connor kissed her on both cheeks, and she sank into his massive frame for a long hug.

Sometimes, Trevor thought she loved Connor as much as her Papa, if not more. Uncle C brought a unique magic into her life. If she never saw him after today, her little heart would break.

As would Trevor's.

He had tried to talk Connor out of leaving, but Trevor stopped when he sensed his brother's commitment. It was a far cry from anything he'd heard in their nineteen years on Amity.

"I've been drifting long enough, T. My life has to be about a higher calling. I'm strong, I'm fast, and I'm smarter than people think. I'm exactly what they're looking for."

"You can see yourself as a soldier?"

He smiled like a man truly at peace with his choice.

"Already am. Just need the uniform and a blast rifle. The rest, they can teach me."

"And they will. But Connor, why not stay here and join Sec Admin? Work with me. You might have heard, but Haven needs a new Second Deputy. You've seen what we're up against."

"I blew that chance a long time ago. This is *your* battleground. Those assholes in Central will see it before long: You're the man to keep Amity safe. I need to fight the bastards wherever Central Command sends me."

"But why the interdiction forces? Their work is dangerous. The UNF offers so many other ways to serve."

Connor sipped the last of his after-dinner drink.

"I'm sure they need folks to keep the air recycling system on their warships in top shape. No thanks, bruv. We lost Mother and Father in the last war. I won't dishonor them anymore. Whatever I can do to stop the next war, I'm there. Please, Trevor. Speak to the Admiral."

The rest was easy. Woolsey's master plan included a vast

expansion to the Interdiction Fleet, which came into direct contact with Black Star forces more often than any division. Trevor offered a glowing recommendation, even as Woolsey said the UNF incurred more than half its casualties in skirmishes with Black Star.

"I'm proud of Connor," Effie told Trevor while they watched him play with Ana. "He's a brave man, like his brother. She is going to miss him terribly, but she's not the only one. If you ever need to talk, Trev, I'm here."

The offer sounded like it was made out of obligation rather than love. Her tender voice was a charade. Would it have made any difference if she knew the truth? What happened at Raison was officially classified. He doubted Effie had any idea about the full scope of the threat. Few on Amity did.

Just as well. They needed distance, except when he visited Ana. The marriage seemed far less important than it did a week ago.

Nonetheless, the Stallion-Labroque clan traveled together to Harmony Spaceport to see Connor off. Ana loved to stand at the viewing platform and watch commercial liners and transports come and go. Trevor brought her at least once a month since she was old enough to walk.

Today, Connor did the honors, pointing out his transport and discussing everything he knew about his destination. Ten minutes before boarding, he hugged Effie then bent down.

"I'm going to talk to your Papa for a minute, then I have to go, Annie-M. You gonna be my best girl while I'm away?"

"Promise, Uncle C."

Connor hugged her as if Ana was his own child. Trevor felt a tear coming on but squelched it. Connor also visibly struggled to hold it together as he led Trevor along the platform.

"I still think there's hope, bruv."

"Hope?"

"You and Effie. She still loves you. Don't give up on that. You're such a great father. Tell her other man to fuck off."

"Yeah. Right. The last time I told someone of importance to fuck off, as you say, I was almost kicked off Amity. Don't worry, C. I haven't raised a white flag. Not yet."

Connor wrapped an arm around Trevor and leaned in.

"Have you heard from Central yet?"

"No. I suspect they'll hold hearings in a few weeks."

"I don't mean about that."

"Oh. Yeah. There's talk of reorganizing Sec Admin, but nothing official. Some days I think Dorrit is looking for a way out. Other days, he seems up for the fight."

"He needs to make the smart move. And if those jackasses don't promote you ... I swear, bruv, I'll come back here with a blast rifle and make them do it."

Trevor stifled a laugh.

"Like you said, this is my battleground. Once you're off station, don't worry about what happens here. You'll have more than enough on your plate."

Connor smirked.

"So, you don't want me to DS every day?"

"No. I just want you to be safe. Be disciplined. Follow orders. Everyone will be fine here. Trust me."

"Always have, T."

This time, Connor's eyes watered. He didn't fight the tears.

"You looked after me your whole life. I've been a perpetual pain in the ass and I let you down a few hundred times. But you never gave up on me. Trevor, I can't tell you what that means. I've always looked up to you more than anyone. Thank you for trusting me at the club. I'll never let you down."

As the Stallion brothers hugged, Trevor's mind went back to Philadelphia Redux twenty-three years ago. Holding Connor beneath that bridge while the war raged above. Wondering if they were about to die in each other's arms.

It's OK. You can let him go now.

He did.

Trevor stood with Effie and Ana, waving as Connor boarded the transport. They stood in silence until it broke seal and flew through the cascade barrier, soon to activate a wormhole.

"I'm hungry," Ana said. "Can we go out to eat? I think Uncle C would like us to."

"Hungry?" Effie said. "Didn't you fill up at the party?"

"Nope. I want a burger."

Effie chuckled. "The real thing, I assume? Not from a kiosk?"

"Of course!"

"Those are very expensive, sweetie."

Trevor stepped in.

"I think it's OK to splurge today. Uncle C would agree."

"Fine. But this time of day, we might have a bit of a wait for a table. You know how things can get at ..."

He wagged a finger.

"Whatever our sweetheart wants, today she gets." He drew Ana close. "But don't start thinking you can make demands. Got it?"

"Sure, Papa."

Yes. It was a good idea. They needed a little fun. He needed a final breather before focusing on the challenges ahead.

Then Trevor's pom vibrated inside his jacket. He flipped it open to see a flashing red comm beacon.

Huh. No incoming ID. Odd.

Could it have been SI? Devonshire certainly would've been capable of bypassing such protocols.

"You two go on ahead. I'll take this and catch up."

He waited until they were clear before answering.

"Trevor Stallion here. Who am I speaking to?"

He heard a long, relaxed sigh.

"Why, I am deeply humbled, Deputy Stallion. To command your attention is truly one of the great honors of my life."

Trevor tried again to ask the caller's name, but the man – perhaps in his forties or fifties, with a lilting, theatrical voice – continued without interruption.

"I have only recently become aware of your fine work on Amity Station. In particular, your brilliant discovery of the Black Star cell in your midst. Your prowess as a detective is surely unrivalled."

"Who is ...?"

"I don't wish to keep you, Deputy. Few things can match the love of family. What a most tragic circumstance for the families of those deceased young people. I am bereft."

Trevor glanced at the call data, searching for evidence of a source.

"Ultimately, I wanted to call and compliment your fine work. We never anticipated an adversary of such skill and precision. Our next maneuvers will require a more deft approach to avoid your cunning and wiles. We will be in touch again soon.

"In the meantime, I must say that even from a far glance, I am so enthralled by your daughter."

His pulse raced. Trevor whirled about in every direction.

"I especially appreciate the way she wears her hair. The curls. A nice touch. I so dearly wish to meet her in the near future. Perhaps you can arrange it. If not, I feel certain my friends will take the initiative. Until we meet again, Trevor Stallion. Farewell."

Trevor's hands shook. He fumbled the pom.

No incoming data.

Effie and Ana walked far ahead, holding hands.

Happy. Oblivious.

What new threats await Trevor, his family, and Amity Station? How will Connor fare as a soldier of the UNF? Answer those questions now in Book 2 of the series: *Shadow Gambit.*

Would you mind rating this book? A short, honest text review would mean everything to me. I love to know what my readers think.

Printed in Great Britain
by Amazon

44018623R00155